A SPY LIKE ME

Laura Pauling

Praise for A SPY LIKE ME

"Move over Gallagher Girls—there's a new spy in town! *A Spy Like Me* is a fast-paced, high-energy ride through Paris that left me almost as breathless as Pauling's hot hero. Super fun beginning, great story, and an ending that won't disappoint.

Gemma Halliday, NYT best selling author of *Spying in High Heels*.

"Oh. My. Holy. Spy. Pants. *A Spy Like Me* is the most fun we've had in Paris since *Anna and the French Kiss*. The perfect mix of romance, mystery and danger, *A Spy Like Me* has more twists and turns than a Paris arrondissement."

Lisa and Laura Roecker, authors of *The Liar Society* and *The Lies That Bind*

Redpoint Press
A Spy Like Me: Book 1
Copyright 2012 Laura Pauling
Second e-book edition, 2013
Second paperback edition, 2013

This is a work of fiction, and is produced from the author's imagination. People, places and things mentioned in this novel are used in a fictional manner.

Summary: After dodging bullets on a first date, Savvy must decide how far she'll go to protect the ones she loves.

Edited by Leigh T. Moore
Cover Design by Novak Illustration

ebook ISBN: 978-0-9852327-1-9
Paperback ISBN: 978-0-9852327-0-2

Visit http://laurapauling.com

Dedication

Thanks to my loving husband and family for all their support.

One

I COULDN'T HAVE ASKED for a more perfect date—the Eiffel Tower, a night in Paris, and holding hands with the waiter I'd been flirting with for weeks. Nothing could ruin it.

"I have a surprise." Malcolm smiled, flashing his dimples. "Close your eyes."

I huffed before shutting them. "Fine."

I'm not really a surprise-me kind of girl. Ever since I'd moved to France with my dad, I'd wanted normal. Cornflakes with heaps of sugar for breakfast, jelly and pepperoni sandwiches at lunch, and a language I could understand. No more *parlez-vous francais.* Give me a healthy dose of swearing, loud-mouthed, impatient Americans, thanks.

"Hey, Savvy." He nudged my arm. "No peeking."

"I'm not. I swear."

Okay, maybe I was a tiny bit. With my eyes shut tight, in almost complete darkness, I could hear the hum of the passing

1

motorboats, the traffic from the road, and the leaves above me, whispering.

Malcolm's warm hand pulled me forward, and I stumbled in the dark. The sounds and smells in the evening air became sharper: the tangy River Seine and the laughter of couples nearby. My imagination went wild. Maybe he'd surprise me with a boat ride. Flower petals would be scattered at our feet, and violinists would be playing on the bank, as we passed, holding hands and locking lips.

I tripped for the third time, straining to hear the lap of the water. "Are we almost there?"

"Soon," Malcolm said.

Grass tickled my ankles, and I gripped his hand tighter. But he let go and pulled away. I heard the unzipping of a backpack. So maybe it wasn't a boat ride. Maybe my surprise would be a hot air balloon flight over the sizzling sunset of Paris where we'd toast to the many romantic nights ahead of us.

"Surprise!"

I opened my eyes and gasped at the sight before me. It wasn't a boat ride or a trip in a hot air balloon, which frankly are probably highly overrated and a bit cheesy. Instead, he'd laid out a checkered quilt with a full spread of sparkling cider and mini-tarts slathered with all kinds of berries and drizzled with chocolate.

I gasped. "Wow!"

"I have a confession." Malcolm looped his fingers in mine.

Oh no. I tensed and pulled away. I should've known it couldn't last. "What?"

He shifted his weight from foot to foot.

"What's the confession?" I urged.

His cheeks turned pink. "I overheard you and your friend talking about your work the other day when I took your breakfast order. I didn't mean to spy on you. And this morning I talked with your dad about a possible job with Spy Games."

"Really." I drew out the word, while my mind raced.

So this whole date was a set up so Malcolm could have an in with my dad and his crazy business of letting people run around Paris pretending to be spies? They at least paid to do it. In my fantasies, this date was about me. Not about a cute boy using me to supplement his income.

"Yeah, I know it was kinda stupid." Malcolm kneeled on the blanket as he laid out fancy cloth napkins and poured the cider. A gentle breeze rippled the sleeves of his shirt and teased the hair above his ears. Cider splashed out of the plastic, fluted glass. He smiled awkwardly and held it out to me.

"Forgive me?"

The tips of my fingers brushed against his when I accepted the glass. "Well, I don't know. Espionage is a serious crime." I paced in front of the quilt.

Malcolm lifted his hands, palms out, in an act of surrender. "Guilty as charged."

I spoke in my sternest most lawyer-like voice. "I want to believe you liked me for me. That you waited on our table because you thought I was cute and you liked the way I laughed."

"Why do you think—"

"Whoops." I put a finger to my lips. "The defense is not allowed to speak. You'll get your turn later. Maybe."

Malcolm sipped his sparkling cider, which I promptly whipped away from him. Some of it splashed out on his jeans. "No cider while on trial."

He snorted, trying to hold back his laugh.

I stifled a grin and continued my interrogation. "I'd hoped for days you'd been building up the courage to ask me out with sweaty palms and an out-of-control heartbeat. The whole shebang."

It's how I felt waiting for him to ask me out. Once I'd admitted it, I couldn't look him in the face. He reached for a strawberry tart, but I slapped his hand.

"No, no, no. No indulging until proven innocent." I spied the cloth napkins. Perfect. "Hands behind your back."

4

He complied with a silly grin. "Do I get my one phone call and a lawyer?"

My heart fluttered, but I stayed on task. Using my famous Spy Games knots, I tied the napkins around his wrists, tightly. My hostages could never escape. I grabbed a strawberry tart, because prosecuting a spy makes one hungry, and continued my attack.

"When asking a girl out on a date, especially in Paris, certain expectations are involved. The boy should spend hours planning the date and picking out the perfect desserts and the right clothes to wear to impress her."

"I object!" Malcolm blurted out. "Hours? That's ridiculous."

I stomped my foot and shouted. "Order in the court room!"

People walking by glanced our way, and even a mime was distracted from his act, so I kneeled and brought my face inches from his.

"Was that an admission of guilt?" I said in a quieter voice. "Did you not put much forethought into the planning of this date? Did you not truly care? And is it true that your only intention and motivation were to get closer to the girl for your career purposes?"

He leaned forward and before I could officially object, he kissed me.

I jerked away, spluttering and gasping, but completely delighted. "The defense is not allowed to sway the verdict. That will be a penalty."

"What're you going to do? Splash more cider on my jeans?" He tilted his head, completely underestimating the girl he'd offended.

I narrowed my eyes, and a grin spread across my face as an utterly evil idea sprang into mind. I sipped the sparkling cider, letting the tart liquid coat my throat. With shaky fingers, I rushed to unbutton his pants and slide them off, revealing navy blue boxer briefs. I pulled off his crisp white tee and let it stay bunched by his hands. Yum. Nice view.

Malcolm spoke in a husky voice. "Are you flirting with the defense, Ms. Bent?"

I ignored the sudden desire to drop the case and pushed forward. "Once you were close to the girl, the plan was to infiltrate her father's company. Do you deny it?"

"There's more to the story," he murmured, his gaze lingering on my lips.

The sounds of Paris at night faded and for a moment I could pretend we were like all the other couples sprawled across the city. Except, we weren't. Boys don't play games with me and get away with it.

"I proclaim you guilty on all accounts for espionage and for asking a girl out under false pretenses. Punishable by death."

He moved to kiss me again, and I was tempted to give in to his tactics. But with a laugh, I stepped back. "The court has decided to let you off with an easy sentence."

He waited for his sentence, but his flushed face told me he was thinking, hoping that I'd come back and kiss him. He'd underestimated me. This whole courtroom drama might be a joke, but inside, I was a bit hurt that this date wasn't really a date. That it was just a way into Spy Games for him.

I cleared my throat in a judicial sort of way. "You are hereby sentenced to fifteen minutes of intense embarrassment by sitting in your underwear in public."

His face turned a bit pale as he realized I meant what I said. I felt only slightly bad.

"*Au revoir* for now," I whispered, and grabbed a smashed tart covered in strawberries because something that good should never go to waste. And then, I was outta there for the full term of the sentence. Almost.

About two steps away and one bite into the tart, I heard a groan. Was he okay? Would his circulation get cut off? Maybe I should loosen the ties. I turned. Malcolm lay in the grass. Just like I left him.

Except for the blood running in rivulets down his arm.

TWO

ALL I DID WAS tie his wrists together and take off his clothes.

For a joke.

A bit of fun revenge.

I swayed, dizzy on my feet. The sounds of Paris rushed around me, swirling into a crescendo. My eyes were trained on the boy, my date, in front of me. Minutes ago he'd kissed me, offered me sparkling cider. He'd smiled and invited me into his world, his life. Now he appeared to be unconscious.

He groaned again, and I ran to his side. Blood gushed down his arm, leaving a trail and dripping onto the grass. No. No. No. How? What had happened? I'd turned away for three seconds! Only a serious injury could cause that much blood.

Like a bullet wound.

But I never heard a gunshot. He was a waiter. I was a nice girl having her first date in Paris. Things like getting shot didn't happen in situations like that.

Following my instincts from watching too many crime shows, I pressed the quilt against his arm to stop the bleeding. But I had no idea if it was working, especially in the growing darkness. Slowly, I pulled the quilt off and peered at his arm. The smell of blood and the protruding flap of skin sent my stomach into upheaval. I quickly covered it up. *DOCTOR,* my mind screamed.

"Doctor! Doctor!" I called out to tourists and couples walking past, but they ignored me.

Some pulled out their phones and snapped pictures. Others saw what looked like a questionable scene and hurried by, not wanting to get involved. And I had no idea how to say in French, "Help! A boy might possibly be bleeding to death!" Or, "I tied him up but I didn't shoot him!"

I knew exactly how this would look to the police. Terrible. Like I was some crazy, gun-happy, screwed-up American teen. Or like I belonged to some secret, ancient society that murdered people for no apparent reason. Right.

I struggled not to pass out. Who would hurt Malcolm? And what if they were still watching? With a gun aimed at us? Or me? *Crap.* I dropped to the ground next to him, huddling close.

"Please, please be okay," I whispered.

"Oh, *now* you want me to be okay," Malcolm mumbled. "After tying me up."

I shook with relief that he was talking and still breathing. I kept pressing the quilt against his arm. "Do you know who might've shot you?"

"Do you have a jealous ex-boyfriend?" he asked. A bit of drool clung to the corner of his mouth.

"This is nothing to joke about," I snapped. "We need to get you to a doctor."

"It's not that bad." His eyes blinked open briefly. He felt his arm, wincing. "It's just a grazing, I think."

"Not that bad? You've been shot!"

I felt past the quilt to the cloth napkin tied around his wrists. The ties had to come off, and I couldn't hide in his shadow forever like a coward. I had to act. And it had to be soon. Before this situation got any worse.

My legs trembled and panic set my skin on fire as I scooted around his body. The barrel of a gun could be pointed right at me, the shooter focused and aiming, waiting for the right moment to pull the trigger. I tugged at the binds, but they weren't called my specialty knots for nothing. Only one thing to do.

"This might hurt but I need to pull you to safety while I go for help." I hooked my arms under his shoulders and pulled.

I heard the ping first and felt the pricks of shattered tree bark against my back. I dropped to the ground. Sobs ripped from my throat, and I curled into a ball. That was why I never heard the gun shot. The gun had a silencer on it, which meant professionals.

"Savvy?"

"What?" I said in a tiny, scared voice.

"Come close and listen."

I inched over to his side so I could see his face. Pain flecked his expression from the set of his jaw to the way his eyelids fluttered shut every few seconds.

"What?" I whispered. I couldn't even hold his hands because they were tied up.

"I like you." A twisted laugh escaped his lips. "I shouldn't. But I do."

"Let me get help." I wanted to reach out and touch his cheek, to comfort him, but I curled my fingers into the grass.

"We need to run," he said. "Help me up."

"What if they shoot again? Or what if you pass out from blood loss?"

He glanced to the right and left as if hoping to spot the shooter. "If they wanted us dead, we'd be dead."

I let his words soak in. This was a warning? For what? Eating too many *chocolat au pains*?

His words puffed out with each breath. "I try. To bring my dates. Home alive. Their dads like that." He held his breath and grimaced with pain. "You run one way. I'll run the other. Eiffel. Thirty minutes."

11

"Shh. Okay. I get it. Don't talk anymore." This time I did run my fingers across his cheek, then I smoothed his hair.

"I'm serious. Go," he barked.

The back of my neck tensed at the urgency in his voice, and I glanced around. The light from the Eiffel Tower and the street lamps still cast a romantic glow but this night had become anything but romantic. Most people rushed past us. We could both stay here all night like sitting ducks, just hoping the shooter would leave us alone. Or I could do as Malcolm wanted and run away.

"Fine." But I didn't move. I was rooted to his side, too scared to go, too scared to stay. I fumbled with the ties. "Let me get you untied."

Then I heard another ping and the grass tore up next to me. I smothered a scream, grabbed my bag, and got to my knees.

"Go! Now!" His voice hitched. "I'll slip out of these knots in two seconds."

I choked back a sob. "Thirty minutes."

Then I ran. I didn't look back, but flew across the grass toward the main road. The thought that a bullet could be shooting toward my back made me run faster than I'd ever run before.

Three

I FLEW ACROSS THE grass, feet pounding, arms pumping. I wove in and out of the trees, cutting zigzag lines to throw off the invisible shooter. A cramp gripped my side, but I kept pushing. What if Malcolm was wrong? What if the gunman had bad aim or sneezed as he pulled the trigger? I zigzagged again.

Benches and tourists were a blur as I zipped past. I wanted to reach out and grab the darkness like a cloak and wrap it around me, but the blazing lights from the Eiffel ruined any chances of melting into the night.

Hide. That's what I needed to do. I pushed harder, almost to the tower. I ducked behind a group of older men out for a stroll, and then after a glance behind my shoulder, I slid behind a cart and a man selling roses. Immediately I slumped to the ground, my chest heaving. Sweat streamed off me and dripped into my mouth. I tasted salt. Tears too?

13

I breathed in and out. What the hell just happened?

Someone touched my shoulder with a soft hand. I scrambled back. A man with corn silk hair offered me a rose. The owner of the cart. I reached out to grab the stem, trying to miss the thorns. He spoke in French, and I nodded.

"*Merci*," I said.

"Trouble?" he asked, his brow crinkling with concern. Light danced in his eyes. He seemed perfectly content to sell roses all day. Just a kind man with probably a simple life, maybe some grandchildren an hour away. I couldn't get him involved.

"No. I just need to rest." I assured him, shaking my head.

He didn't seem to understand and went back to selling roses. I lifted the bloom to my nose and let the soft petals brush against my skin, the sweet smell giving me a false sense of security. Was I safe? Had the mad man with a license to kill gone home? Or was he after Malcolm? Damn it. When would thirty minutes be up? I let my head fall against my knees and tried to ignore the guilt. If I hadn't been all cute and flirty and tied Malcolm up, he'd be much better off. He might not have gotten shot. Wait a second. Why did he get shot? I wasn't sure I wanted to know.

With each painful minute, I pictured Malcolm, running, falling, getting shot. And then the silent movie would start again and the scene would play over and over. After what

14

seemed like an extremely long time, I pushed up and peeked around the cart. My legs cramped and my shoulders felt tight and sore. I had to be safe, right? I hadn't heard any gunshot pings since I ran away, since Malcolm got shot, since our date got ruined.

With a slight limp, I walked the perimeter of the Eiffel, searching for Malcolm. It would be hard to miss a guy in his underwear. With every flash of brown hair, my heart leaped. But it was never him. I rubbed my shoulders, ignoring the fear squeezing the breath out of my chest.

Finally, I leaned against a tree, letting the crowds of people blur in and out. The boisterous sounds of the late-night crowd faded into white noise, and the nice man closed up his cart and left for home. I wasn't sure how long I stayed or if I even nodded off here and there, but he never came.

Malcolm never showed.

I convinced myself he decided to seek medical help, or that he found the shooter and wrestled him to the ground and turned him over to the police. Or that it was too much for him to make it to the Eiffel, and he was safe at home, wherever that was. Why hadn't I gotten his phone number?

Clouds passed over the moon, casting a shadow over the city of lights. Shivers racked my body. The crowds thinned. Thirty minutes had passed several times, and I had to go home.

The next morning, I woke up in a haze. My head pounded and my heart ached. Somehow I'd made it home last night, past Dad who'd fallen asleep reading a Dan Brown novel, and into the shower. But no matter how hard I'd scrubbed, I couldn't wash away the memory of what happened. I'd stayed up late into the night, worrying.

Throwing aside any dirty clothes, I dug around in my closet and found the box. The one full of different spy gadgets—gifts from Dad, of course. A beginner's code-breaker book that I hadn't even cracked the spine on yet, an obnoxious flower pin that doubled as an audio recorder, and I couldn't possibly forget about the black ski cap Dad wanted me to wear as a Spy Games' staffer. I was hoping to find a bulletproof vest or weapon of some sort. Not that we needed weapons for Spy Games. The wannabe spies were placed in groups and traipsed across Paris together. I handed out coded clues at the Louvre and later tortured the hostage. Pretty boring, actually. But people seemed to love it.

Malcolm. Thoughts of him hovered in the room, not letting go, not leaving me alone. I liked Malcolm. I liked the lopsided grin he wore when he took my order every morning, already knowing what I wanted. I liked his polite and kind words when he waited for Aimee and me to finish chatting before he presented us the bill. And I especially liked that he was a cute boy who could speak English.

Leaning against the wall, I breathed deep and tried to calm my beating heart. Why did I act so impulsively last night? I could've at least asked him some questions first or talked about my hurt feelings in a rational way. Not put him on trial. What had I said? Punishable by death?

I had to tell Dad. He might wrap me in bubble wrap and metal armor to keep me safe, but he'd know what to do about Malcolm. I entered the kitchen. Dad was buried in the morning newspaper, his legs sprawled out to the side of the table. He had no idea I'd almost died last night. I peeled a banana, took one bite, then threw it away. Instead, I poured coffee and drew comfort from three extra sugars.

Finally, he peered over the top of the paper for a second, his wave of dark hair slicked to the side. "Morning, Savvy."

I had to get his nose out of the newspaper. "We need to talk."

"Sure thing, what's up?" But he kept reading, as usual.

"It's serious." More serious than whatever drama he was reading about.

He folded the newspaper and looked at me with scared eyes, scared in the way that he might have to buy tampons or something. My mouth went dry and I struggled to find the right words.

"Savvy?" He put the newspaper down, his full attention on me.

"Right. Something kinda happened last night."

"With Malcolm?" Dad sat straighter and his voice became sharp. "If he so much as touched a hair on your head—"

"Whoa! Calm down." I held up my hands. "Malcolm didn't do anything."

Warmth spread through my chest. Dad hadn't shown he cared this much since I lost my luggage on our flight to France. I'd freaked out because it had the scrapbook my friends made me as a goodbye gift, and he'd been so concerned. I looked at a clump of dried gel hanging from a hair above Dad's ear, anywhere but at his eyes. I didn't want to see his reaction to me getting shot at.

"We were walking near the Eiffel Tower. He had this wonderful picnic—"

Dad lowered his eyebrows until they practically touched his nose. "Did you say the Eiffel Tower?"

"Yeah, um." I searched for the right words but they wouldn't come.

"There was a shooting last night by the Eiffel. Did you see or hear anything?"

"Pff, No." Crap. That was my chance to tell all. Why did I blow it? Maybe Dad knew something. "Did anyone get hurt? Were any bodies found?"

"The news didn't say, but I'm glad you're safe. Maybe you should stay home today and skip Spy Games." Dad picked up the paper again like the decision was made.

I knew right then I couldn't say a word about what happened. Not if I ever wanted any kind of social life again. I'd have to take care of Malcolm myself. Somehow.

"Oh, man, but I was so excited for Spy Games today!"

"Really?" Dad perked up. He'd been trying to get me excited about his new line of work since we'd arrived. He must have recognized my less than enthusiastic interactions with the wannabe spies, I mean clients.

"Definitely."

"Well, okay. But I want you to be careful." His eyes narrowed as if suddenly deciding to be interested in my life, my real life, not just what he saw on the outside. "So what happened on your date?"

"You could say it was an adventure." More like a horror movie. But I didn't even care anymore why Malcolm asked me on the date. I cared if I'd accidentally had a hand in killing him.

Dad straightened the paper. "Ah, here it is. The shooting. Right next to the stories about some big pastry extravaganza contest and a dog show. Oh your mom would've loved the dog show, all the fluffy dogs prancing around...."

His voice trailed off and the white elephant (a.k.a. Mom) that had wedged itself permanently between Dad and me made its appearance. He gazed off, memories of past times flashing across his face, times when she was around. My legs jiggled up and down, fighting off the dread. I missed Mom too, but I had to know Malcolm made it.

"Dad? The shooting?"

"Oh, right. The paper says the police found evidence of a shooting and lots of blood. But nothing else. No sign of anything. They're combing the Seine for a body."

Did that mean Malcolm might have died? Maybe someone killed him, wrapped him up in the quilt and threw him in the river? My face prickled and fear spiraled up through my chest. I leaned over and fiddled with my shoelaces. *I left a guy half-naked by the Eiffel Tower last night, alone and bleeding.* I wanted to rush the three steps across the kitchenette and hang my head over the sink and puke my guts out.

Four

"YOU LOOK PALE." Dad sounded like he cared. "Are you feeling okay?"

"Yeah." Except I'd made a huge mistake. I never should've tried to play the role of the flirty date. I never should've tied him up. What had I been thinking?

"I've been meaning to talk to you." He folded his newspaper twice over, which always meant the talk was serious. Usually it meant chatting about my future, especially since I was eighteen. This year I was exploring my options before college, in other words, helping my dad with the business, while experiencing a new culture.

"Can we talk later?" My words came out kind of breathless, like I'd run ten miles. "I'm meeting Aimee early this morning." *And I had to see about a body.*

He clasped his hands together. "I guess. We'll talk later then."

I nodded while under the table I dug my fingernails into the palms of my hands. I had to know if Malcolm was okay. Maybe he'd gotten home last night, wrapped up his arm, and would be at work today. I hoped.

"Okay, but be careful. Stay with the crowds." He pushed back the chair and it banged into the cupboard. He dumped the rest of his cold coffee into the sink. "You up for the fiver or the tenner this afternoon?"

"Maybe tomorrow." And then I felt worse, if that was possible. I hadn't run more than a mile since we got to France.

"Great. I'll be at the warehouse preparing for the debriefing at nine sharp. I'll see you there."

I nodded and downed a glass of water before slipping outside. Resting my head against the front door, I traced my fingers along the grains of wood. Dad wanted to talk to me, really talk to me, and I'd said no? What if he'd wanted to tell me about Mom? Or say he was sorry? That had to wait. My priority was finding Malcolm.

I turned to leave and tripped over a brown paper package on the step. Every piece of mail we get addressed to Mom makes her absence that much worse. She should be here to get them herself. I kicked it off to the side and it landed behind a bush with a satisfying thud. The birds singing in the trees needed to be shot. I sprinted to the corner before slowing to a jog. Prayers slipped from my lips, me making a deal with God. Something about Malcolm being alive and at work, and me never eating cookies again.

Aimee waved ecstatically from the far corner of *Les Pouffant's*, our favorite café. I speed-walked through the black wrought iron tables searching everywhere, behind every person and pillar. No sign of Malcolm.

"Oof!" I walked right into a big somebody.

"*Excuse-moi, Madamoiselle!*" His big round belly puffed into me, knocking me back, and his long, curly grey beard had bits of frosting stuck in it. Cinnamon dusted his shoulders. He frowned at me, his shaggy eyebrows almost touching his nose.

"I'm so sorry," I mumbled, then rushed past him. Aimee had already ordered for me: an extra-tall latte and a croissant filled with strips of chocolate.

"Oo la la, you look terrible!" The sun gilded Aimee's blonde frizzy hair and speckled her blue eyes. "You know that was the Pouffant of *Les Pouffant's* who you just bumped into."

I waved my hand. I had bigger concerns than poofy pastry chefs. As soon as my butt hit the chair, I opened two menus and propped them at the edge of our table. I leaned forward and nibbled on my croissant.

"What is up?" she asked.

I wrapped my hands around the warmth of the cup. "I don't think I can do Spy Games today."

She crinkled her nose and laughed. "You are never in the mood. Have you talked to your papa about this yet?"

"No." I poked my finger into the melting chocolate, which I'd normally be devouring. "But have you talked with your grandmother about backpacking across the world yet? And touring ancient castles?"

Aimee puckered her lips to the side. "No. That is different."

Customers streamed in and out of the café, a sea of strangers, but none of them were Malcolm. If he didn't walk out of the café in the next minute, I'd scream.

After tapping the side of her cup and staring intensely, Aimee squealed. "I can not stand it anymore."

"Stand what?" I tested my latte before taking a sip.

"Your date! With the cute waiter?"

"Shh." I didn't want to talk to Aimee about my date. Her friendship was too important. What if she wrote me off as a total jerk? And then slowly backed out of our friendship? I couldn't handle losing my only friend.

Aimee waved her hand. "Put away the menus. He did not show for work this morning."

I gagged on my drink and spit it out on the patio. "What?"

"He did not show. I already asked."

Images of Malcolm being pulled from the bottom of the Seine flashed in front of me, his body deathly white, eyes vacantly staring at me. I groaned.

"I have heard that groan before. After you used your papa's spy equipment to see if he ever talked to your mother and he caught you."

I fiddled with the menu and sipped my latte. I tried to focus on the good parts of last night: the picnic and the effort Malcolm took to make it romantic, probably spending the last of his money for the week. I remembered his quick kiss. I remembered his fine-looking bare chest. But the color red bled into my images and ruined the memory.

"Share now, before I make a scene." Aimee stared me down, her grip tightening on her cup, and the blue flecks in her eyes turning stormy.

I whipped the cash out of my shoulder bag and slammed it on the table next to a small metal tray. "We've got to go. Now!"

"Something must be terribly wrong if you leave half your latte." Aimee placed her hand on my arm. "What happened?"

I combed my fingers through my hair and tried not to hyperventilate. "I'll tell you on the way. Let's go." I grabbed the tray from the table, and while Aimee fiddled with her chair, I shoved the tray up my shirt. A girl can never have too much protection.

We half ran, half walked toward the Eiffel. When we were almost there, I breathed a bit easier. Within minutes I'd know whether or not my date took a big drink in the Seine.

A little out of breath, Aimee said, "Start talking."

That's what I loved about her. Ever since we met, she always cared. Wanting to know what was wrong without wanting anything back. I took several deep breaths then summed up the previous evening.

"Beautiful sunset. Sparkling cider. Fruit-filled pastries. Great conversation. A kiss."

Aimee clasped her hands together with a dreamy look on her face. "Sounds romantic."

Then I told her the rest, almost. I talked about his admission of guilt and the mock trial. And the part where I tied him up and the fact that Malcolm wears boxer briefs, not tighty-whities. When I tried to talk about the shooting and that I didn't know if he was dead or alive, my throat closed up. I couldn't do it.

At first, her face showed nothing. Then her lips twitched, and her eyes crinkled. She lowered her head while her shoulders shook. Several times, she tried to rein it in and act casual but to no avail.

"Go ahead. Laugh. I get it. I'm an idiot." But the truth was nothing to laugh at.

She stopped giggling, wiped at her tears, and then grabbed my hand. "Oh, Savvy. How do you get into these messes?"

"No clue. I just need to know he escaped." A part of me wished I'd told her the truth.

"I'm positive someone found him last night after you left. I'm sure." She cocked her head and suppressed a grin. "Almost sure."

At the Eiffel Tower, I sprinted toward our picnic spot, with Aimee right behind me. The cops were already gone. The river searched. Not even a bit of yellow police tape was visible. The dewy grass soaked my sneakers, and I shivered at the bite in the air. He was nowhere.

"You sure about all this?" Aimee asked, a hand on my arm.

"Yeah, I'm sure." I slumped to the ground, not caring that my homemade bullet-proof vest jabbed into my stomach or that the wet dew was seeping into my pants, and I'd have a spot on my butt for the next hour. What if he was lying in a foreign hospital or tied up as a hostage? I couldn't let myself think he might've died. "What if something terrible happened?"

"I doubt that." Aimee crouched next to me. "Do you like him?"

"Heck, no." Even if I did, what did it matter? He'd gone missing and could very well be dead. And I had no idea why or what he was mixed up in.

Aimee nodded as if to say, yeah right. Then she tapped her watch. "You might not get fired from this job because your dad is the boss, but I can."

She stood and slung her backpack over her shoulder. The whole ride on the Metro, I tried not to think about Malcolm. We got off at our stop after throwing out all sorts of conspiracy theories like my dad being overprotective and sending his goons to shadow us or Malcolm working for the Mafia. But I had bigger things to worry about.

Like what the hell happened to Malcolm.

Five

AIMEE AND I ARRIVED outside the dirty white warehouse known as Spy Headquarters seconds to nine. Weeds spilled out of the cracked pavement and black and red spray paint dripped down the walls. Overall, it was kind of creepy— exactly what Dad wanted. I gripped the metal handle, and the door opened with a familiar screech. Once the door closed behind me, I felt safe from any random, unexplained bullets.

In one of the office-turned-dressing-rooms, we rushed to change our clothes, put on our gear, and then get in position for our grand entrance. When Aimee wasn't looking, I ditched my armor, but it wouldn't be for long. Every noise that sounded close to a ping or ricochet sent fear coursing through my veins. A serving tray could possibly save my life. Maybe.

Aimee climbed the steps on the side of the warehouse, and I followed. Newly spun webs clung to my face and neck. I brushed them off with one swipe. At the top, Aimee and I helped each other hook the zip line cables onto our belts and tighten the safety straps. Then step-by-step, keeping my eyes focused on the back of Aimee's head and not the fifty-foot drop, I sidestepped a rafter to our position. My fingers dug into the support beam.

"You can do it!" Aimee whispered.

As we inched closer to our take-off spot, I watched my coworkers perched like pigeons, waiting patiently. Gray Chalston, Dad's right hand man, always coordinated the staff and made sure the games ran smoothly. Frankie Newtz, the eccentric guy in his twenties who still wasn't sure what to do with his life, played a great psychopath, miscreant, hostage, murderer, whatever the games called for. His wild red hair and acne scars just added to it. Nancy Jergen, a housewife from upstate New York who loved to wield a gun, (thank God they were never loaded), played the double agent. And then there was Aimee and me, the lowly informants.

They all nodded hello. Dad had strict orders—no talking in the rafters. My palms grew sweaty, like last time. This was our second round with the "grand entrance," and the drop scared the crap out of me.

The spies trickled in, timid at first at the large empty space and the cold cement floor. No chairs or tables or water coolers were in sight. Or free, tasteless coffee.

"Look at them," I whispered.

A group of balding men walked in wearing trench coats. True wannabes. They wore sunglasses and carried backpacks probably filled with spy gadgets they'd bought off eBay. I couldn't look down for long because my stomach felt queasy and vertigo hit me like a sugar high. Aimee had no problem standing on the roof rafter; after all, she was the one who wanted to climb mountains. Not me. I rubbed my arms. It was damp and the chill started in my toes and coiled around my body until I was shivering like a naked spy on a rooftop in January.

And then this macho man breezed through the entrance, full of swagger, wearing leather pants and sunglasses. He posed in the middle of the room, ready, willing, and waiting for danger.

The ultimate spy.

I made a mental note to stay away from him. His stomach pouched over the edge of his pants as if he'd eaten one too many donuts, and when it came to hair gel, he was my dad's twin.

The beam beneath my feet creaked. I swayed and clenched my teeth to hold my breakfast back. The smell of bat excrement made me feel positively sick.

Aimee nudged me. "It is about to start."

A light sweat formed on my body as our time to plummet towards the cement floor drew near. I checked and rechecked my cables and attachments. A cold draft sent goosebumps down my legs. Maybe I'd end up in a hospital next to Malcolm. Or the morgue.

Aimee whispered, "You can do this."

"Doesn't mean I want to."

Gray gave us a stern look to stop talking.

As soon as Dad strode through the side door, his boots echoing on the cement, everyone quieted. Kind of like when God created the earth, I imagined. Dad evoked this kind of scary presence when he was in full Spy Games mode. By his long stride and the swish of his leather pants, the sway of his shoulders and his slicked-back hair, they would never know that six months ago he sold herbal remedies to constipated old ladies. Unfortunately, his dramatic efforts worked on everyone but me. That was because I'd seen him in his sweats, singing to Barry Manilow, while he burned our instant mac and cheese.

Dad took full advantage of everyone's gawking stares. He glanced around as if a hundred men in black suits with ear buds were about to burst through the door. It was all part of the act.

"We have a serious situation." His deep booming voice bounced off the walls and echoed between the rafters. "A high profile executive has been taken for ransom. It's your job to follow the clues and save him. Before it's too late."

The warehouse door screeched open, and everyone looked. Malcolm entered.

Malcolm? He was alive! Joy burst through my veins and flooded my body. A zillion-ton weight lifted off me, and I felt like I could float off the beam if I let go. We needed to throw confetti and drink lemonade because I wasn't a murderer after all.

Malcolm strode across the room and I drank in the sight of him, his moving limbs, his chest rising up and down as he breathed! He settled into the back of the crowd, cool and composed.

The instantaneous burst of joy over the fact I wasn't a murderer faded, and my blood went from simmering to boiling. All this time, I believed he could've been dead. He could've called, texted, or thrown pebbles at my window. Anything! He probably didn't show up to work at *Les Pouffant's* just to torture me.

I leaned slightly forward to catch a look at his guilty face. I felt a spinning sensation before I realized I was falling forward. I desperately reached for Aimee, swinging my arms wildly. She caught the edge of my shirt, but gravity ripped it from her hands. Air whooshed around me and I forgot all proper form in free falling. My stomach dropped. Images of me going splat on the cement floor flashed through my mind.

My whole body jerked, and it felt like my arms were going to be ripped from their sockets. I stopped, suspended in the air about ten feet from my rafter, high above the heads of the wannabes who were so into my dad they didn't notice a thing. I swung back and forth, dangling from a wire. Gray held the line, and I silently pled with him to pull me back up. Clearly, he needed to develop his skills of telepathy.

Sweat tickled my armpits and dotted my forehead as the cement and the heads of the people swung back and forth in my vision. Malcolm became a blur. I was stuck until it was time to drop. I'd look like a loser, but I didn't care. Solid ground. Nice, hard cement under my feet. That was all I cared about.

Dad continued with his speech, obviously not aware that with one slip of Gray's hands, his one and only daughter could become a floor decoration. "You'll have to work together or it will be very hard for your team to succeed—"

I blocked the rest out. I just wanted to stop swinging like a monkey.

"And here's the staff to help you with your spy mission today. Give a hand to Nancy!"

Crap.

Nancy swooped past me to the cheering of the crowd. Dad boomed out their names as they dropped down. Frankie. Then Aimee. Of course, they all performed perfectly. One leg down, one leg bent in the wire hook, one arm holding on, and one arm out (kinda cheesy if you asked me). They all landed with grace and style.

And then there was me.

Six

Dad cleared his throat after an awkward silence. Blood rushed to my face, mostly because I was tilting forward.

"And folks, here's Savvy," he said

Gray slowly let out the line and my body lowered, one painful yard at a time. My limbs hung useless, the halter riding up between my legs. I begged the spy gods to whisk me away, somewhere, anywhere.

The ground drew closer, and I tried to get my feet to land first. But I just ended up flopping around like a fish on a hook. After minutes of ultimate humiliation, I hovered inches from the ground, close enough to kiss the dirty cement. A part of me wanted to, and I swear I heard a snicker. Maybe it was Malcolm.

Aimee helped me to my feet and guided me over to the rest of the staff. I walked past the macho man and noted his name: Cliff Peyton. Frankie winked at me. I refused to look at

Malcolm, and I didn't have to look at my dad. Disappointment rolled off him in Tsunami-like waves. I wanted to burst out that I'd tried, but the guy I thought I'd killed just showed up alive.

I grabbed the easel and paints for my next part of Spy Games and left before anyone could tell me what a spy dork I was and that I should set up a cart and sell friendship bracelets for the rest of my life.

As I traveled to the Louvre, I needed a release, something to focus on besides the major-Malcolm-rage ripping through me. That distraction came in pieces of colored candy. After shoving a handful of Skittles into my mouth and stuffing the package back in my bag, I strode into the humongous courtyard of the palace of medieval kings. It surrounded me on three sides, with turrets, arched entranceways, and fancy stone work that made me want to wear a bustle and carry a parasol. Every time, no fail, it sent a thrill through my chest, but all I could focus on was the metal tray pressed against my skin.

My homemade bulletproof vest.

That's right. After my humiliating fall from the rafters, I shoved that baby right back into place before leaving the warehouse.

A wind blew through, and I held the beret against my head as I gripped my art supplies. Every few seconds, I couldn't help but glance around for anyone suspicious holding a sniper rifle. I hurried through the early crowds and into the glass pyramid, smack dab in the middle of the courtyard, which leads downstairs to the information desk and into the museum. A special tag allowed me to bypass buying a ticket. Sweet deal.

Aimee and I played informants. At the Louvre, I passed off an envelope to the spy teams filled with crucial information in exchange for money. She worked the Eiffel. There was something very satisfying about collecting stacks of green. It wasn't real money, of course, but it looked it. If someone found a stack lying on the side of the street, they wouldn't know it was fake until they were tracked down and thrown in jail for counterfeiting.

Walking through the hallways that would soon be bustling with tourists, I headed to the Vien Room on the second floor. In a flash, my easel was set up, canvas ready to go, and paints in hand. I loved being the first in the large room, enjoying the company of the masterpieces on the wall. Only a small bench with black padding decorated the room. The paintings more than made up for the lack of fancy furniture. These quiet moments alone were the hardest because inevitably they gave me time to think. And the only thought crossing my mind was that someone shot at me the night before.

Inspired by the old masters and with a shaky hand, I added a few brilliant strokes to my half-finished masterpiece of a naked angel with wings—a cherub kissing the forehead of a half-clothed female. I blew it a kiss. "Magnifico!"

"That's bloody nice work," a male voice with a hot English accent said behind me. "Been working on it for a long time?"

I peeked over my right shoulder. A young man with long bushy hair covering his eyes set up his easel near mine. Great. A real art student. He'd never understand my job. And I wasn't in the mood to explain.

"If you need any tips on the naked part, let me know. Maybe I could be of help." He didn't even try to hide the innuendo. Perv. I bit back my retort and focused on the wings, squiggling my brush down the canvas, and I hoped he wouldn't spot me for what I was—a total fake. He turned his back to me with a toss of his scraggly hair.

With my eye on my watch and my arm poised to paint, the first spy group entered the room. They stuck out like a finger painting next to a Van Gogh, their rainy day trench coats and sunglasses screaming *wannabe*. Huddled in a group by the opposite doorway, they searched for the struggling art student (a.k.a., me). By the end of the four hours they'd be knocking out bad guys in a cutthroat race for the prize.

"Oo la la! What a gorgeous painting!" With a dramatic flourish, I finished off the wings. "Just being here among the masters fills my soul with love."

"Do they always dress like that?" The art student nodded toward the amateur spies as one of them crossed the room. He pushed his hair away from his face and revealed his familiar face. Malcolm! He was wearing a wig!

"What are you doing here?" I muttered out of the corner of my mouth while keeping my eyes glued on my wing, which looked slightly like a burnt marshmallow.

He stopped painting and turned his gray eyes on me. "Not even a 'glad to see you're alive'?"

"Glad to see you're alive," I managed, controlling my rage. While I thought he might be dead, he played jokes!

At that point, I almost reverted back to kindergarten coloring and painted a bright yellow sun in the sky, because the spy team had split up and were asking anyone with a scarf wrapped around his neck, the prepared question. How could they not recognize the girl who fell from the ceiling with the safety straps riding up her butt? I was right in front of them.

I pulled out my ponytail to help them recognize my long dark hair and jacked my voice up an octave. "I study painting under the great Gloria Van Deusel. And she is ze most wonderful teacher. I just love painting and being an art student so much."

Malcolm snorted. "You might want to work on that accent."

"Your fake British accent isn't much better." I shot back. I wanted to ask him how he managed to escape the night before and if his arm was okay, but I couldn't stop the angry words from spilling out. "I thought you were dead."

He narrowed his eyes but didn't have time to explain because a wannabe spy approached him and not me. All my arm waving and mixtures of Italian and French had been pointless.

The older woman, with long, graying hair up in a bun, tapped him on the shoulder. *"Excuse moi?"*

Malcolm thickened his accent and branched off into the subtleties of shadowing techniques. The lady glanced back at her team and shrugged. They waved her on and pointed toward me.

And then because I was afraid Malcolm would screw it up, I leaned over and said, "I can help you, Miss."

She read from a note in her hand. "Do they sell blueberry scones?"

I gave my scripted line. "No, but there is a café nearby where you can find a cream puff."

Then I dug into my satchel and handed her an envelope. I dropped my satchel on the ground behind me and continued to paint while she dropped the money rolls into my bag.

She rushed back to her group, waving the envelope in the air. Good thing our national security wasn't on the line, or we'd all be dead. Something to talk to Dad about.

I smoothed down my artist's smock and worked on mixing the right shade of green for the grassy hillside. "I can't believe you followed me here," I whispered. "Haven't you caused enough trouble?"

"Me?" Malcolm didn't look at me but mixed his paints. "The least you could do is say you're sorry. I'm pretty forgiving."

With each stroke of my paintbrush, my rage simmered, bubbling, ready to explode. "Seriously? After the stunt you pulled this morning, I'm not the one who should be apologizing."

After that we both turned to our easels. I painted the same blade of grass over and over, basically ruining my painting, and Malcolm's arm whipped back and forth across the canvas in jerky movements.

The next team that came through did better, until they shoved the money roll into my satchel. As soon as they turned to leave, Malcolm jabbed his paintbrush at me. Pecan brown splattered across my face.

"What stunt?" he demanded. "At least I didn't take your clothes off and tie you up."

I ignored the slam. "What stunt?" My throat ached but I held back the sob. "The one where you told me to run from the shooting and then never met me again. I didn't know if you were dead or alive. You didn't show up to work and then sauntered into Spy Games like a king. That stunt."

I had to completely turn away before I throttled him. Tears burned.

The hard tone in his voice softened. "I didn't realize you cared."

"Of course, I cared, I left my date bleeding to death with some madman on the loose."

"I told you it was just a grazing." His voice dropped lower and he nudged me with his elbow. "Admit it. You think I'm cute, don't you?"

It was my turn to splatter him with paint. "Hardly."

"Though you do have an odd way of showing it." He rubbed the red marks on his wrists from the ties.

I refused to feel guilty. "At the time I had my reasons."

He placed his oil paints onto the stool next to him and stepped closer to me. "Aren't you the least bit interested in what happened?"

"I'm glad you're alive. But no!" I grabbed my bag from the floor and used it as a shield.

A guard sauntered across the room, close enough to listen.

Malcolm put his hands on the bag and tried to keep me from backing away. "You can at least let me explain!"

I pulled back, hard, and pushed him away with my right foot.

"Never!" Tears burned and the emotion of the night before and this morning caught up to me.

He fell back on his butt, except he never let go of my bag. I lunged for the handle, and we fought in a tug-of-war. With one final yank, I ripped it from his hands. The momentum pulled me back and I flailed my arms for balance. Green bills fluttered in the air as I lost my hold.

Tiny rainbow-colored pebbles seemed to float in the air around us. Shock crossed Malcolm's face and he paled. The guard raced forward. I cringed as the candy hit the floor like an avalanche and skittered across the tiles to the far reaches of the room.

"I'm sorry," Malcolm gasped out. "You had food? In the Louvre?"

I could have sworn the whole room, even the walls, gasped, and the angel in the painting smirked.

Damn.

Seven

ACK! I'D FORGOTTEN TO throw out the rest of my Skittles. I
dropped to the ground, scooping up the money by armfuls
and shoving it into my bag. Before I could pick up the candy,
the guard stepped up to me.

"*S'il vous plait.* Come with me."

Great. One more spy team was set to come through, and I
was screwed. Or they were because their informant wouldn't
be here. I gathered my stuff, collapsed the easel, and flashed a
scathing look at Malcolm.

On the way down to the museum offices, I texted Aimee
asking her to switch spots with me, quickly. Thirty minutes
later after lots of hand motions because my French sucked,
and after the guards found my dad's phone number in their
files, they kicked me out. For good.

As soon as I stepped from the pyramid-entrance into the
courtyard, a blast of wind hit me.

"Savvy!" a voice called.

I peeked through my Medusa-like hair to see Aimee waving furiously as she ran toward me. I yanked the artist smock over my head. "Here! Quick change."

She ripped off the burnt-orange pea coat and handed it to me. "You'd better hurry."

"I know. I know. Can we meet up later at *Les Pouffant's*?"

"*Oui*, see you there."

Aimee flew into the pyramid clutching the easel and satchel, just as Peyton and his group arrived in the courtyard. Talk about good timing. They pointed at the turrets and stone arches, oohing and aahing, then Peyton rushed them into the Louvre.

I left the fledgling spies and Malcolm behind, hurried across the courtyard, and grabbed a taxi. At the Eiffel I threw a bunch of bills at the driver, and then hoped they weren't the Spy Games counterfeit ones. I sprinted across the grass, dodging tourists, and passed the first leg of the tower. I flashed my special Spy Games pass and bypassed the line for the elevator on the ground. Weaving in and out of the tourists, I raced to the first floor. All three hundred steps.

With my chest heaving and my breath shooting out in short gasps, I waited in a shorter line for the elevator. After the ride up, the doors slid open at the tippy top, and I burst out. I pulled my coat together and folded my arms. If I thought it was windy at the Louvre, here at the top of the world, it quadrupled a million times.

A narrow walkway circled the top of the Eiffel, and the city of Paris was spread out before me. Crisp air filled my lungs as I entwined my fingers through the mesh cage. The Seine snaked across the land, and the bridges looked like Lego pieces. Tips of skyscrapers poked at the sky in the distance. But what always amazed me was the wide expanse of blue, like I was overlooking the entire world.

After taking a few deep breaths, I turned and leaned my back against the wire cage. Tourists passed me in a blur. My eyes went out of focus until I caught a flash of blue go by. I recognized it, a scarf with threads of a paisley blue and yellow, and the lady had brown hair. I squinted and my heart dropped straight to the ground floor.

"Mom?" I whispered.

The lady slipped into the crowds like any other tourist. It had to be her. Mom had shoulder-length brown hair that she claimed grew one inch every ten years. I followed blindly, weaving in and around tourists, probably pissing them off, but I had to know. I followed the memory of my mom's hazel eyes, her smile, her laugh. I followed the few happy memories I had and the crazy wish she were here, looking for me.

"*Excuse moi?*" Someone tugged on my coat, but I brushed them away. The blue and yellow scarf teased me, bobbing in and out of the crowds.

And then I heard a desperate voice. "I found the scones but where can I find a root beer float?"

The words yanked me back into the real world. I stopped and turned around. Recognition flashed across the woman's face. She tucked a strand of graying hair back into her bun.

I whipped open my bag. "Take the clue."

The Eiffel Tower clue was a basic code that sent them off on a treasure hunt through the most famous historical sites of Paris. For them, that was when it got fun, because Frankie shot blanks at them in empty alleyways. He got their adrenaline pumping.

She seemed a little unsure, so I nodded. As soon as she had the clue, I took off after the lady with the scarf. I'd probably lost her for good. After circling the lookout tower several times and handing out another clue, my energy petered out and I sagged against the mesh cage. I'd always imagined Mom visiting and walking with me through the Louvre. We'd quiz each other on which painters went with which paintings. And then after we'd toured the Eiffel and had our fill of culture and history, we'd go find some off-the-grid patisserie and sit for hours, sipping lattes.

And I could ask her why the hell she left.

Obnoxious laughter carried on a breeze. Cliff Peyton. Great. I so wasn't in the mood for his 'tude. Peyton pointed in my direction. I closed my eyes, to center myself. This was a job. He was a regular guy who would be out of my life in fifteen minutes. Then I could look for Mom.

He sent a youngish woman from his group over to me. Her blonde hair fell right below her chin and swished back and forth. I put my hand on my bag.

"Excuse me, I mean, *excuse moi?*" Her voice was just above a whisper.

I nodded at her.

"Do you know where I could buy some root beer?"

Oh, crap. I hated when they screwed up the line. Dad had strict orders to not help them out. At all. Period. "Sorry, I don't." I walked away.

She tried again and still messed up. She said something about a Dr. Pepper float. Jeez.

The lady with the blue scarf passed us.

The Spy Games client tried again. "I found the scones—"

I cut her off in the middle of her sentence. With not so gentle a nudge, I pushed her aside and sprinted. No games this time. Paisley-scarf lady was only a few feet away, just out of reach of my fingertips. I dodged an older woman with a baby and grabbed my mom.

She turned, and the fringes of her scarf hit my cheek. I stared, mouth agape, as French flowed from her mouth in angry currents.

Mom couldn't speak French to save her life. And I know the last time I saw her she didn't have green eyes or a large mole on her chin with two black hairs sprouting from it. Ew. Even so, it was Mom, and she pretended not to know me.

Her look softened and she grasped my hands. "My dear, are you okay?"

Before she could let go of my hands, I babbled out some words, sounding like a nervous twelve-year-old about to give an oral report. "Where have you been?"

She leaned closer and whispered, "Did a package arrive for me?"

Hot tears filled my eyes, but I refused to let them fall. That was all she could say to me? "What's going on?"

Discreetly, she whispered, "If and when it arrives, don't open it. Hide it in a closet or better yet, burn it. Can you do this for me?"

"Where are you staying? You've got to call Dad, let him know you're here."

"Savvy, this is important. You must follow my directions. I don't want you getting involved."

"Sure, I got it."

She glanced to the left and right and squeezed my hand. "They probably already know you are in France. Please," her voice grew desperate, "don't do anything out of the ordinary. Act like a teenager. Eat croissants. Shop. Sightsee." Then she started mumbling and I wasn't sure if she was talking to me or not.

"Mom?"

She snapped out of it. "Shh. They could have spies watching us right now. They already took a dear friend of mine. I won't let them take you too."

"Huh?"

"Listen." Her words rushed out. "In a couple weeks there is a big pastry event near the apartment. Near *Les Pouffant's*. Meet me there. I'll find you. Promise?"

"I promise." What had gotten into her?

She walked away like she didn't even know me.

"Mom!" I called. We had a museum to visit and lattes to drink. And damn it I wanted an explanation. She turned back toward me with a finger to her lips and fear in her eyes. She shook her head and disappeared into the crowds.

What had happened to my business-like mom who wasn't scared of anything? The one always rushing off on trips for her scrapbooking business or locked away in her bedroom, working. I didn't know the mom who wore disguises and told me to burn packages. But after years of

51

being so busy with work, she needed my help. After leaving Dad and me two years ago, did I want to help? I wasn't sure, but I did know one thing. I couldn't wait to get home and open that package.

Someone gently shook me, but I couldn't move from the mom-stupor that had fallen over me. Another shake.

"Savvy!"

I snapped out of it. Aimee's hair looked a bit on the fritz, windblown strands falling in front of her face. Her eyes, wide with panic, darted left and right.

"What's wrong?" I asked.

"Never mind that. We have got to get out of here. That guy is crazy." She tugged on my arm and dragged me toward the elevator. "I messed up. It happened so fast, and I was not sure what to do."

An angry voice pierced the air. "I can't believe you!"

Aimee groaned.

I gritted my teeth and nodded toward Peyton, who stormed toward us. "You mean that guy?"

"*Oui*," Aimee whispered, inching toward the door while holding my arm in a death grip.

Eight

PEYTON'S EYES BURNED into me like they were lasers and I was a metal wall he was trying to blast through. He pointed to his right. "This woman from my group managed to say the right words and you completely ignored her."

"I...I'm sorry." How would Peyton understand that I'd seen my mom and then received a strange message from her? He wouldn't. I gave him my mean, terrible, you-should-be-scared-of-me look.

"As staff, you are supposed to do everything possible to fulfill our spy experience. Not only did you both screw up at the Louvre, but—"

My eyes widened.

"Oh, yes. I know all about that. Not only did you fail there but you did here too." He put his face inches from mine. Spit hit me as he spoke. "Your friend here was not allowed access to the museum, so we couldn't get our clue." He whipped his head toward her. "And then she refused to give it to me. I had to call Mr. Bent."

Aimee half-sobbed, her fingernails jabbed into my arm. "I am sorry. I was not sure what to do. I wanted you to have the full spy experience. I thought Mr. Bent might have an alternate plan for you. And then the guards led me away."

I cringed. Not good at all. Completely by accident, we'd sent this man over the edge, although he must have been pretty close anyway.

Cliff Peyton kept his face inches from mine. His breath made me gag. He would never understand about my mom. And what could I say? The Louvre was my fault. And Malcolm's.

Aimee's grip loosened on my arm, and she moved between Peyton and me. After clearing her throat, she said in a loud, shaky voice, "You need to leave, Sir."

He jabbed a finger into her chest, pushing her into me. "You were both probably in on it. Is that what you do for fun? Pick one guy in the room and screw up his day?"

I slipped my hand into hers, squeezing. "You need to find your group."

With one last grunt and glare at Aimee, he strode away. Clearly the guy had more problems than just us. He acted more like a teenager than we did. At the door to the elevator, he turned and pointed at us. "This isn't over!"

As soon as he was gone, Aimee turned and hugged me. "Oo, I am so sorry. I made things worse. I should have given him the clue."

I placed my hands on her shoulders. "This was not your fault. I started it when I brought candy into the Louvre."

Aimee shook her head. "You made a mistake. That is no reason for him to lose it."

I tucked her hair behind her ears. "I have to head on over to the hostage site so I don't screw up that too. Why don't you go home and soak in the tub and eat your grandmother's cookies. I'll explain everything to my dad."

"That would be nice, but no." Aimee set her jaw and the fear left her eyes. "I am going to follow him."

I pulled her off to the side. "But why? He's totally psycho. No telling what he'll do."

"I will be fine. I want to make sure he treats the rest of his spy group okay. If not, then I will have proof against him if he causes problems for us later."

She didn't need to say it. She wanted proof so my dad wouldn't fire her. I knew better than to say anything.

"Good luck and stay safe," I said, and after a quick hug, she left.

I waited while the few tourists we'd attracted got bored with staring. I needed to shrug this off. I had a hostage to torture in a couple of hours, but I couldn't forget about the package. It wasn't like Mom was asking me to kill someone, but it was contact. Still, I wasn't sure I was ready to accept it with no explanations.

After handing out the coded messages at the Eiffel, I shifted my armor back into place and headed to the hostage site—a small room in the back of the Galagnani bookstore along the Jardin des Tuileries. The spy teams would arrive after a couple hours of breaking codes and finding clues hidden among famous churches, gardens, and historical hot spots. The first team to free the hostage would win the game. Unfortunately, all we could offer were cheap trophies as prizes.

The past few times, I'd arrived early and Frankie and I'd played card games. I've beaten him at War like five times. I entered the bookstore and navigated the narrow aisles with books towering on either side of me. They let us use a small storage room in the back.

Frankie nodded when I entered, his red frizz just long enough to flop in and out of his eyes with every nod. Freckles dotted his arms and face. He already had the cards set up on an overturned crate. First, I strapped on my belt and gunned the electric screwdriver, which is great for prying secrets out of scared hostages.

"Oo, scary." Frankie mocked.

"That's right," I said in my most threatening tone. "Don't ever think about crossing me."

My cell phone vibrated. "*Bonjour*," I said, happy to be in torture mode and forgetting everything else. Hopefully, the caller was Aimee telling me one of the groups was on their way.

"You in position, Savvy?" Dad asked.

I gulped. Cliff Peyton had called my dad. A client had never called my dad on me. I flashed back to the crazy look in Peyton's eye and the anger rolling off of him over what was a minor offense. So I screwed up. I admitted it. But something was totally off with him. Dad really needed to do background checks or something.

"Just strapping on my belt," I said.

"Have any of the groups made it there yet?"

Maybe he was going to let the whole Cliff thing drop. "Not yet."

"Mr. Peyton called me twice. He was extremely volatile."

Crap. "And?"

"Are you okay?"

The hint of concern in his voice caused mine to shake. "I'm fine. Just getting ready to torture Frankie. Why?" *And did you know I saw Mom?*

"Stay there. I'm stuck in traffic. Maybe you should—"

"Dad?" No answer except the empty silence of a lost connection. Great. I sensed a huge lecture in my near future.

I shut the phone and jammed it into my bag. I'd tried. I'd given them the best spy experience I possibly could, but there was no way I could've foreseen the complications that came with someone like Cliff Peyton. If Malcolm hadn't shown up to harass me at the Louvre, none of this would've happened. Malcolm again. It seemed to always come back to him.

Frankie and I squeezed in a few games of War. I lost. Twice. It was hard to focus even on a game that required no strategy. In the middle of our third game, Frankie jerked straight and cocked his head. "Did you hear that?"

I tapped the crate. "You can't fool me. Don't try and get out of losing. I'm about to kick your butt. I can feel it."

We played a few more cards.

Frankie stopped again, poised to listen. "I'm serious. Something's going on up front."

"Fine." I kicked my stool back and pressed my ear against the wooden door that opened into the shop.

I'd recognize that voice anywhere. Peyton. And he wasn't singing show tunes either. He'd probably wheedled info out of my dad so his group could get here first.

"Told ya," Frankie said.

"Get in the chair," I answered.

In a flash, I whipped out the rope and tied him up with one of my famous knots. I'd barely put on Frankie's blindfold and stuffed the gag in his mouth when the door burst open and slammed against the wall with a bang. Peyton towered in the doorway, but no group. Not a good sign that he split from his team. His once-slick hair stuck up in several directions. Where was Aimee? She was supposed to be following him.

"You can't stop me now!" I ran the electric screwdriver and faced Frankie, but I really needed a chainsaw because the tiny buzz didn't do anything to hide my shaky voice.

"Little late to start playing the game, don't you think?" Peyton sneered.

With slow, in-control movements, I placed the screwdriver on the crate. Frankie struggled against his ropes. He must've sensed the tension. Facing Peyton, I drew in a deep breath. "You're supposed to stay with your group. I'm sure they need your help."

He puffed out breaths while cracking his knuckles. "They probably do, especially since you screwed up everything for us."

My hands wouldn't stay still and kept clasping and unclasping. Desperate to send him on his way, I practically begged him. "You still have time to follow the clues and make it back here in first place. I'm sure of it."

Peyton snorted. "Right."

I didn't need an inner spy sense to tell me I was in trouble. Behind me, Frankie mumbled something but I couldn't focus. I wished like hell I didn't know how to tie such a good knot. I'd have loved it if my hostage could slip out of his binds and save me right now.

I kept my voice low and calm. "I'm sorry about the Louvre. I'm sorry about the Eiffel. I wish I could change what happened."

Peyton's eyes darted around the room, taking in the crates of old books, the cobwebs, and the hostage. "I could've won this game." A vein pulsed in his neck. "Thanks to you and your friend I won't even finish. With a little convincing, she told me where to find the hostage."

Aimee? She'd better be okay. I choked down a nervous laugh.

"You think this is a joke?" He stepped closer, his chest rising up and down as if he'd run a marathon.

"No. I think in the Spy Games handbook it says—"

He shot back, "I know what the handbook says. I read it."

"Oh," I said meekly and then moved behind Frankie.

Frankie muttered through his gag, "Untie me."

I fumbled at the knots, but Peyton took two steps, grabbed my arm and yanked me away. "Don't even think about it."

"Look. I'm sorry." I decided on a personal approach. "I know life can be hard sometimes."

He shoved me up against the wall. The rough wood jabbed into my back but I refused to show any pain to this bully.

"I don't need you to tell me about my life," he snarled. "Got it?"

"Yep," I squeaked.

"Don't you touch her!" Frankie threatened, struggling against the ropes.

Peyton ignored him and focused on me. "How are you going to make up for your big mistake?"

This guy might as well have been a wild grizzly bear holding a red-hot poker and threatening to skewer me for dinner. I had no idea what to say to him. If I were a real spy with any good instincts, words would have slipped out and cooled him off. I would've known what to say to reflect his accusation and get out of this.

The door to the storage room slammed shut.

Nine

MALCOLM. HIS HAIR WAS mussed and his cheeks were flushed like he'd run here. For what? To save me? Ha. More like to take his revenge.

"Leave her alone!" Malcolm rushed across the room and punched Peyton in the gut. The big man doubled over then two seconds later he rammed into Malcolm. I grabbed the screwdriver and jabbed Peyton in the arm. He backhanded me. Pain shot through my head, radiating out from my cheek. Two seconds later, Malcolm punched him in the face with a solid right hook.

Frankie shouted through his gag, "Untie me! What's going on?"

Peyton regained his footing and gasped at my reddening cheekbone. Horror filled his eyes but they hardened when he saw the screwdriver in my fist. "You should've stayed out of this."

Malcolm gripped the back of Peyton's neck and squeezed. Peyton dropped to the floor, writhing in agony.

"What's going on in here?" Dad kicked the crate out of his way and approached Peyton. Cards fluttered only to settle on the wooden floorboards. Awe for my dad grew. Yeah, he was tall and a bit of a spy geek, but right then the gel in his hair made him look tough, like a member of street gang.

Malcolm stepped back, and I sneaked a peek at him, trying to figure out why he came to my rescue after all that happened.

"Peyton?" My dad repeated.

As soon as the sorrow appeared in Peyton's eyes, it disappeared, replaced by a steely determination. "You don't understand. She ruined everything."

Not taking his eyes off Peyton, my dad grabbed him by the arm. "Leave. Now. We'll talk later about refunds."

Go, Dad!

Nancy and Gray both arrived, breathless and with flushed faces. Immediately, Gray strode over to Frankie and removed his gag and blindfold.

After a moment of tense silence, Peyton said, "Fine. You'll be hearing from me." With a grunt, he strode from the room.

Dad smoothed my ruffled shirt with a gentle touch and traced my cheek with the back of his fingers. "Are you okay?"

I nodded, all words trapped in my throat. Is this what it took for Dad to act like he cared? Muscles in his jaw twitched. Blood rushed to my face, and the room felt about a hundred degrees hotter. He cared but he was still mad.

Gray, Nancy, and Frankie tried not to look at me, shuffling their feet, fixing their hair. Malcolm picked up the cards scattered on the floor.

"Savvy," Dad said in a clear but firm voice, "why don't you take the rest of the afternoon off. Get some ice on your cheek. I'll see you at home."

His face turned into a mask, but the lines on his forehead seemed deeper. His shoulders slouched, and I could tell he blamed me. I grabbed my backpack, hiding the tears, and ran from the room. I didn't stop running until I got to *Les Pouffant's*.

"Where were you when I needed you," I whispered to the stone angels with curved wings that stood at the side of the doorway. Waiters dressed in black and white moved in and out of the café like they were in a choreographed dance. I loved this place.

Inside, I ordered a latte. The counter and the pastries behind the glass case became a blur. Maybe Dad would ship me off to boarding school. I highly doubted he'd believe today was my best effort. And if I was honest? It wasn't. When I had the latte in my hand and took the first sip, my mind cleared a bit. Aimee must have forgotten to meet me here. Time to go home. And open the package Mom told me to burn.

I trudged up to our door, and the back of my neck prickled. Something was off. The front door moved in the breeze. As the director of Spy Games, Dad was the guru of safety precautions. He locked the doors, changed the bulb for the porch light, and left a light on when we were gone. He would never leave the door unlocked, much less open!

I crept up the steps and nudged the door open with my foot. If I were a real spy, my heart wouldn't be knocking against my ribcage and sweat wouldn't be breaking out on my forehead. I'd burst into the room, pull out my gun, and the intruder would run for his life. A weapon! That was what I needed. I grabbed Dad's umbrella by the door and tiptoed across the room.

The couch pillows were on the floor, and Dad's papers on the kitchen table looked mussed. But I saw no overturned tables or fallen lamps like on television. Still, I couldn't breathe easy until I checked the rest of the apartment. For a few seconds, I stood with my arm above my head, umbrella poised, listening.

A noise came from the down the hall in my bedroom. Peyton's angry face flashed in my mind and my legs shook. What if he knew where we lived? With light steps, I headed down the narrow hallway. My bedroom door was open. A draft ruffled the ends of my hair.

I heard it again. A clicking sound.

Enough. I wasn't going to tiptoe around my own home. I eased open the umbrella and charged into the room with a war cry. I spun around to confuse any intruder. I stopped and swayed, a bit dizzy. The clicking noise was my open window. The shade moved back and forth in the breeze, hitting the windowsill and making a slight click each time. I let out a breath and closed the umbrella. The person was gone, but someone had definitely been here. I slumped onto my bed. What would someone want from us? My fuzzy socks? My measly piggy bank? Or maybe a package! I sprinted back to the front door.

There it was, the package I'd tripped over and then kicked behind the bush earlier today. I brought it inside. Mom had a strict rule. No one was allowed to touch her mail or go through her things. Again, at the Eiffel, she'd told me to burn this. But Mom wasn't here, was she? I ripped it open.

Inside, I found a clunky camera, like an old Polaroid, wrapped in tissue paper. But more importantly I found a note, typed, with no signature.

Sign up for the Pouffant Pastry Extravaganza.
Take a picture of Jolie Pouffant.

That was it. I mean, that was it? That didn't tell me anything about my mom, where she'd disappeared to, or why the only time she'd talked to me she wore a disguise. And it didn't tell me anything about who sent it, like where he or she lived or why the hell they needed a picture of Pouffant.

Tips of green stuck out so I dug under the layers of tissue paper protecting the camera. My fingers brushed against the clean feel of printed bills, lots of them. I started pulling them out, more and more, until green covered the table. More money than I'd ever need in my life, or maybe a year. Now that told me something.

Mom was into something big. Like maybe she worked as a secret photographer for an entertainment magazine doing an article on pastry chefs. Or maybe this Pouffant fellow wasn't just a pastry chef. Whatever it was, Mom didn't want me to know.

But in a situation like this, I had to follow the old rule: Follow the money. And if it wasn't a rule, I just made it one. And in order to follow the money, I'd need to sign up for the pastry thing. A.S.A.P. Good thing I knew where to find Pouffant.

The front door rattled, and I froze. Voices floated in from outside. Dad chuckled and talked, and I heard Frankie and Nancy and Gray. The whole Spy Games staff was outside my front door, and I had thousands of dollars spread out on the table.

I shoved handful after handful of money back into the package, grabbed the camera and the note, and sprinted back to my room.

The whole crew moved into the kitchen and shuffled chairs around for a staff meeting. Why here? Dad never brought them to our house. I didn't have a good feeling. I shoved everything into the back of my closet and waited to make my entrance. What would I say to everyone? "Oh hi everyone, yes, I'm the boss's daughter who pissed off a client today. And what is that? Why yes, I did get kicked out of the Louvre." Insert fake laughter. "Yes, I'll be packing for boarding school because my dad is kicking me out. Anything else you want to know?"

After procrastinating as long as I could and hoping the meeting was almost over, I entered the kitchen. The whole Spy Games staff was crammed into our kitchenette, sitting around the table drinking instant coffee.

"What's up?" I asked casually. Now I was terrified of not only getting fired but of getting shipped away somewhere as well.

"Glad you could join us, Savvy." Dad barely acknowledged me.

Maps of Paris covered the table. Dad posed a question to the group every few seconds. Gray took notes and punched numbers into a calculator. Hunched over the table, Frankie sipped the instant coffee. Nancy nodded, but her whole body drooped.

One person was missing, and I knew she'd never ditch a staff meeting. The job was too important.

"Where's Aimee?" I asked.

Frankie flashed me a bored look, and then went back to stirring another sugar packet into his coffee. Nancy looked at me with sympathetic eyes that said, "Oh, you poor thing." Like when your dad eats your last piece of Halloween candy.

Peyton's last threat echoed in my mind. He couldn't have gotten to her. Could he?

Ten

"DAD?" I TUCKED THE same piece of hair behind my ears over and over because it wouldn't stay in place. "Where's Aimee?"

The only evidence he'd heard me was the higher pitch of his voice and the way his fingers gripped the pencil. He whispered to Gray. Frankie's legs twitched like he wanted to bolt and avoid the confrontation.

Basically, Dad ignored me.

"Except for that one incident, we got mostly positive feedback." He glanced over his notes. "I'll be working on a new route. There are many terrific tourist sites in Paris. In no time at all, we'll have a new mission mapped out and ready to go."

I ducked my head in epic shame, biding my time as Dad closed. I tried not to think about Aimee. Maybe she had to run errands. Maybe she got the stomach bug. There were lots of perfectly good reasons for her absence.

"Thanks, everyone," Dad concluded. "Go home and relax. It's been a long day."

The staff gathered their stuff and filed out. Gray nodded to me. Nancy squeezed my shoulder, and Frankie winked at me.

"Good luck," he whispered.

Not a good sign. Maybe I'd gotten Aimee fired, too? That was why Nancy looked at me like I'd have to live with the guilt. I held the door and said goodbye, ignoring the increased pulse thrumming through my veins.

Finally, they were gone. Our apartment felt huge. Nowhere to hide. No cracks to slip into and disappear for a while, like a month or two. I decided to start first.

"I can explain. Just give me a chance."

"Savvy." Dad's voice sounded a bit impatient.

"No, really. I was doing great at the Louvre and then Malcolm messed up everything. He got me kicked out."

"Did you or did you not bring candy into the Louvre?"

I couldn't lie my way out of this one. "Kind of."

He tilted his head to the side.

"I didn't do it on purpose. And no one would've known if it hadn't been for Malcolm."

Dad sighed in exasperation. "Malcolm asked to observe Spy Games before officially applying for a job. I told him to shadow you!"

"What? Why didn't you tell me?" This would've changed everything.

"I tried. You ran out of the debriefing so fast I didn't have a chance. And then you must've had your phone turned off."

"Oh."

"We had a strict contract with the museum. We were only allowed to use it for Spy Games as long as we didn't cause any trouble."

I couldn't look him in the eyes. "And spilling candy constitutes trouble?"

"Unfortunately, yes. We've broken the contract."

Part of what drew customers was incorporating big tourist spots like the Louvre.

"I'll go back and explain," I said. "I'll apologize. I'll write them a letter. I'll get down on my knees and beg. I'll scrub their floors for a year."

The words tasted bitter on my tongue. The apology was only a habit. I always apologized, hoping to smooth over the tension in the house. Not that it ever worked.

"It won't matter." With a sigh, he closed the file folders spread on our kitchen table. After stuffing them into his leather briefcase, he stopped and studied me. "Are you that unhappy?"

"What?" And I thought I'd hid it so well.

He paused, and in that moment I could see the heartbreak written on his face. He missed Mom just as much as I did.

"Because I can't have you working for Spy Games if you can't take it seriously. I know you mock some of the clients. I know you slack off at times. I've overlooked a lot of it, but as my daughter, how you treat the job in front of the staff is a reflection on me."

Oh, the shame! How do parents know everything? He must have planted bugs in the rafters, in my bedroom, in the kitchen; or slipped trackers in my shoes. I shriveled up and wanted to crawl away and hide in a sandbank.

Dad moved to the brown leather loveseat. He motioned for me to sit down, but the stubborn side of me refused. He rubbed his temples. "It's about Aimee."

I stepped back. "No way. You can't do this. The Louvre wasn't her fault. It was mine. You can't fire her too. Please! She takes care of her grandmother and counts on this job."

"Savvy!" Dad's voice was sharp, and I stopped babbling. "Aimee isn't fired, and neither are you."

I plopped on the couch even though a part of me wanted to run away. "Where is she?"

Dad pulled out a letter and handed it to me. "I found this taped to the door."

I held the paper. My hand shook a little bit as I quickly read it. The note was from Aimee, and it said something about taking some time off to backpack across Eastern Europe. It said how sorry she was for the short notice, and that she'd be in touch when she got back. The words blurred on the page, not making any sense.

As if Dad sensed my doubt, he said, "Hasn't she always wanted to travel?"

"Yeah." I read over it again, but I didn't believe it. Not for one second. "Don't you think it's odd that she didn't give it to you in person? Or talk to you about it? Or talk to me?"

"A little. But it was probably awkward for her."

"What about her grandmother?" I reminded him.

This isn't over. Peyton's words pounded in my brain and spread into my heart like poison.

"Aimee is very responsible," I continued. "She'd never leave without making alternate arrangements."

This isn't over.

"What about Peyton?"

Dad waved his hand. "I don't think he's any trouble. He was letting off some steam. I'll give him a refund, he'll pack his bags, and he'll head back to the States."

"But he threatened us earlier." I bit my lip and flashed back to the scene in the Eiffel. Yes, I made mistakes, but he overreacted. Then it hit me. Maybe he'd found her following him and after extracting the hostage site from her, he took her hostage? I stifled a gasp.

I'd failed Dad today but this was my chance to make up for everything. We could work on finding Aimee together. We'd be spies. Real spies. He'd love it. He'd always wanted me to get into the whole spy thing. We could work together on a mission, and he'd be so happy. Hope bubbled up in my chest.

"Dad, I have a strong feeling she did not go backpacking. You've always said to follow our instincts. We could work—"

He zipped his briefcase. "I admit her leaving is a bit strange. But instinct is different than an overactive imagination. You're too close to this to see properly."

His words cut through my excitement like a knife through the last piece of birthday cake. Why wouldn't he believe me? Dad had done everything possible to get me excited about Spy Games, from the box of spy gadgets to the spy hat. And when I gave him the chance to work on a real mission with me, he shrugged it off as an overactive imagination?

"Did you put ice on your cheek?" His stress level was rising. I could tell by the multiplied number of lines on his forehead.

"Yeah, sure." I traced circles on the arm of the couch.

Dad rubbed the scruff on his jaw. He stood up from the couch, looking like he'd aged about twenty years. His shoulders were hunched over. He started to say something, then stopped. Then he finally spoke.

"I'm going back to the office to work on the new route."

And then I was alone. And felt it. Aimee was the first person hired on staff and we were friends from our first shared latte and triple-layer cake. But it felt like someone had taken a fork to our sweet glaze and smashed it into crumbs. We'd dreamed so much together. I couldn't believe she'd just take off. She'd at least call.

My arm jerked with the revelation. I ran over to the front door and dug out my phone from my jacket pocket. After sending her a text, I went back to the couch, rehearsing in my mind all the conversations I'd had with Aimee over the past weeks. I didn't remember any mention of a trip. Nothing made sense. A year ago I would've agreed with Dad and squashed any doubts. But this wasn't about me. It was about Aimee. I'd follow through with the Extravaganza and do a little investigating at the same time. By myself. Without Dad.

No turning back.

Monday morning came, and I woke with a major Spy Games hangover. I rolled out of bed and searched for a tee to throw on over my cammie. Coffee. I needed a shot of caffeine.

Hopefully after a cup, my head would clear and I would accept that my crazy suspicion Peyton had done away with Aimee was just a crazy suspicion. I wanted to be wrong. I wanted the letter to be a prank. I wanted Aimee to meet me for a latte this morning as usual. And I needed to find out about this pastry Extravaganza thing.

With my fingers running along the wall, I stumbled down the narrow hallway and into the kitchen. I smelled the coffee. Hazelnut. It must be Dad's way of making me feel better, but I'd rather him write a note or do the dishes because his coffee tastes like dishwater. My eyes were beginning to clear, and I noticed the shape of a blue coffee mug sitting on the counter. I leaned against the kitchen counter and rubbed my eyes. The blurry reflection in the toaster of a dark shape caught my attention.

What the hell?

I studied the reflection but it was too blurry. It wasn't my dad. Could it be Peyton?

I might have a hard time waking up in the morning, but there's nothing like an intruder to get the mojo flowing. I inched my hand toward a drawer and wished like hell I were wearing one of those sleepers with the feet instead of a T-shirt with my pink panties showing.

After a pretend stretch, I pulled out a butter knife from the drawer and flipped around.

Eleven

MALCOLM.

Relief flooded my limbs. I remembered how mad I was at him and how mad he might be at me, so I held the knife up and ready. We didn't exactly leave on the best of terms, and yesterday I made it worse because I had no clue he was shadowing me.

Malcolm sat relaxed in Dad's kitchen chair, legs crossed, fingers tapping away on his laptop, eyes glued to the screen. Like he was alone in his bedroom or something.

"Hey! What are you doing here?" I waved the knife. I'm known to be pretty loquacious but I couldn't quite find the right words to express my shock. Normally, I loved when Dad left early for work. Today, I wished he were about to stumble from his bedroom.

Malcolm smiled, his eyes glued to the screen. "Where else would I be?"

Oh crap. He wanted revenge. I tugged on my T-shirt, trying to stretch it past my knees.

He jotted notes on a small notepad on the table beside his laptop. "If you have a flash, I can download any documents."

What was he talking about? The whole shadow-me-for-a-day thing was over. What kind of revenge would an angry but still-cute waiter want? I had to get him out of our apartment. "My gosh, will you look already!"

His gaze flicked up and locked on the knife. He snorted and moved his laptop as if it were a shield.

I slashed the knife through the air like I was a sheik from Arabia. "Maybe you didn't get the clue the other night that I'm not interested in you."

He closed his laptop. "Hope the coffee is right. I know you like it strong."

My hand wavered and so did my confidence. I mimicked his casual approach. "I can't argue that you didn't take time to get to know me before our date."

He smiled. "As a waiter, I notice these things."

"Right." What else had he noticed? I was determined not to show that his surprise visit had me rattled. Why had Dad let him in? He sipped his coffee, his eyes still on mine. I tried to zap some common sense into my brain while staying in control of the conversation, but I fell silent and rested my hand with the knife on the counter. Thoughts of Aimee were constantly with me, hovering in the back of my mind.

"What's wrong?" he asked.

His cocky self-assuredness was gone and in its place was genuine concern. For me.

I managed to swallow. "Just waiting to hear back from a friend."

He took his mug over to the sink and rinsed it out like he'd been living here for a year, then he rubbed his hands together. "Anything I can do to help?"

"Not really. Unless you have a crystal ball or a magic wand."

"Sorry." Malcolm shrugged. "Where do we go from here?"

"*We* are not going anywhere."

I wouldn't consider me almost getting him killed the start of an epic romance. The silence grew heavy with expectation as I struggled to find the right words. Maybe if I apologized he'd forget about the whole underwear thing. I was sure he was trying to lure me in for some sort of big revenge.

"Hope you don't mind spending a lot of time with me," he said with mischief in his smile.

I remembered the kiss. Again. His soft lips. But I don't date anyone based on a kiss. Okay, screw that. A hot kiss totally makes me want a second date. It was what happened after the kiss that ruined everything. Who was he to waltz into my kitchen at this time in the morning? Why did he keep acting like we worked together?

"Why are you here?" I asked.

His eyes widened and understanding flashed across his face. I waved the knife in the air to show I meant what I said. I mean, I really didn't know anything about this guy.

He stood and took a step closer. "The note explains everything."

Trust in my knowledge of the situation disappeared.

"I thought you knew I was here." He glanced at his watch. "It's almost ten o'clock."

"Oh." How could I have slept that long? And with Aimee missing?

He smiled and glanced down at my lack of clothing. "That explains the outfit."

"You think I entertain all guests this way?"

He smirked and opened his mouth to speak, but I cut him off. "Don't answer that."

His face grew serious. "Your dad was supposed to leave you a note."

"I'm sure you noticed by the way I stumbled into the kitchen I'm not in the habit of looking for notes by my bed."

He raised his hands as if to show his innocence while closing the gap between us. My hand shook.

"I met with your dad this morning. One of his employees left suddenly and he needed a quick replacement. I wanted an exciting job for some extra cash. It sounded perfect."

He might as well have taken the knife and plunged it into my heart. A replacement for Aimee already?

"Don't sign any contracts yet," I said. "Because we still don't have confirmation she really left. Hate to disappoint you."

"Already signed on the dotted line. I start training today. With you. Mornings only because most afternoons I still have to work at *Les Pouffant's*." He took the final step and grabbed my wrist. With his other hand, he gently eased the knife from my grasp and laid it on the table. "Sorry about your friend."

I tried to pull away, my hopes crashing. How could my dad sign someone so soon? He didn't even wait a day.

Malcolm pulled me closer, his fingers loosening their grip. My eyes lingered on the tiny flecks of charcoal in his eyes, the faint blush to his cheeks, and the way his hair fell just below his eyebrows. Okay, working with him might not be that bad.

"I could really use your help with this whole spy thing. Please?"

Damn. He was good.

Twelve

I FOUND THE NOTE confirming Malcolm's story. Fine. I'd train him but I'd look for Aimee too. The first stop would be *Les Pouffant's* to sign up for that Extravaganza thing. Even though she'd never texted back, I clung to the small shred of hope she'd be waiting for me with the sun sparkling off her hair, smiling and waving.

At the café, Malcolm and I hovered at the edge of the outdoor patio. I searched the flow of customers but Aimee was nowhere to be seen. Malcolm babbled on about espionage in a newbie sort-of excited way, something about night vision goggles.

I placed my hand on his arm to shut him up. "I'm going to check inside. You keep watch. I'll be right back."

I walked into *Les Pouffant's* and strode over to the glass case. No one noticed me because some woman was crying and babbling in French into the arms of Pouffant himself. He snapped his fingers and the *maitre d'* scurried over with a steaming cup of cocoa. Watching him listen and care for her made me feel a bit empty. I missed my friends and my mom.

The official Extravaganza sign-up was taped to the front counter. Prize money would be offered to the contestant who made it to the finals a month from now. The preliminaries were in less than two weeks. Mom's words came back to me about meeting at some pastry thing. This Extravaganza was it.

I signed up then hurried back outside.

Malcolm was leaning against a lamppost with his legs crossed, so casual and relaxed. He held a cup of coffee in his hands. "Is this part of the Spy Games route? You and your friend came here often enough."

I took up guard next to him, my eyes glued on the moving faces. "It's not part of the route, but we started every morning here." I felt like a robot, shooting out the answer to his question without any thought. Muscles in my arms and legs tensed, willing Aimee to appear. Strangers weaved through the tables, and I wanted to scream at them to move out of the way. I couldn't leave until I was absolutely sure.

"How do you start a typical work day? After coffee and croissants, that is."

"We meet at the warehouse, my dad introduces the mission, the staff does a bit of training. Blah, blah, blah." I couldn't stop glancing at the table where Aimee and I usually sat, hoping she'd appear. Just yesterday morning, before the start of the games, I'd told her about my date with Malcolm. Maybe I'd been so busy talking about myself, I'd never given her a chance to talk. Maybe she couldn't break through my blabber to tell me she was leaving.

"You want to talk about it?" Malcolm interrupted my thoughts.

"Right, the debriefing. Wear long johns because it gets kinda chilly hanging from the rafters. Don't forget gloves for the bat poop."

"I meant talk about whatever it is you're worried about." His head tilted to the side and it was like every fiber of his being was focused on me.

"I was thinking about Aimee."

"The friend you meet here?"

I nodded. "The one who supposedly quit the games to travel the world."

"But you don't believe that." He blew on his coffee, meeting my eyes over the rim of his cup.

"Not really." I longed to hold a latte, feel the warmth on my hands, a simple distraction. But I probably wouldn't enjoy another one until I found Aimee.

"Sometimes people make impulsive decisions. Ones they might regret later." Malcolm emphasized the word regret and didn't take his eyes off me.

Inch by inch, the slow burn of embarrassment crept across my neck and face. By the tiny quirk of his lips and the glimmer of mischief in his eyes, I knew he was referring to me. Time to get this out in the open. "Yeah, um, sorry about the other night and you almost getting killed. That usually doesn't happen on my first dates. And thanks for helping me out with Peyton."

Malcolm pressed his lips together and paused, as if to stretch out my ultimate humiliation. "Apology accepted. I just wish the kiss had lasted longer."

My face turned the color of a crimson sunset, or that was what it felt like. I tripped over my words, until I managed to ask the question burning on my mind. "How'd you get home?"

"I can't tell you all my secrets." He leaned into me and whispered, "But I am known to like a bit of revenge."

As soon as he said that, he pulled back. Was he flirting? I couldn't tell, so I changed the subject. "Enough." I wanted to pin him to the floor and hold a butter knife to his neck until he took our problems, my problems, seriously.

He tipped his head back for the last drops from his cup.

I grabbed a small metal serving tray off a table and hit him in the stomach with it. "Let's go."

I started to walk away, but Malcolm didn't move. The tray was in his hand.

"Well?" I asked. "Slide it up your shirt for protection."

"Er, right."

I straightened my back and tucked my hair behind my ears. "As your official Spy Games mentor, I'm responsible for your safety. Now it's time to get started."

Malcolm grabbed his backpack. "I'm ready for anything, boss."

Our eyes locked, and I tried to see past his charcoal-flecked ones to find the truth. Did he kinda like me? Or was this some big game to him? Why was I even thinking about that when my best friend was missing?

I whispered, "There's one exception to the rule."

"What's that?"

"Always listen to your gut."

My gut still didn't have a read on Malcolm's feelings for me, but it was definitely telling me that Aimee didn't leave on a fun holiday to Eastern Europe.

I shook it off, stepped back, and grabbed my bag filled with spy gadgets. "Let's go."

Thirteen

MALCOLM WHISPERED IN MY EAR. "Does some super-secret evil villain live here?"

I elbowed him in the gut. "Somehow rose trellises and flower boxes don't say evil to me." I loved the old-time feel of Aimee's family's cottage, the paint chipping off the sides and the old stone chimney and crumbling walkway. I was a bit jealous of the stability of living in the same place for so long.

"I'm trying to figure out how this is training," Malcolm complained.

I approached the door, trying to ignore the guilt of not following Dad's instructions, but then I remembered how he blew off my conspiracy theory on Aimee. Someone had to find her.

Over my shoulder, I said, "You're shadowing me, following the lifestyle of a Spy Games staffer. Deal."

Before I could knock, a shrill voice yelled at us in French. Aimee's grandmother, Marie, stormed across the neighbor's tiny yard.

"What's she saying?" I whispered.

Malcolm raised his eyebrows. "She's basically telling us to scram. Who is she?"

I looked at Marie and stared back at the cottage in front of me. "I've got the right place."

Malcolm muttered, "She's on the attack."

Marie stopped in front of us. Her wispy white hair was held up by bobby pins and she wore a faded, flowered smock that looked like a relic. She scolded us. In French.

"Marie?" I coughed and spoke louder. "It's Savvy. Aimee's friend?"

A look of understanding and a bit of apprehension crossed her face. She switched to English and pasted on a smile.

"What was I thinking? I did not recognize you. It has been far too long." She held out her arms and gathered me into a hug and kissed both my cheeks. "*Bonjour*, Aimee's young friend."

That was what I loved about Aimee and her *grand-mere*. They both spoke English. In fact, that was probably why Aimee and I were friends—because she could talk to me.

"I keep asking Aimee when you are going to visit again."
She released me and noticed Malcolm. "Who is this? A special
man in your life?" She kissed both his cheeks. "Marie."

"Malcolm." He didn't hesitate for a second when Marie
enveloped him in a hug too.

She opened the door and entered the cottage with a
wave of her hand. "I was visiting next door. You must come
inside for some tea. A bit of young love is just what I need."

"Yeah, about that." If I didn't straighten out the story,
she'd have us married before we left.

Malcolm put his arm around me and squeezed. "I was
lucky to find such a gem." He leaned over and planted one on
me.

He slowly let me go, and I had trouble finding my breath.
I didn't know whether to belt him one or throw him to the
ground and kiss him back.

Marie clapped. "How wonderful. It is your lucky day. I
made gingerbread cookies and the kettle is on. I keep telling
Aimee she needs to find a good man and settle down. Maybe
you can talk sense to her."

We followed Marie into a tiny sitting room off the
kitchen. Herbs growing in pots on a windowsill scented the
air, and a giant fern filled most of the room. Tiny chairs
surrounded an equally tiny glass table the size of a
checkerboard.

"Looks great," I said. "I like the new furniture."

"*Merci*. Take a seat and help yourself. I will be right back."

As soon as she left, I kicked Malcolm in the shins. "What were you thinking?"

He rubbed his shin. "I couldn't disappoint an old woman. She probably lost her husband in a war long ago. Would it kill you to make her day?"

"Unfortunately," I said while giving him my darkest look, "we aren't exactly coming with the happiest of news."

He reached for a cookie. "All the better to brighten her day with our *young love*."

"Fine, but let me steer this conversation. Consider this part of your training in role playing and how to question a subject."

Marie cut our conversation short when she entered with a kettle and poured us tea. Her hand shook, and I worried she would drop it.

Malcolm stood. "Let me do that for you."

Marie smiled and crinkled her face up with tiny lines. She winked at me. "And a gentleman, too."

I distracted myself with a tiny thread unraveling from the cloth napkin. The more I got to know Malcolm, the more I liked him.

When the tea was poured, and the cream and sugar added, Marie settled into her chair. "To what do I owe the pleasure of your visit?"

Malcolm leaned back with a cookie, an amused look on his face.

I licked my dry lips. How exactly do I tell a grandmother that her only living relative is missing? "We were in the neighborhood and thought we'd drop by for a visit. Is Aimee here?"

Marie lowered her eyebrows. "Aimee should be at work. Is everything okay?"

Malcolm kicked me under the table as if to say "good one."

"Um, my dad gave certain staff the day off to rest."

Marie put her teacup down. "I hope he's not thinking of letting her go, because we really depend on her earnings."

"No, no, nothing like that. Aimee is a valued part of the team."

A light sweat broke out on my forehead, and I could feel a nervous rash spread across my neck. I decided on a more direct approach. "Did Aimee tell you where she was headed today?"

"I have not seen Aimee since she left for work yesterday morning."

Fear bloomed in my chest, pressing against my lungs, making it hard to breathe. It was hard to laugh and act like nothing was the matter.

She clasped her hands in her lap. "Should I be worried?"

I waved my hand and laughed, probably a little too loud to be convincing. "No, not at all. She slept at my place last night and um, er, left early this morning. She borrowed a sweater of mine last week. Do you think I could take a look in her room?"

If Aimee was on any kind of innocent trip, her grandmother would know about it.

"Sure, dear. You remember. First room on the right."

I excused myself from the table, needing to be alone.

"Do you need help, sweetie?" Malcolm asked.

I mustered the most sugary voice I could. "I've got it, pumpkin. Be right back."

I was at the stairs when I heard Marie encourage Malcolm to go with me. She needed to clean up in the kitchen, and even though she wasn't young, she wasn't that behind the times either. I begged to differ with the flowered apron.

I took the stairs two at a time. In the doorway, I looked over the room before poking around.

With a warm hand on my waist, which I tried to ignore, Malcolm said, "Good one down there. You almost sent her to an early grave. Was I supposed to learn from that?"

"No one's perfect." I kept my eyes on the room. It looked different and I wasn't sure why. I couldn't remember if the pink and green flowered wallpaper, cracked and peeling in places, was the same or not.

"What's our next lesson, boss?" His breath tickled my ear. Shivers rippled down my spine. In a good way.

I promptly moved into the room, desperate to find proof she *was* on vacation. I strode over to her jewelry box. Most of it was gone except for a necklace. I picked it up and let the beads poke into my skin before letting them slide from my fingers. I threw open the doors to her closet to find half of her clothes gone. Except for a pair of hiking boots. She'd never leave without her hiking boots.

Malcolm fussed around in the room behind me. "No ticket reservations or books on Europe or hotel reservations. You might be right."

The reality that my best friend was most likely kidnapped hit me in the gut. I slumped to the floor and leaned against her dresser.

Malcolm sat next to me. "I'm sorry."

He rubbed my shoulders, easing out the tension, then he wrapped his arms around me. Slow-burning warmth spread through my chest. I enjoyed the comfort of his body close to mine a little too much, but did he think I was going to break down and cry or something? Hardly. I whipped out my cell and sent an email to my home computer, reminding myself to check up on Marie next week. Until Aimee returned, or I'd rescued her, I'd make sure Marie was okay.

I shook off the temptation to call Dad with proof that Aimee could indeed be missing. He'd already screwed up his chance to work with me, and he'd probably find some way to trivialize my evidence and point out all my overreactions.

"What now?" Malcolm asked.

We stood as I answered. "When we make a mistake, we do everything in our power to fix it."

"Mistake?"

"If Aimee was kidnapped, it's my fault, and I'm going to find out what happened."

I was ninety nine percent sure I knew who'd done it.

Fourteen

THE NEXT MORNING, I whipped off the covers as soon as Dad left. I changed into my favorite spy jeans, the ones with the stylish rips right above the knee, and a grey long-sleeved shirt. I had a mission. I was ready to spy—I mean train a spy.

After waiting a few minutes to make sure Dad wasn't coming back, I opened the door and searched our non-existent yard. Malcolm stepped out from behind the hedge.

I cracked up. He wore black jeans, a black shirt, and a black ski hat pulled over his dark hair. He also carried a small black backpack.

"What?" He pulled an innocent baby face quite effectively.

"Are you trying to get arrested for robbing a bank?"

"You said to wear spy clothes."

"Yes, I did." I motioned him inside. "We don't have much time. My dad will take like an hour running, and I want to be gone before he gets back."

"I have a few essentials like candy bars in case we get stuck or trapped." He stepped inside, and I realized why spies dress like that in the movies. Because it's totally hot. Dang, he looked good in black.

"What now?" he asked.

"Right." I shook it off. "Follow me." I headed back to Dad's office/bedroom, which he leaves unlocked. I strode across the room to his private filing cabinet.

"No coffee this morning? Or perhaps a stroll to the patisserie?"

I scowled at him and pulled a paper clip from my pocket. Then I proceeded to untwist it. "Lesson for the day. How to pick a lock."

Malcolm glanced back at the door. "But this is your dad's office."

"Yeah, so?"

"Why are you spying on your dad?"

I'd like to say my dad is a high-profile spy and this is where he hides the world's best-kept secret. But I'd be lying. "Client files."

On my knees, I wiggled the end of the paper clip into the small keyhole of the bottom drawer. Malcolm crouched close by. Sweat broke out on my forehead when I didn't hear the click. After several minutes of jiggling, I handed it to him.

"Okay, I showed you how to do it. Now it's your turn."

"I don't feel right about this."

"This is the only way to find Aimee. Trust me."

Malcolm leaned over and jiggled the paper clip in the lock. He bit his lower lip and stared at it. After a few minutes, I heard a click and the drawer opened.

"Okay, move over. Keep watch out the window for my dad."

I flipped through the files and found *P* quickly. Peyton's file was the first one. I opened it and scanned it, my heart in my throat. I'd never realized how many personal questions Dad asks. Maybe to tailor the games to the clients' needs? I wasn't sure. But Peyton hadn't filled out any of the questions about his life, his family, or his job. Maybe he'd gotten fired or divorced. Even so, a crappy life wasn't a ticket to Jerksville.

"Your dad!"

"Impossible!" I crushed the file on Peyton in my grip. "He could only have gotten in a few miles."

"Maybe he cut it short. But he's across the street and he's booking it."

"Crap." I grabbed a pen from the desk and scribbled the address on my hand.

The door opened and slammed. His footsteps pounded in the hallway. The phone rang.

"Double crap. Under the bed." I gently closed the file drawer and then dove under the open futon where Dad slept. "Hurry up," I whispered.

Malcolm crawled in behind me, and seconds before Dad walked in, I yanked his comforter farther off the bed to hide us.

Dad answered his phone a little breathless. He must have had a teleconference and forgotten. Just my luck. If he found us, not only would Malcolm be fired, but Dad would never trust me again.

As he chatted, I became very aware of the wannabe spy lying behind me. His breath hit the back of my neck, causing me to shiver.

"Admit it," he whispered. "You couldn't unlock the filing cabinet."

"It was part of your training."

Dad stopped talking for a second and I didn't dare say anything else. I prayed he wouldn't need to get into his client files. I'd put myself in a dangerous position, but it was all for Aimee.

"I was hoping we'd have a bit more time to pay off those loans," Dad said. "The business has only been running for a few months."

Malcolm faded into the background.

Dad's voice grew tense, like when he'd argue with Mom. "Most small businesses need at least five to ten years to pay off. I need more time."

Strand by strand, I pulled microfibers from the rug. Money trouble?

"Yes, I understand the economy is hard. I'll have the first payment by the end of the month."

Spy Games was popular and doing well, wasn't it? This was Mom's apartment, but I never knew we lived here because we couldn't afford anything else. I gulped. What about all the money I wasted on pastries and lattes? Malcolm seemed to sense this and placed his hand on my arm. I remembered the Extravaganza I entered. Something on the advertisement mentioned prize money. I thought about Mom's money stashed in the closet. Maybe I could truly help out, instead of screwing everything up.

Malcolm found my hand and entwined his fingers with mine. I closed my eyes and listened to Dad's words. "I'll find the money somehow. I can sell off some assets."

Assets? Like our house in Pennsylvania? I blocked out the rest of the conversation. Instead, I focused on the softness of Malcolm's hand and the warmth of his body, wishing I could snuggle into him. I hoped the penned address on my hand wasn't getting smudged, because finding Peyton was next on my list.

An hour later, we were crouched in the prickly bushes outside Peyton's rented apartment. The tall brick buildings were built for tourists and quick money. Not exactly high class, but it was still in Paris.

Malcolm focused on the front of the building. "Do you think Aimee could be here?"

"I doubt it, but at some point she probably was." My voice caught, betraying the state of my nerves. I wasn't exactly a pro at breaking the law. "You saw how psycho Peyton was yesterday. When you, um, saved me."

"Was he mad at Aimee too?"

I stayed quiet when a young family burst from the front door in a babble of excitement, ready for a day of exploring. A young couple entered the building, then I whispered, "He was mad at both of us, but it was mostly my fault."

"Are we going to scale the wall and break in through a window?" Malcolm broke a twig in half that was sticking into his back. "Because sitting in this bush kinda sucks."

"We're not superheroes." I yanked the ski cap off his head and threw it behind the bushes. "Watch and learn." I waltzed up the front walk and right through the door. I took the stairs to the third floor, with Malcolm at my heels.

"There are two different ways to enter a room when we're not sure what we'll find," I whispered. "There's the 'button hook,' which is just bursting into the room. We're going to 'slice the pie.' Normally, we'd need three people for this. One, to keep an eye on the hall, one to open the door, and one to peek in and look for any danger."

Malcolm pursed his lips to the side and took a step back. "But we have only two."

"I'll open the door, and you peek in. I don't think we're in too much trouble in this apartment building."

"What if he's in the room?"

"It's prime tourist-time. He's probably out soaking in more of the Eiffel before leaving for home."

I couldn't help but feel a twinge of guilt. It quickly disappeared when I thought about Aimee, possibly tied up and stuffed in a closet. On tiptoes, I approached #307 and pressed my ear to the door. Silence. Good for us, but possibly terrible for Aimee. From my backpack, I pulled out a flat-sided hairpin and poked one end into the lock. My hands shook as I wiggled it. I poked it into the hole, and I prayed.

After a few minutes of intense humiliation, the lock clicked. Malcolm turned the knob and opened the door a crack. I stuffed the hairpin in my back pocket, relieved. I held up fingers, counting to three. Each breath sounded like a freight train in my ears. Breaking and entering went against every moral fiber in my being. Okay, peeking at Dad's files didn't count.

I gently kicked open the door. This was for Aimee.

Fifteen

MALCOLM PEEKED IN FROM the side. He gave a thumbs up, and we entered. A tiny kitchen with a table for two opened into a living room with a plaid couch and a matching chair. I smelled bacon. My heartbeat felt like gunshots going off in my chest.

"You check the kitchen. I'll find the bedroom. Look for anything that might be a clue—tickets, receipts, maps, anything."

I ran down a hallway that branched off the living room and went back to the bedroom. I whipped open the closet door. Nothing. It was a long shot and would've been way too easy. Not knowing how much time we had, I opened drawers, looked in suitcases and searched under the pillow and bed.

Cliff Peyton was kinda boring. On his nightstand was a Breathe-Right nose strip, a detailed map of Paris, and Sydney Sheldon's *If Tomorrow Comes*. Nothing too suspicious. In the nightstand drawer was a tin of breath mints and tickets for the Eiffel tower.

"I might've found something." Malcolm stood in the doorway, a coil of rope dangling from his hands.

"That's not good." I dropped onto the bed.

A rope? Maybe he had already used some of it on Aimee. I hadn't planned on taking extreme invasive measures unless I found something suspicious, and I had. Or Malcolm had. He sat next to me on the bed, which sagged and pushed us together. The mattress was probably from the 1800s.

"This isn't a Clue game," I said. "That could be for anything."

I zipped opened my backpack and reached inside. "We'll know for sure in a couple days."

Amazement spread across his face and he glanced at the door. "Are those—"

"Trackers? Why, yes, they are. Fancy you should ask." I dropped three black button-like trackers into his hand. "Add them to his clothes. I'll put them in his shoes." I sounded way more 007 than I felt.

"How?"

"Don't you ever watch the movies? Rip open the seam a tiny bit and shove it in. He'll never know."

"Where did you get these?" He ran his finger over them. "Isn't this illegal?"

I pulled out a pair of sneakers from the tiny closet. "It might be, but I have strong probable cause. Get to work."

For the next ten minutes, we worked in silence. The quiet built up in my head, warning and whispering that I could get caught any second, and my shaky fingers made it that much harder to finish my task. Finally, I shoved the last one into a tiny crack in the sole of his sneaker.

"Let's get out of here," I urged.

We rushed to the door and opened it to find ourselves face to face with Peyton.

Damn.

In a matter of seconds, he went from eyes-wide-open shock to jaw-clenching furious and back again. His eyes darted between Malcolm and me, and he backed up a few steps.

My heart shot into my throat and pulsed, sending tiny sparks of fear into my body, from the sweat on my scalp to the itch in my toes that told me to run like hell. Could we go to jail for this?

Malcolm gripped my arm and held me back. "Breathe," he whispered. "I'll take care of this."

"No way," I muttered and took a few steps back, dragging him with me to give Peyton space. I had to show him we weren't the bad guys. "Hey, how you doing?"

He stood still, his fingers twitching at his sides. "What the hell are you doing in my room?"

"We thought we'd stop by and chat and noticed the door was open." I said it as casually and friendly as I could.

"And you decided just to let yourselves in? Is this how they do things in Paris?"

Malcolm muttered, "I can tell you've got this."

I didn't bother to give him a dirty look. "Remember me? From Spy Games? The Eiffel Tower?"

Complete annoyance settled in his eyes. "How could I forget?"

"I guess we got off on the wrong foot."

All the meaningless words from Peyton's file flashed in my memory. Nothing that would help me.

"That's one way to look at it." He stepped closer. "You ruined everything!"

Malcolm moved in front of me. "Why don't we talk about this? Peyton, right?"

It was tempting to hide behind Malcolm and let him smooth things over with his charm and good looks, but I refused to play the coward. I pushed him back.

"I did not ruin anything," I argued.

Peyton snorted like he didn't believe a word I said. My fingers curled into a ball, and I remembered the look on his face, his out of control behavior.

"I don't have to explain anything to you. Not my actions, not my words. Not when you are completely psycho!"

"Good one." Malcolm grabbed my arm and rushed toward the door.

"What's your problem?" Peyton asked.

I whipped away from Malcolm's grasp. "A Spy Games staff member is gone." I pointed a finger at him. "After you threatened us."

Color crept up his neck and across his face. "You think I had something to do with your friend's disappearance?"

"I know you do." I followed Malcolm's lead. "I came to check out your place for any clues."

"That's crazy." He pulled out his phone from his pocket and started stabbing at numbers.

I didn't stay for coffee, and ran out the door. Malcolm followed.

"That's right, coward. Run! Because soon the police will be after you. Enjoy your last days of freedom!"

I slammed the door as something crashed against the other side of it. Probably a vase or lamp.

"Let's go," I said. "This is how to leave a scene when you've been compromised."

We booked it out the front door, Peyton's words ringing in my ears. The police?

Sixteen

AFTER RUNNING SEVERAL BLOCKS, I finally slowed down. My lungs burned. Malcolm started to talk but I cut him off. "I don't want to talk about it."

He nodded, any hint of a smile disappearing.

I turned down one street and then the other with no direction in my mind. Aimee and I often roamed Paris, talking until we found a spot we liked. But she wasn't here. And by tonight I might be in jail.

Malcolm kept his eyes trained forward as if he were obsessed with the large red rose on the lady's hat ahead of us. I'd pissed him off, but I didn't care. It was better he knew the real me—the sweet, the silly, and the crab. For the umpteenth time that day I had to fight the urge to pull out my phone and text Aimee.

Malcolm quickened his stride. "We completed our mission. Hopefully, Peyton will lead us right to Aimee."

"Yep," I said.

I remembered the time Aimee and I'd wondered how many cafés we could visit in one day and still get our work done. We'd sampled about every croissant, tart, and scone in Paris. Then we'd spent the next week eating nothing but celery to lose the extra weight.

"What's the next plan of action if Peyton ends up a dead end?" Malcolm asked.

He pointed to a cute café with a blue-striped canopy, signaling us to stop. I shook my head and kept walking. That day with Aimee, we'd forgotten which shops we'd visited, and when we tallied our list at the end of the day, we'd had five repeats.

Malcolm spoke louder. "Because we still can't be one hundred percent sure that Peyton is our man."

I glared at him. "Thanks for the professional analysis."

I kept walking, leaving him with the sting of my words. Why did I feel like such a crab, pincers and all? Pretty soon, a dirty grey shell would start growing over my back and antennae would sprout.

"If Peyton is our man, will we go to your dad or the French authorities? It's not like Peyton is French. The French police might just laugh in our faces."

"Probably," I answered.

Malcolm's frustration was increasing, and right when I was listing in my head the different punishments the French could throw at me for breaking and entering, he gripped my arm and pushed me up against the glass front of a cute but super-expensive boutique just for hats.

His flushed face was close to mine. "You're supposed to be training me for the next Spy Games, but instead you're walking aimlessly around Paris."

His lips tightened and a muscle twitched in his jaw. He was millimeters from my face. All I had to do was pucker up, and we'd be smooching like French lovers. He could grow a twirly mustache and wear a beret, and I could whisper *Je t'aime* and forget about all of this.

"You're the trainer. What's the lesson here?" he asked.

He needed an answer. I could've told him that to live the life of a spy, you had to deal with people's idiosyncrasies, with wandering the streets and missing the people you loved like moms and best friends. I blinked away my tears and hardened my face. My words came out as a whisper as my throat closed up.

"After especially hard or draining missions, it's important to relax and refuel."

He didn't move back, and we stood there face-to-face, lips almost touching, both of us breathing a bit abnormally. The crowds of people passed us by. The bell above the boutique door jingled. A baby cried. A slight breeze stole between us. Thoughts of Peyton and prison time faded, and I curled his hair around my finger.

"You know, you're awfully cute when you're ticked off," I said.

Malcolm tilted his head, and his face softened as if suddenly he understood the female brain. He traced his thumb across my lips.

"And you, Savvy Bent, are sexy when trying to act like you don't give a damn."

With both hands on his chest, I pushed him away and broke the spell. I didn't want to feel that close to someone who would just leave me later.

"Don't you have to go to work?" I asked.

He smiled a warm and cocky grin. "Why yes, I do." Then he leaned in and whispered, "someday you'll have to admit you like me," before he turned and walked away.

"I'll text you about our next training," I yelled.

"Whatever." He didn't look back.

Two days later, I woke up a total grump. I wasn't even close to finding a creative pastry recipe for the Extravaganza. Peyton's trackers showed nothing unusual, and I had no clue what to do next. I stayed in my flannel nightgown, which I'd dug out of the bottom of my dresser after walking in on

Malcolm in my kitchen. Flannel nightgowns are highly underrated, soft and comforting. I didn't shower or brush my hair, and I raided almost every single carb we had stored in the cupboard. Dad left early for Spy Games business, so looking like a granny, I pondered how uncooked rice would taste. I checked the remote showing the position of Peyton's trackers. Again. Each hour gnawed away at the faith that I'd find Aimee.

I finally showered and threw on my dad's oversized white T-shirt that said "pastry chef" and a pair of jeans. I spent a few hours whipping egg whites into a meringue, dicing strawberries, and attempting to turn confectioner's sugar into frosting. All combinations of ingredients failed epically. This was crazy. How in the world of French pastries would I beat out top chefs? Insanity. I wished a best selling recipe had been included in the package.

Underneath the superficial worries about what frosting to use were thoughts of Mom's package I'd opened. Why did I have to take that guy's picture? What was it really all about? My gut said it was more than it seemed, and I needed to demand she tell me everything.

Finally, after my second failed attempt at making the perfect tart, I kicked the wall. It was so useless. Following stupid instructions didn't bring me any closer to Mom. I didn't even know if I wanted to be close to her.

"Savvy?"

"Dad? I didn't hear you come in." I didn't want to talk to him about any of this.

"Is everything okay?"

"Um, yeah." I waved at my face. "It's just hot in here."

Dad shifted from foot to foot and glanced toward his office, his escape, and then back at me like he knew he should say something. He stepped closer.

"You know, sometimes the more time that passes, the more we feel the effects of a different culture."

I nodded like the dutiful daughter. Yeah, I guess that could be part of the problem, but ever since I'd seen my mom, the feelings about her that I'd pushed down had gurgled up like air bubbles in a cheesecake. And I didn't even know if cheesecake could get air bubbles.

"Why did Mom leave?"

"Your mom would have to explain that."

"Mom's not here. Try."

He sighed. "Sometimes people need a break to figure things out. She'll be back."

I didn't dare glance up because I didn't want to see the truth. "So the split isn't permanent?"

Dad's silence told me everything. Finally, he said, "Only time will tell." He wiped a smudge of frosting off my nose. "Why the sudden interest in cooking?"

I didn't want to tell him I knew Spy Games was struggling or that if I won the contest I could go on to try for the prize money.

"A hobby to keep me busy between Spy Games."

"Good idea." He put his finger under my chin and lifted my head up. "You can do anything you set your mind to, whether you ever make the perfect croissant or not."

I blinked back the tears blurring my vision. Wow, the second time in a week Dad had talked to me about something other than Spy Games. I bit my lip, then spoke.

"Bet I can beat you in chess?"

A light that I hadn't seen in weeks flickered in his eyes. He glanced at the table and I could sense the flooding memories. Happy ones. When Mom, Dad and I were a family.

The light faded, and he cleared his throat. "Not tonight. I've got some paperwork to catch up on."

He turned his back to me, his shoulders hunched. I struggled to hold back the words churning in my mind. Dad expected me to take his brush-off in stride and go read a book or something, and the daughter he knew and had lived with for eighteen years would've done that. I didn't want to be that girl anymore. That girl wouldn't be searching for her best friend. That girl wouldn't dare stick up for herself. And that girl wouldn't challenge her dad.

"You can't ignore me forever!" I shouted.

Dad stopped. Slowly, he turned and faced me, his face worn and weary. "Savvy, I'm not ignoring you. I'm trying to get this business off the ground and provide for you."

"Sure, right."

Why did I feel guilty for wanting to spend time with my dad? The next few hours sucked. I pulled out our travel pack of games—checkers, Backgammon, and chess—and played against myself. I imagined the conversation I could've had with my dad where I'd learn all of Mom's past secrets, especially the one about her penchant for dressing in costume and her problem with paranoia.

That could be why I never noticed the knock on the door or the fact that someone had entered without me even knowing it.

Seventeen

"HELLO? ANYONE HOME?"

I jumped from the chair like I had a rocket strapped to my back.

"Whoa, it's just me." Malcolm entered the tiny living room.

I drank in the sight of him, his quirky smile and the familiar glint in his eye like he knew something I didn't. Was it something about Aimee? I'd been checking up on the trackers and so far Peyton had been a very boring tourist. Feelings rushed through me and I couldn't tell if it was excitement that we might have a breakthrough on the case or because Malcolm was standing so close to me.

Dad entered the room. "Oh, Malcolm. I forgot you were stopping by."

He coughed and his eyes shifted to the right like he regretted leaving his office. I directed my glare of complete evil between the two of them.

Dad flashed a cheesy grin. "Sorry, Savvy. I forgot to tell you."

"Tell me what?" I sensed a conspiracy and didn't like it.

Dad started cleaning up the chess game for me. "Malcolm called earlier and said you'd missed a couple days of training."

Dad raised his eyebrows and peered at me. I hid my face and got busy cleaning up the rest of the games.

He continued, "Which I'll forgive. But he also shared that things were a little tense between the two of you, so he asked for another day off."

"I wanted it to be a surprise." Malcolm stepped closer to me. "I thought if we were going to be working together, we should have an afternoon of just plain old fun in France. Your dad agreed."

"How come I wasn't involved in this decision?" I played the role of the crab while searching Malcolm's face for the sly wink that told me there was more to this.

Dad backed away with his hands in the air. "Uh, I just remembered a teleconference I have in a couple minutes. Have fun." He practically sprinted back to his office/bedroom.

I fumbled with the zipper on the game package, deciding to fish for some answers. "I have to come up with an entry for the Extravaganza."

"An afternoon off might help. The best ideas come when we're not looking for them." Malcolm crossed the room and grabbed my hand. "And I wanted to say sorry for being a jerk the other day. Next time we can pass a hundred shops if you want before choosing one."

"I wasn't exactly a princess either." I drew closer and whispered, "What's going on?"

His lips curved up, showing the dimples I couldn't resist. He shrugged. "Wait and see."

"Fine." I relented. "I'll be right back."

I headed to my bedroom to change, heart fluttering, pretty sure Malcolm had breaking news on Peyton or some kind of clue that would help.

As we headed up the stairs to Malcolm's apartment, my excitement grew. He had to understand I wasn't here to bat my eyelashes at him and that my focus was on finding Aimee. I tried to make my voice low and menacing. "I hope you're not planning an afternoon of flirting."

"Darn." He flipped around on the stairs, brushing up against me. "There go all my plans. You might as well go home."

He had to be just fooling around, but still, I felt annoyed that he could joke when I could barely crack a smile. I tried to shake it off. Time to prove I wasn't about to fall apart. I could be relaxed about this too.

He unlocked the door and we entered. His apartment was pretty sterile, a word that usually made me think of hospitals, needles, and green scrubs.

"I totally get it."

"What?" he said, as he dug around in the smallest closet in France.

I ran my finger across an empty bookshelf hung on the wall. The counter had nothing on it. The couch didn't even have a pillow. Not even one candle. "Why you don't invite girls up here."

He caught my eye and my stomach fluttered. "Atmosphere has nothing to do with romance."

He went back to digging, and in that moment, I believed him. Boy, did I ever.

"Aha! Found it." He pulled an ugly green gym bag from the depths of the closet.

"Hmm. That looks suspicious. Are you going to divulge our afternoon plans?" I'd hoped he had a crystal ball that would reveal how to find Aimee.

"Peyton's on the move." He unzipped the bag and pulled out what looked like material from Marie's scrap bag.

119

"What?" My face heated up. He did know something! I rushed over. "Tell me."

As I waited for his answer, I allowed myself a brief daydream. I'd smash a lock and break down the door. The stale smell of an abandoned house would greet me but I'd push through. I'd call for Aimee to hear her struggle from a back room. It would only take seconds for me to find her, slice through her ropes and rescue her. On our way out, I'd take down a couple bad guys.

"Haven't you been paying attention to the trackers you planted?" He separated the quilting scraps.

"Yeah," I huffed. "He's not moving. And I've been up to my eyeballs with Spy Games stuff." If I tried, I could find a connection between chocolate peanut butter ice cream and Spy Games.

"I've been doing a bit of spying myself. He's been on the move for a couple of hours. I figured you'd want to be all business today without your dad knowing."

"Of course, duh." I snorted. I knew it. I could tell from the moment Malcolm had walked into my living room. The flutter in my chest had told me great things would happen today.

He pushed the pile of cloth toward me along with a wig that looked like the end of a mop with silver and gray hairs wrapped up in a messy bun. "Get dressed."

I gave him my dumb blonde look. Yes, even us black-haired beauties have our moments.

"Your disguise?"

I blew air through my lips. "Of course, I knew that."

An hour later, Malcolm and I hobbled, arm in arm, to the Metro. He wore faded old man corduroys and a plaid flannel shirt, even though it was warm outside. A derby hat sat on top of his grey head, and he had a long wizard's beard. I'd never seen this side of Malcolm, all business and no play. But I liked that he was helping me.

"So, Dearie, you up for some square dancing this week?" I pushed my mop of grey hair out of my eyes then smoothed down the ugliest dress ever. I swear I was a walking commercial for patchwork quilts, and not in a cozy cottage kind of way.

Malcolm leaned on his cane and shuffled his feet. He whispered, "Do I look like I could dance?"

Oh, right. "I guess we'll have to spend our days taking care of the grandkids then."

He tried to hide a muffled snicker. "You're not very good at this, are you?"

I stopped and pulled my arm away. "I'm fine. Just so you know, I was the understudy for Aunt Spike from *James and the Giant Peach* in a third grade play."

He slipped his fingers through mine. "Let's go, Hilda."

We didn't say much on the ride underground per Malcolm's orders. I guess lots of old married couples don't talk when they reach a certain age. Kind of like my mom and dad. Except they're not that old yet. Off the Metro we crossed the street, a bit faster than our age should've allowed, and headed toward a big gate.

"Parc des buttes."

I burst out laughing, but when we entered the park, my mood shifted. I lost any desire to joke about parking our *derrières* on the benches. Aimee and I would have a good time with that one—when I found her. I picked up my pace. Peyton was on the move. In this park.

I could be moments from rescuing my friend.

Eighteen

MALCOLM GRABBED MY HAND. "Slow down, dear. Let's enjoy the day."

What he really meant was, "Stop running through the park like a schoolchild when you're supposed to be 70 years old." I couldn't help it. It had already been too long. What do they say? After twenty-four hours the chance of finding someone decreases?

His eyes darted back and forth along the perimeter of the park, but the only somewhat suspicious movement was a mime performing for a big family picnic and a young couple riding a tandem bike. I pictured me and Aimee riding on the bike, dodging squirrels in the path until we'd give up and walk. Or coming here with her grandmother, who could fill us in on the history behind this place. Because every place in Paris has a history.

After shuffling through the winding paved paths that rolled with the landscape, he stroked his long beard—quite convincingly I might add. "I bet I know where he's headed."

He led me down narrow paths overhung with tree branches and ferns, and with no one around, we jogged. The smell of damp earth and leaves brought me back to working in my dad's herb garden and walking through the woods behind our house. But those memories were safe ones, and there was nothing safe about what we were doing now—following a potential madman.

We turned a corner and a humongous rocky bluff jutted into the sky. Ivy clung to its side, crawling toward the gazebo-like temple at the top. I shivered a bit because the cliff towered over a lake. Even though the water sparkled in the sun and seemed pretty harmless, it was a long drop from where we stood. A wooden-slat bridge that didn't look very safe seemed to be the only way across. It started a few feet ahead of us, way too far up for me to consider crossing. I swayed with dizziness just looking at it, and I gripped Malcolm's cane. "I need this more than you."

"Did you see him?" Malcolm pointed and peered across the bridge.

I followed his gaze, fearing and hoping that he'd seen someone. "Who?"

"A man just ducked into the woods over on the cliff." He cupped his hand to shield the sun from his eyes. "I think it was Peyton."

"Why, what did you see?" Maybe I needed glasses. Dark shapes moved in between the trees.

"Tall, dark hair, an obnoxious swagger. Sound like him?"

Sounded exactly like Peyton. "Are you sure?" Adrenaline rushed through my body. "Oh my gosh, an island would be a perfect place to hide a hostage." Aimee could be tied up under a tree, hidden by long willowy branches, she could be shivering from cold and shaking from starvation, she could be terrified thinking no one would ever find her.

"Stop and breathe." Malcolm rubbed my back.

After gasping a bit, I stepped onto the first wooden plank, swallowing down my breakfast and refusing to look below.

"We can cross the safe and legal one." Malcolm grabbed my hand, trying to pull me in the other direction.

"It would be too late." I growled and ripped out of his grasp. "We cross now and have him lead us to Aimee."

Ignoring the sign with a big circle and a line through it, I started across the bridge, my eyes on the temple. The wooden slats creaked and swayed under my weight. I didn't care about the rules or the danger. I wanted to find Aimee, and I couldn't give Peyton any more of a head start than he already had.

Halfway across, Malcolm stopped and the bridge creaked. I groaned, my fingers digging into the railing. Through sheer determination of will I made it, and then dropping the granny act, I sprinted across the top of the rocky cliff calling Aimee's name. The leaves and ferns brushed my face and arms. I found nothing but fox dens or rabbit holes. After looking under every rock and tree, my adrenaline crashed. Nothing.

Malcolm called out, "I found something. Over here!"

With a surge of energy, I ran through brush and ducked branches until I found him, standing by a tree, holding back the big drooping branches. The heartbreak in Malcolm's eyes told me everything.

"This doesn't mean she was here. This could be anything."

Underneath lay the scattered remains of what could've been Aimee's meager captivity, frayed rope and a power bar wrapper. I pulled out the tracker and we both looked at it.

Malcolm blew out a breath. "Sorry. He's leaving the park."

The leaves and rope blurred in front of my eyes. It couldn't be. Some pieces of trash weren't real clues. But then why did I feel my hope slipping away? I couldn't stand there, next to Malcolm, so I ran and ran and ran until I couldn't breathe. I needed to be alone.

I arrived at the other bridge—the safe one—and slumped against a tree, welcoming the jagged bark piercing through my shirt into the skin of my back. Pain was good, a reminder that nothing should matter but Aimee.

Malcolm was soon with me, gently lifting me up by the arm. "Honestly, I don't think she was ever here. I should never have pointed it out. That could've been anything."

"Or it could be everything. Wasn't that the same kind of rope we found in Peyton's apartment?"

"Possibly. It's pretty common rope." He held out his hand. "Let's go back and regroup. He'll be on the move again and we'll find him."

I sighed not wanting to give up, not wanting to admit that I was failing, not wanting to tell Malcolm to stuff it when he was just trying to help. We'd find him? When? How? I wanted answers.

We crossed the safe bridge. The green of the trees blurred against the blue sky and the slight breeze moved my granny dress against my legs.

Malcolm stopped halfway. "You might as well take in the view. We did tell your dad we'd have some fun."

Geese flapped their wings and skittered across the lake to settle near the edge. Large tree branches dipped their fingers into the edge of the water. Aimee would've loved it. I leaned my head against his shoulder, refusing to give in to tears. I didn't want Malcolm to know how much it was getting to me.

"So, dear, my memory is getting a little fuzzy," he whispered, his breath kissing my cheek. "Tell me again about our wedding day."

I stiffened a bit when he put his arm around me. Very easily, I could've slipped into this role and forgotten. Pretended that all was well, and felt safe and loved with the warmth of his arm draped across my shoulder. Except I couldn't muster the energy to play his game.

"You can quit trying to cheer me up. It won't work."

"I remember now," he said. "We got married under the Arc de Triomphe at sunset. It was almost perfect, except for the flock of pigeons that pooped all over our family and friends. We, of course, were safe under the arc."

I relented and couldn't help but smile. "Did we enjoy our honeymoon?"

Malcolm didn't say anything but traced his fingers down my back. My legs grew weak, and I leaned into him a little bit more.

He kissed the side of my head and whispered, "Oh, yeah."

I just about lost my breath when he said that. For once I didn't have anything to say. My heart was lodged in my throat. He ran his fingers down my arms and goosebumps quickly followed. He laced our hands and pressed his face into the crook of my neck.

"I'll play out any fantasy for you, Savvy Bent, if it will keep a smile on your face." He gently kissed my cheek.

If my life were a movie, that would be when the music started, and Malcolm and I would've engaged in one of those long kisses that made all the girls swoon. Maybe even some of the men if they were being honest. But we didn't. Instead, tears slipped down my face. I couldn't remember the last time someone had gone out of his or her way to try and make me smile again, and all it took was a few simple words. It was much more than that. Without any complaints about the lack of training, he was helping me in every way he could. Maybe, just maybe, I could call him a friend. I didn't have many.

A shot rang out, ripping a hole through the fantasy.

Birds burst from the trees like fireworks. Malcolm wrapped his arm around my waist and slammed me to the bridge. I hit the wood with a muffled clang. All my breath shot out my mouth, leaving me gasping. I was inches from the edge. My vertigo maxed out. I stared at the water far, far below us, just waiting for a victim to fall into its clutches.

"Are you still wearing that stupid tray?" Malcolm asked.

"It's not stupid if it saves my life, thank you very much."

Malcolm moved to get up, then swore, and we watched the black tracking box falling toward the water.

"Forget about it," Malcolm said. "When I say three. Run. Off the bridge. Don't look back."

My heart pounded for a completely different reason. "What about you?"

"I'll be right behind. THREE! Go now."

Another shot shattered the air.

I scrambled to my feet, gathered my skirt and sprinted. My granny shoes clicked against the bridge, until I finally kicked them off. I pumped my arms and tucked my head, hoping my wig wouldn't fly off. I tore down the winding paths, ducking the tree branches, and leaping the cracks in the pavement. My lungs were screaming when I finally stopped near a bench and sucked in air, doubled over.

"Quick, follow me." Malcolm dove under the nearest sweeping tree branches.

My whole body shook. The muscles in my legs quivered like I was trapped in a room with a mountain lion. I gripped the bench to stop the shaking in my arms. Who would shoot at us? Peyton? He was mad, but was he completely psycho? I hoped not for Aimee's sake. And mine.

"Come on! Now!" Malcolm urged.

I froze wanting to dive under the tree and wanting to sprint toward the entrance and make my escape. The crunch and snap of branches breaking behind us motivated me to take the dive. I squeezed in next to Malcolm, trying to keep my breath from sounding like gunshots.

Nineteen

WE WAITED.

I didn't dare move.

I tried my best to peek through the leaves of the branches but couldn't see much. Hopefully that meant whoever was on the outside couldn't see me.

"Who—"

"Shh. No talking," Malcolm reprimanded.

Minutes passed. I huddled close to Malcolm, trying to shrink from sight. My mind seemed incapable of logical thought, and all the sounds around me became extremely loud. The rustle of the leaves. The wind moving in the branches. The geese on the nearby lake. Malcolm's breath on my neck. Footsteps on the gravel path.

Footsteps? Oh, crap. Oh, crap. Oh, crap. Oh, crap. I closed my eyes as tight as I could and held my breath. I didn't want to hear those footsteps coming closer and closer. I didn't want to see a gun poke through the branches.

I wasn't sure how much time passed but I needed to breathe. So ever so slowly I let air escape out the side of my mouth.

"It's okay to breathe," Malcolm whispered. "Whoever was on the path didn't see us. They kept walking."

The rest of my breath came out in a big whoosh. I took several deep breaths, trying to steady my shotgun heart and shaking legs. I held back a sob.

"It's okay," Malcolm said, "I think we're out of danger."

My voice trembled. "I don't dare move. What if he's waiting for us to come out of hiding? What if he's still searching?"

"We can wait a bit then."

Malcolm wrapped his arm around my waist, and I'd never been so thankful for human contact. I pressed into his warmth, but my thoughts stayed on the fact that I'd gotten shot at twice. I couldn't believe Peyton would try to shoot at us. At me. I screwed up at the Louvre and the Eiffel but my actions hardly deserved sudden death. Who could it be? My body stiffened.

"What's wrong?" Malcolm asked.

I was glad I didn't have to look him in the eyes. "What if this wasn't Peyton?"

"What do you mean?"

I thought about my mom's disguise at the Eiffel, her directions to burn the package, and her fear when she'd shushed me. She did not want to be found. Then I'd opened the package anyway and went through with the instructions to sign up for the Extravaganza. And all that money. What if this was about the money?

"Savvy?" Malcolm asked again.

"This might be about my mom." I spoke the revelation before realizing it.

"What do you mean? About your mom?" His voice rose as if he were suddenly interested.

"This is the second time we've been shot at and we didn't know Peyton the first time."

"It has to be Peyton. I saw him on the other side of the bridge." Malcolm shifted his body and sat up. "After I dropped the tracking device into the lake, he must have circled back."

I didn't want to talk about my mom, or share about the package. My gut told me to keep it a secret, so I played along with the Peyton theory.

I faced him. "Right. He must've. And the hostage site." I couldn't forget about the food wrappers and frayed rope, possibly the same rope that matched the one I'd found in Peyton's apartment. My stomach growled, interrupting us. I laughed. "Glad he's not walking past right now."

"Aha! That's why I came prepared." He pulled off the spy backpack that I'd made fun of when I first saw it.

"You don't happen to have a Hawaiian pizza in there, do you?" A girl could hope.

"Sadly, no. But maybe this will do?" He pulled out a handful of chocolate bars, crackers, and two small bottles of water.

My eyes widened. "You're the best!"

I leaned forward and kissed his cheek right above his old man beard before realizing what I was doing.

"I didn't say I was going to share it. You're the one who's supposed to be training me to be the ultimate spy. Where are your provisions? What did you do to be prepared in the face of danger?" He covered the food with his hands and waited for an answer.

I scrambled. "Well, it is important to be prepared, but it's also important to have the stamina to go without food in case of imprisonment."

"Good cover." He handed me a chocolate bar.

"Thanks." I unwrapped it and smelled the milk chocolate.

For some reason, I felt as if I were sitting by Willy Wonka's chocolate river, only this tasted even better. As we munched on the food, our conversation dwindled and awkwardness settled in.

"So, tell me your biggest fear." Malcolm guzzled his water, then looked at me with honest eyes. "Since we've been shot at together. Twice. Maybe we should know each other a little bit better."

I bit my lip. My biggest fear? That was easy. "Black crickets."

Water came out Malcolm's nose when he laughed. "Crickets?"

"What? Not what you expected? Black crickets freak me out. Especially when there are hundreds of them covering my yard, hopping around like they can't wait to get in my house and jump into my bed." I shuddered. "Your turn."

Malcolm played with the cap of his water bottle and studied a pile of dirt. After a few minutes, he looked up. "My biggest fear is failing my dad. That during this year away from home, I won't be able to meet up to his expectations."

He fell silent, lost in thought.

"A year away from home?" I asked.

"It's a tradition. When we turn eighteen, we have a year to live on our own and prove ourselves before we're welcomed into the family business. First my brother did it and now it's my turn."

Wow. Talk about pressure. And failing parents? I knew something about that. His confession made my black cricket phobia look like a joke, or like I was afraid of being close to someone or had a problem sharing my deepest thoughts.

"If it makes you feel any better," I said, "I already failed mine, both of them." Why else would Mom have left? And why she didn't trust me enough to talk to me?

"No way. Your dad loves you. I can tell."

"He has a funny way of showing it." Time to change the subject. "What's your most embarrassing moment?"

"That's easy. There was this one time. I was on a date with this cute girl."

"Oh." For some reason, I didn't like the idea of Malcolm on a date with anyone else.

"And, well, because of a misunderstanding, she got really mad at me."

I narrowed my eyes at him, hoping he wasn't talking about what I thought he was talking about.

"And to my great surprise, she tied me up, took off all my clothes, and then left me in my underwear. But that wasn't the embarrassing part."

I clasped my hands together and fiddled with my fingers. This was my most embarrassing moment, for sure. "What was it then?"

He put his finger under my chin and lifted my head so I was looking into his eyes. "That I went behind her back and made it look like I was on the date for other reasons. She didn't trust me, and when we got shot at, I couldn't protect her."

I tried to lower my head, but he wouldn't let me. Instead we locked eyes, and I felt my breath slowly squeezing out of my lungs. Gray flecks swirled in his eyes and I fell into them, head first. Moments passed, and we didn't say a word. The breeze hugged us, pulling us closer together. I leaned forward. He leaned forward. My heart quivered just before our lips brushed like the soft sprinkling of sugar on a donut. Sweetness. The breeze swirled, and for a moment, I forgot everything. But then he stiffened and pulled away, the honesty in his eyes fading.

"We should be okay to leave."

"Right." I brushed off the hurt and confusion and helped him pick up the chocolate wrappers.

Minutes later, we trudged up to the gate. He grabbed my hand but then let go as if he made a mistake. "Let's go. Enough excitement for today."

On the Metro ride home we didn't say a word. The whole being married pretense was dropped and even though he sat next to me, he didn't touch me. He stared out the window at the blurred underground walls.

My body moved with the sway of the train, but he leaned away from me at every turn. What had changed? Maybe he'd decided I wasn't worth getting shot over. Some friends are willing to die for each other but our friendship was new, just budding, needing sunlight to grow. Possibly being killed moved a big ole cloud right over us. I shivered in its shadow.

Somehow I knew I'd wind up on my own trying to find Aimee. I had reached that dead end. The trackers hadn't worked, and the device was at the bottom of the lake. I had absolutely no other clues. I wanted to ask him what to do next, beg him to sit down and brainstorm with me, but the words wouldn't come.

Hands shoved into his old man pants, he said, "I have to work at *Les Pouffants's* this weekend. Next Monday, then?"

"Sure." I was officially on my own.

Perfect time to check on Aimee's grandmother and maybe snag some gingersnap cookies. I wanted to check out Aimee's room again. Something hadn't felt right the first time. I'd missed something, some clue, important to finding her. Or maybe I just wanted to feel close to her.

At Marie's house, right away I knew something was wrong. The once happy blooming flowers in the window boxes drooped. A shadow seemed cast over the house and the cute little cottage looked a bit forlorn and neglected.

I knocked on the door. No response. I knocked a bit harder. "Marie?" No answer. Not even a scuffle of footsteps.

Twenty

MY GUILT OVER AIMEE and not being fully honest with Marie the last time got to me, so I twisted the knob and gently opened the door. I expected the smell of cinnamon and ginger because Marie always baked. But there was nothing. Not one hint of spice or warmth.

No one seemed to be home, but I really wanted to check Aimee's room again. Call it my budding spy sense, but trespassing uninvited seemed the best option. I wasn't going to eat any cookies, just take a peek inside. I walked through and closed the door, hoping a neighbor hadn't seen me. The floor creaked. Was it that loud last time? I quickly made my way up the stairs to Aimee's room.

At first, I stood in the doorway and observed. The room looked the same as when Malcolm and I were here. The fading wallpaper, her bed, her jewelry, the half-empty closet. What was it? I stepped in the room and made my way over to her dresser. I ran my fingers over the beaded jewelry. If Aimee left on a hiking trip, she wouldn't bring necklaces. I turned to the closet. But hiking shoes she'd bring. So why were they still here?

I sat on the bed and closed my eyes, letting my mind drift. Maybe if I relaxed and stopped trying to figure it out, the answer would come to me.

Minutes passed.

Memories faded in and out of the few times Aimee and I had spent in her room, which granted wasn't a lot because she lived outside the city. The faded smell of her perfume barely lingered. I remembered the laughter and her crinkly smile. This was where the clues I was missing would magically appear. But nothing.

Except for the creak downstairs, which wasn't part of any memory.

My meditation came to an abrupt end, and I sat straight and listened.

Another creak. Was Marie home? Wouldn't someone walking into her house make more noise? This intruder sounded like me. Sneaky.

Damn.

Somehow I had to leave the house, and I couldn't use the stairs. Why didn't I think to bring rappelling hooks? I crept over to the window and pushed it open. A breeze drifted through bringing fresh air to the stale room. It was my only escape route.

Slowly, so I wouldn't make any noise I brought one leg over the windowsill and let it dangle. This was crazy. I wasn't the kind of girl to jump out of second story windows. Maybe I should hide in the closet?

I heard footsteps on the stairs. My heart raced. I threw the other leg over. If I hung from the window and then dropped, the fall wouldn't be that big of a deal. I hoped. Gripping the bottom of the window, I let my body scrape against the wood as I slowly lowered it. I had no idea how far of a drop it was but the cottage wasn't that tall. Right?

The bedroom door creaked. I couldn't drop. What if the person heard me? I held on for dear life and hoped the person couldn't see my hands. Sweat broke out all over my body in a rush of heat. What were they looking for? Aimee wasn't a criminal who stored cocaine or top military secrets in her closet. I prayed the person would leave because my fingers were cramping. I couldn't hold on much longer.

The door creaked again. Whether or not that meant the intruder had left the room, I didn't care. I let go.

The impact shot up through my legs and forced a groan from my chest. My feet ached but I dove into the nearest bush. I sat and massaged my fingers while waiting for my body to stop shaking. But spies don't stop in the middle of a mission because their fingers hurt. I crawled along the side of the house until I got to the kitchen window. If the intruder was leaving they had to come this way.

Inch by inch, I raised my head until I could peek into the kitchen window past the ruffled curtains. The intruder seemed to have vanished. I sank back down and stayed crouched by the side of the house. Who could the intruder have been? Who else was interested in Marie and Aimee?

I didn't dare move. Mysteries swirled around me as if all I needed to do was reach out and catch the answer like it was a leaf on a windy day. Marie's front door slammed, and I jumped up to run like crazy. A middle-aged woman with mousy hair rounded the corner. I couldn't catch one word of her French it was flowing so fast. I nodded. The woman grabbed my arm and dragged me to my feet, while continuing the scolding.

"Sorry." I breathed deep and tried to call up a smooth response. I'd seen enough spy thrillers with my dad. I should be able to get out of any situation. "Just visiting Marie's granddaughter, Aimee."

The woman narrowed her eyes then glanced to her left and right and brought her face inches from mine. Her eyes held a hint of fear. She spoke in choppy English. "No one lives here." She let go and turned abruptly.

"Wait!" I called out and caught up to her. "What are you talking about?"

She slowly faced me and shook her head no, then hurried into her house.

"What about Marie and Aimee? You must be mistaken!" But the lady was gone.

Her words stayed with me. And then it hit me. Knickknacks. Framed photos. Dirty clothes. That was what was missing. The lived-in feeling of a teenage girl's room. I had no idea why, and I wasn't any closer to figuring out what had happened to her.

Except, I knew there was more to Aimee and her life then she'd led me to believe. And that was never a good sign.

Twenty-one

FINALLY, THE BIG DAY arrived. Pouffant's Pastry Extravaganza. I'd not only find out the secret behind Mom's secret assignment but I'd see her again. And trust me, I had a list of questions. A long list.

I lied to Dad about needing a day of shopping then slipped out. The crisp morning air kissed my cheeks in the typical French greeting, and I headed off to the Extravaganza, backpack slung over my shoulder, balancing a covered tray of cupcakes on my right arm. I know. Lame.

I walked the streets, a pile of nerves. The mystery of Aimee and Marie and their house gnawed away at the back of my mind. And what about the piles of money stashed in the back of my closet? What the hell was my mom getting paid to do? Why was taking a picture of Pouffant worth that much money? I wasn't sure if I wanted to know the truth.

Leaving the main traffic area and entering the blocked-off side street used for the Extravaganza was like entering a different time, like I'd been transported a hundred years into the past. *Les Pouffant's* was transformed. Men with berets and women with their hair rolled up in buns stood by their carts of freshly baked bread, hunks of homemade cheese, and fresh tarts. A group of older men with beards and violins played classical music. Excitement pulsed.

But no sign of Mom. Yet.

Important-looking men strode through with clipboards, ruining the romantic atmosphere. TV cameras flooded the place, setting up around the big, sure-to-win chefs. I approached the registration table. The smell of sweet frosting and cinnamon laced the air. I bumbled through beginner French to get my number, then searched for the corresponding table.

"You, little girl."

I ignored this statement because why would anyone call me a little girl? I guess older men consider teenagers to be little.

"*Excuse moi*! Girl."

I stopped and turned. No way. Pouffant, with his grey hair curling at the sides, peered down at me from atop his throne. His big old belly protruded out and if he swung at the right time he could take someone out with it. But his eyes freaked me out. I'd never noticed them before. Crystal-clear blue eyes as translucent as the Mediterranean Sea. A creepy chill crawled across my back. He seemed to look right through me as if he knew all my secrets. I forced myself to remember how he took care of the upset customer in his shop, and that he had kindness inside somewhere. I hoped.

"Are you stupid, girl?"

I should whip out my camera and snap his picture, but my cupcakes were already in danger of slipping and crashing to the ground. I glared then turned my back to him, which caused a rippling gasp to spread throughout the crowd surrounding him.

A female reporter nudged me. She spoke in French, so I just nodded my head and said, "*Oui.*"

"*Vien ici.* Come here."

I was content to ignore him, but the gap in the crowd closed and people inched forward, pushing me back toward him until there was nothing to do but turn around.

Pouffant leaned close. "I applaud your efforts, girl. Entering a contest this big with professionals." He said professionals as if the word was synonymous with royalty.

"Whatever."

He stepped in front of me and put his cracked and stubby fingers on my collar. "Do you know who I am?"

"Kris Kringle?"

He burst out with a jovial laugh, and I swear his belly jiggled like a bowl full of my dad's homemade grape jelly. The throng of adoring fans all laughed too. He pulled me close.

"You can joke, girl, but I promise, no one pulls a fast one on me." He dropped his voice low so only I could hear. "I know who you are and why you are here. A word of warning. No one crosses Jolie Pouffant and lives to tell about it."

And then he let me go like I was a street urchin. I backed away. He knew about the camera? And the money? He couldn't. What else could he have meant? Shaken, I stumbled away until I found my table. The layout was simple but breathtaking.

On top of a white paper tablecloth spread from one side to the other were different pastries and cakes in the layout of a small village. Small tarts were cars. Larger square cakes were in the shape of cottages, and it was all for me. I double-checked my number against the table number. Yep. It was mine. The instructions had failed to mention that I didn't have to worry about my entry. I shoved the cupcakes under the table.

With a silly grin, I stood behind my masterpiece. It didn't take long for my smile to fade as people pretty much ignored me. I didn't care. The judges had to taste my entry—even though I hadn't made it—and that was all that mattered. My hardest trial was not snacking on the tasty tidbits spread out in front of me. And keeping my mind on my mission. And waiting for Mom.

Every older female who walked past with longish brown hair wearing a scarf or a hat, I hoped would signal for me to follow. Or drop a note by my side stating a time and place to meet.

It never happened. Was she okay? Maybe she wasn't just paranoid. I gripped the bag over my shoulder, feeling the lumpy form of the camera against my side. My palms grew sweaty, and I fiddled with my ponytail. Why a special camera? My heart rate increased exponentially. Is that so the film couldn't be traced back to anyone? Why the secrecy? My mission became a reality. Just a picture. I could do this.

I grabbed the camera from the bag and headed toward Pouffant. The crowds drifted around me. I breathed in the heavenly scents, wishing I could dip my finger and sneak a swipe of a delicious-looking cake, but I didn't want to get kicked out. I neared Pouffant's table and lifted the camera to my eye. My vision blurred and my hands shook. I zoomed in on his table overflowing with samples from his bakery. An army of tarts and croissants surrounded his entry. Frosting of multiple colors decorated the tops with fancy lettering and ribbons. Special glazes glinted in the sun.

Then I focused on Jolie, his curling hair, wiry beard, and old-man nose. I pressed the button on top of the camera. The force of something leaving the camera pushed my body back.

Two seconds later Jolie Pouffant fell headfirst into his pastries, obliterating the tower of flaky goodness and the surrounding army.

Oh, crap.

Twenty-two

THE FLOOD OF TELEVISION crews swung their attention to Jolie spread-eagled on a bed of pastries, and it was all I could do to swallow the vomit rising in my throat. I shot someone. Holy crap! I murdered a famous pastry chef in a foreign country. Or I seriously hurt the guy. I didn't want to stick around to find out.

My legs gave way, and I stumbled backward. If someone had noticed my presence and the backfire from the camera-turned-weapon, I could end up in prison. All my dreams of college, becoming a rock star, and someday baking the perfect chocolate chip cookie disappeared. The cold reality of prison bars, orange jumpsuits, and stale bread crusts sank into my bones. I shivered. But I had my answers.

Mom was possibly a cold-blooded assassin.

My mom, the one who baked cookies on occasion, the one who put Band-aids on my cuts, the one who'd left years ago. She was a killer. And now I was too.

Like mother like daughter.

No wonder she wasn't here. Or if she was, it was just to make sure I finished the job. Not to chat with me.

I needed to take the money and run. Far away. But where? I had no clue. I only knew I couldn't stay here. I turned and strolled back to my table, arms swinging like I was taking a walk in the park, like I didn't just possibly murder a man. Back at my table, I shoved the camera into my bag and slung it over my shoulder. So far, no one was after me.

Except my highly trained Spy Games eye caught a man slithering through the crowds. He wore a white apron, a poofy chef's hat, and he carried a tray. When he neared the entrance to *Les Pouffant's*, he slipped inside. Extremely suspicious since the shop was closed.

Maybe killing Pouffant was a distraction so he could break in. If I was about to go into hiding, I wanted to know why. Someone had used me. Did Mom know about all this? Or was she an unsuspecting pawn simply following directions? After a quick glance around to make sure no one was looking, I hurried away from the chaos and toward the shop, following the man in the apron.

I ducked under the flowered trellises hung over the doorway. The shop was closed due to the Extravaganza, and the man wearing the apron had broken the lock. I slipped inside after him.

The succulent, sweet smells were deceiving. A place that held such wonderful pastries like cream puffs, layered cakes, brioche, and macaroons couldn't be the backdrop for murder. The shop was quiet and dark. I crept into Pouffant's lair and searched under tables and in the cleaning closet but nothing seemed out of place. Where did the man go?

I walked around the glass cases and into the kitchen. A door to the right was cracked open. I tried to convince my heart to leave my throat and go back to my chest, and then I opened the door all the way. Stairs. A musty smell tingled my nose. The hairs along my arm rose. With light footsteps, I went into what felt like the underworld with no clue what demons I would find.

I held my breath on the stairs, afraid of creaks, but then let it out at the bottom. A narrow hallway, dingy and filled with cobwebs, led to a door at the end. It was open. I crept down the hallway but stopped abruptly at the smell curling from the open door. I shuddered at the dank atmosphere that reminded me of scary movies and zombies. What did a pastry chef like Pouffant keep in his basement that was worth thousands and smelled like that? I wasn't sure I wanted to know.

Voices echoed from beyond the open doorway. One voice stood out in particular, a voice that I'd grown accustomed to, one that had nudged its way into my heart. Malcolm's. I knew he worked here but what the hell was going on? What did Malcolm know? Was he the chef who'd sneaked into the shop?

Their voices drew closer, and I sprinted back the way I came. I hightailed it up the stairs, and back in the shop. I had two paths. Out the front door, entering my life as a fugitive, or hiding in the shop and finding answers. Crouching low, I darted across the room and ripped open the nearest door and slipped inside. Man, it was heavy.

A shock of freezing air engulfed me. Hairs instantly stuck out across my arms and down my legs. An endless supply of signature cakes frosted to perfection waited on shelves to be delivered to some gala event. I turned to open door number two, but voices filled the room.

I was stuck in the freezer.

With the door open a crack, I held onto every wisp of warmth I could get. I kneeled and peered out the opening. The *maitre d'*, dressed like a butler with a ponytail and narrow face, smoothed the collar of his tuxedo with precise movements. He stood by a pillar with ivy wrapped around it and faced Malcolm. Wasn't the butler always guilty? If he found me, he could smother me with decorated cakes. Or worse, he could lock me in a freezer.

"*Zut alors!*" he said, and then a flood of French spewed from his mouth.

Malcolm spoke in low tones, his voice barely reaching me. I couldn't hear the words, never mind understand the French.

The butler's voice rang out, harsh and angry. Did he work for Jolie, too? Did either of them know about Jolie? Images of him unmoving on his bed of pastries sneaked into my conscience. I might've killed a man. In cold blood.

They continued to talk. Columns of my smoky breath rose in the air and dissipated in front of me. I searched boxes on the shelves, and they all had the same name embossed on the sides. Jolie Pouffant. The guy was the French version of Betty Crocker.

Their words shot through the air like gunshots pinging back and forth at each other.

The butler eventually had to stop and take a breath. He switched over to English. "And what about the prisoner?"

Prisoner? As in Aimee? My spine tingled. Or my mom?

Malcolm growled. "I'll persuade the prisoner to talk. Isn't that why you hired me?"

The butler grumbled in French first, then said, "And what about the girl?"

Malcolm interjected, speaking clearly. "Trust me, she's an innocent in the whole thing."

Were they talking about me? My heart contracted so fast it pounded against my chest. I was sure it would echo into the other room and possibly down the street. Even in the freezer, a hot flush spread across my skin, causing goosebumps to rise on my goosebumps.

The butler spoke, "*Oui, oui.* You say that but wasn't this Peyton fellow supposed to keep the girl distracted and away from here and Jolie? You planted the fake evidence. You led her to the cliffs. Yet she is here."

My body turned rigid. My fingernails dug into the palms of my hands, breaking the skin. Peyton? Everything rushed back. In Peyton's apartment, it was Malcolm who brought me the rope. At Parc des Buttes, it was Malcolm who found the prisoner site with the same frayed rope. Had he set me up? I remembered his brush off. Was that guilt?

They switched back to French, and I desperately wished I'd paid more attention to my French lessons in high school. I tried to pick out what few words I might recognize. With my eyes closed, my brain struggled to understand and remember. One word repeated. *La mere.* As in mother. Were they still talking about me? And my mom?

My mind whirled, and I had to suck in air in shallow gasps so they didn't hear me. I pressed my head against the

156

icy metal of the door. The numbing cold spread. I wished I could turn off my heart and hide it in layers of ice.

What would they want with my mom? Or me?

The butler spoke again, in a cold clear voice. "Get the information from your girlfriend. Or I will."

My teeth chattered. My fingers and toes were slightly numb. The walls of the freezer seemed to close in on me. If they didn't leave soon, I'd have to open the door and reveal myself. And if I did that, I shuddered to think. They'd probably stick me in a box labeled cream puffs and leave me to freeze.

Please, please, I prayed. *Leave.*

As mini icicles formed off the tip of my nose, chairs scraped on the floor. My eyes flooded with tears and I sent a silent message to my pinky toes to hold on for just a bit longer.

At last, when they left through the front door, I clumsily crawled onto the wooden planks of the floor. Heat wrapped around me, but the shivers came from deep inside. I rubbed my stiff hands across my arms and legs, but I didn't have time to lay here and thaw. I had to run. Fast.

I stumbled through the streets for home. Moments with Malcolm tore at me. Tender moments, laughing, and flirting. He'd acted like he liked me when clearly it was all a ruse. Anger rose above my fear. My eyes widened, breaking the frozen tears that were still in my eyelashes.

Malcolm had transformed from cute waiter to clueless spy to double agent, hired to gather information on me. And they must have kidnapped Aimee to do it.

The next day, I was downing my fifth cup of coffee when someone knocked on the door. On a normal day, a knock at the door wouldn't freak me out, but yesterday Pouffant had hinted I was getting troublesome, and he didn't seem to be the type of person to fool around. I grabbed the largest frying pan we owned and crept toward the door.

With one hand on the doorknob and one on the ultimate weapon of death, I called out in a shaky voice, "Who is it?"

"Hey, it's Malcolm. Open up."

Did I welcome in a cute guy who had been hired to spy on me? Duh, no. But if I didn't act normal, he might suspect I knew and then...what if they sent someone to snuff me out early? No way was Malcolm a hired gun. He wouldn't hurt me. He couldn't. I might be just an assignment to him, but he wouldn't take my life. I hoped.

I opened the door, letting in a blast of cooler air as Malcolm walked through. I quickly shut the door and gulped.

"What's up with the pan?" he asked.

I flipped it around, a gigantic smile on my face. I looked back and forth between the pan and Malcolm. "Eggs. Scrambled eggs. I was hungry."

"Right."

Totally lame answer, but it was better than the truth that I was prepared to take someone out with it. I crossed the living room into the kitchen and eased the pan onto the stovetop, then positioned myself behind the kitchen table. Distance. I needed to keep our distance so I could think clearly. "What brings you here? Did my dad ask you over again?"

He showed me his stuffed backpack. "Thought we could head to a quiet little park somewhere."

"Yeah, not in the mood. Sorry." I stayed behind the table. "And we don't have a real good history in public."

"True. We can stay here." He turned his back to me and reached into his backpack. Two seconds later, he twirled around and blew into a party horn, the loud blast knocking apart my suspicions. "Heard you made it through to the Extravaganza finals." He grinned.

What? Surprise must have showed on my face.

"You didn't stick around long enough to hear the results?"

"No. Not with the big commotion going on. I got out of there." *And I was freezing my ass off while learning you were a spy. That was all.* "So what happened anyway?" My voice cracked. Images of Pouffant landing on top of his pastries popped into my mind, the squished cakes, the smeared frosting, and the gasping crowds. This was where I'd learn if I was a cold-blooded murderer or not.

Twenty-three

MALCOLM LOWERED THE PARTY horn and plopped his pack down.

"Oh, right. Pouffant. I guess someone in the crowd shot him with a tranquilizer gun." He zipped open his pack. "I can't believe you didn't know you'd won."

Won? The words floated, hovering nearby, but I couldn't quite catch them to speak. Relief flooded my arms and legs, and my body sagged. I wasn't an assassin. Better yet, my mom wasn't an assassin.

Malcolm caught my arm. "Are you okay? Honestly, winning that contest is about impossible. You beat out top pastry chefs."

"Just luck," I murmured.

"No such thing as luck in that contest. Congrats." He pulled a soft blanket from his pack.

Of course he was right. I certainly hadn't created my entry. Someone with the skills had helped me win. But why? What would I have to do at the Extravaganza finals? Not sure I wanted to know.

"The finals are in two weeks. For now, let's celebrate." He pulled out grapes, bread, cheese, and champagne. Hopefully it wasn't drugged with truth serum.

I watched with a keen eye as he set up everything on the floor of my living room. If he were to question me would he wait until before or after the champagne? And if I didn't answer what would he do? I shook off my paranoia. I was just an assignment to him. Not a target.

He patted the blanket. "Come on. I promise I won't bite."

I'd heard those words before. "Are you sure you want to do the whole blanket/picnic thing? It didn't work out too well for us the last time."

"I thought we were past that. I'm offering you a chance to redeem yourself." A crafty look played across his face. He brushed his hair out of his eyes and smoothed the edge of the blanket.

I half-smiled at his show of nerves and joined him on the blanket—at the farthest edge.

Malcolm popped a grape in his mouth. "So, Savvy Bent, tell me about yourself."

Obviously he was going with the not-so-subtle approach to questioning. I relaxed, a little. "What do you want to know?"

"What about your family. I know your dad. How about your mom?"

I was right. They had been talking about Mom. I could play his game. "In ninth grade, she was a state-champion in Chinese checkers. She tried to teach me the higher levels of strategy for the game, but I never had a real interest."

I took complete pleasure in watching Malcolm's facial expressions go from excited to frustrated at my trivial answers.

He flashed me a fake smile. "What else did she like to do? Any hobbies?"

I bit into a hunk of bread and held up my finger, so he had to wait while I chewed. After sipping on champagne, I finally answered. "She wasn't like normal moms. She was extreme about her exercise regime."

"Really?" He tilted his head and gave me his full attention.

"Oh, yeah. She got up before the crack of dawn to run like fifteen miles." I tried to act as sincere as I could. "She'd sprint across the nearby cow pastures and hurdle hay bales. I swear she was psycho. I loved her but I would've appreciated more chocolate chip cookies straight from the oven."

That was true, but it wasn't because she was playing leapfrog with hay bales. It was more like business trip after business trip. Malcolm did a fairly good job of hiding his excitement at the info, but his hand trembled as he downed his glass of champagne. I poured him another.

"What else?" he asked, ripping off a chunk of bread.

I tapped my head. "Let's see. My friends always thought she was kinda weird because she'd spend hours in the backyard, shooting at targets. I had to stop inviting them over because she'd scare them away. I don't even want to talk about the knife throwing."

He moved behind me and rubbed my shoulders. "Sounds tough. I know a little bit about obsessive parents."

I bet he did, if his story was true about his year on his own to prove himself. As he rubbed my back and ran his fingers through my hair, I didn't know how to feel. Did he like me at all?

I continued my story. "It was all good until I figured out the reason behind her obsessions."

He stopped rubbing and slid his hands down the sides of my arms. Again, they were trembling a bit. I wondered how much he was getting paid.

"And what was that?" he asked.

"Oh, I don't want to bore you with details. Let's talk about Jolie. I can't believe someone knocked him out."

Malcolm stiffened for just a second then leaned back into a casual pose, one leg crossed over the other. "Probably some jealous competitor."

"Yeah, probably. But I think he's bad."

"Savvy, he's one of the most loved figures in France. Why would you think he's bad?"

I turned and faced him. It was my turn to pump him for information. "I'm serious. And I don't think Peyton had anything to do with Aimee disappearing. I think Jolie did."

Malcolm choked on a grape. He pounded his chest, tears in his eyes, until the coughing attack stopped.

"Who knows?" I continued. "He may have shot at us at the park and possibly on our date." The more I thought about it, the more likely it seemed. Pouffant clearly didn't like my family or me.

After breathing deeply, Malcolm raised an eyebrow. "But that was a week before the Extravaganza. He wouldn't even have heard of you."

"True, but still." On the outside, Malcolm's rationale made sense. I mean, a week ago, I hadn't even heard of Jolie or the prize money. But I also knew that from our very first date Malcolm had an interest in my family and Malcolm worked for Jolie. Heck, he probably kidnapped Aimee so he could take her job. Clearly, Pouffant knew about me, and they both knew something about my family that I didn't, or they were delusional.

"You're right. He couldn't have known," I said.

He gently pulled me into him. My head rested in the crook of his neck, and he twirled my hair between his fingers. I breathed deep. Control. Nice and easy. Would anything distract him from his mission? I lifted my head slightly and brushed my lips against his neck. His vein pulsed and his breathing quickened. As expected, he gently pushed me away.

"You're killing me," he said.

"*Moi*?" I asked innocently.

"What did you discover about your mom? What was the reason behind her obsessions? You can't leave a guy hanging."

I planted small kisses on his neck, moving up to his jaw. "Hmm. You don't really want to talk about my parents, do you?"

He responded by lifting my chin with his finger. His gray eyes searched my face, moving from my eyes and lingering on my lips. He moved closer until our lips were inches apart. "Sure I do."

I gave in and whispered, "After she returned from a trip, I looked through her stuff and found some secret documents. I think she was some kind of," I paused as his eyes grew wider, "spy."

"Did you find anything else?" He gently kissed me as if he really didn't care about my answer.

Each brush of his lips against mine was turning my brain to mush. Tiny sparks of heat spread from the touch of his fingers on my skin. Was he feeling anything? I struggled to find the right words, because I didn't want to burst his spy bubble, but I also didn't want him spreading lies about my family.

I kissed the soft spot below his ear and mumbled, "Actually, I'm just joking."

He jerked away, breaking from our light kisses. His hands dropped from my arms as if my skin were poison. "What do you mean?"

Before answering, I decided it was wise to move within grabbing range of the frying pan. I'd gotten the information I needed. He didn't care about me, and that stung.

"My mom isn't a spy." I forced a giggle. "She was like every other work-consumed mom in America. The only thing she ever exterminated were the dust bunnies under our couch."

"Good one."

The next thirty minutes, I kept the banter as light as I could, considering I was miserable and wanted to tie him up and leave him somewhere butt naked. Finally, he packed up to go, stating he had to work at *Les Pouffant's*. More like go back and report.

"What? Leaving so soon?" I said. "We haven't even talked about my dad yet."

I bit my lip right after the words left my mouth, and we locked eyes, the silent questions coursing between us, both of us wanting to know what the other one knew and willing to do anything to get it. I had info the *maitre d'* wanted. And if the *maitre d'* worked for Jolie, then that meant the great Jolie Pouffant wanted to know. That was when I decided it was my turn to spy. On Malcolm.

He might hold the answers.

Twenty-four

WHILE GRAY RAMBLED ON about the business, I hid behind my latte.

We were huddled around a big white plastic table in the warehouse, and the chill rising off the cement floor and leaking in through the windows set my teeth to rattling. I rubbed my arms and blew into my hands to warm my fingers. Though chilled on the outside, a fire burned in my belly. I felt like a large black cauldron with all the memories of the past couple weeks churning, bubbling, and boiling. The lies. The messages. The trickery. I had lost touch with the truth. And Malcolm sitting across the table looking oh so suave and knowledgeable just added fuel to the fire.

My head pounded. Clues, images, and snippets of conversations swirled in and out of my brain. What had happened to Aimee? And what did that have to do with me?

Her grandmother's cottage was abandoned, the neighbor warned me to stay away, and I had no leads.

As Gray finished up his end of the meeting, Dad shuffled papers ready to embark on a long list of to-dos.

"So." My voice echoed in the large room but still sounded small and wimpy. I cleared my throat and spoke louder. "I don't think Spy Games' clients are all that impressed with our dramatic entrance."

Frankie smirked. Nancy gave me her motherly smile. Gray ignored me. So did Dad. Malcolm studied me.

"Your dad explained it to me," he said. "Sounds like fun. I bet clients love it."

I pictured Malcolm tied up in a chair while bat turds dropped from the rafters into his hair. With that image in mind, I said, "I had a conversation with a client and she mentioned it was kind of show offy."

Okay, that conversation never happened, but no one had to know.

Dad cut in. "The entrance stays." He rambled on, but I quickly lost interest.

I pictured walking over to Malcolm with a power drill in one hand, ready to torment him, and the fear on his face when he broke down crying, admitting his guilt. Every once in a while, Malcolm tried to catch my eyes, but I refused to play his game. I refused to be another toy in his chest.

"Savvy?" Dad asked.

Everyone was staring at me. "Yes?"

"What do you think? Will that work?"

A blush crept across my skin. I had to cover. I couldn't disappoint him. "Yup. Great idea."

A part of me wished I knew what I was agreeing with. Dad can brainstorm some pretty wacky ideas. Like dropping from ceilings. But I couldn't ask him to repeat it. He wanted me to be the perfect Spy Games staff. Enthusiastic. Attentive. In control.

The rest of the meeting, I imagined different ways to torture Malcolm. Except, it made me miss Aimee, because she would have had great ideas. I'd never felt so far away from helping her as I did right then, sitting through a meeting, with her replacement at the table. It was like she'd been erased from the earth and no one cared.

"Does anyone here even miss Aimee?" My voice was louder than I meant it to be.

Dad took control. "Savvy, of course we do, but we're happy she's living her dreams."

"You believed that note?" I looked into the eyes of my co-workers, pleading for someone to take my side.

Gray spoke up. "Why wouldn't we?"

I pushed my chair back, causing a terrible screeching noise that sent shivers up my back. "Because she never said goodbye. She never talked about it and that's not like her."

"How long did you know her?" Malcolm asked.

In my snootiest voice, I said, "Six months."

Malcolm leaned back. "It takes years to know someone. Most people are putting up a front of how they'd like people to view them."

"What? Did you take psychology?"

He seemed embarrassed to be fighting over words with me. "Actually, I've taken two courses online."

Great. We had something in common.

He looked around at all the staff. "Given that six months is only a fraction of the time needed to fully understand someone or have them share secrets, we have to assume Aimee is telling the truth."

Dad rubbed the scruff on his chin, clearly impressed. My limbs trembled. How could Malcolm betray me like that? I'd told him all about Aimee. We'd spied on Peyton together and searched Aimee's apartment. I thought he'd agreed with me. But that was before I knew he worked for Jolie, before he set the kidnapping up to look like Peyton was guilty, and before he tried to exact information from me over a living room picnic.

How could Dad believe Malcolm over me? Tears threatened. The embarrassing kind. I couldn't take it anymore.

I slammed my hand on the table, then instantly regretted it as pain shot through every finger. "Aimee's in trouble." I turned and left before Dad could put me in chains and ship me off to Siberia.

I spent the next day fuming that Malcolm had tried to seduce me for info on my family and then jerked me around at the staff meeting. So not cool. While silently cursing him, I prepared for Operation Take Down Malcolm.

"Where you going, Savvy?" Dad asked from his slumber on the sofa.

Not sure how dads do that. Mine can snore away, mouth open, drool spilling, and still know what's going on around him.

"Heading out for a run." *And a little bit of espionage.*

I smoothed down my black shirt over my black pants. I looked a little bit like the wannabe spies I mocked, but I wasn't going to dwell on that.

"Okay. Sounds good. I'm going to, um, continue working." He picked up a folder to review.

Yeah, right, I laughed to myself. "I might stop by Malcolm's to review some Spy Games rules."

"How's he coming along? Will he be a good replacement?" He lowered the file, his eyes fixed on me. "I had a good feeling when I hired him. We were lucky."

Right. Just the word *replacement* turned Aimee into a piece of Tupperware. "He'll be just peachy."

On my way to the Metro, I let the cool air clear my mind. I'd give anything to talk to Aimee. She'd tell me in a flash if this were ludicrous or brilliant. She'd laugh at the irony. Of me. Spying. Not only on Peyton, but now on Malcolm. For so long I'd ignored all the times Dad tried to chat up the Spy Games life, and here I was, going off on another spy mission.

Looking for Aimee could be considered spying, but I'd never felt in any real danger. This Pouffant guy, on the other hand, was obsessed enough with my family to plant a spy in our lives and to shoot at me—or hire someone to shoot at me. Twice.

Malcolm's darkened window mocked me. What does a guy like him do in his spare time? I hadn't really talked to him since he'd tried to question me about Mom, which had totally flopped on one hand, but on the other hand, revealed his true colors. A shade called double agent.

After walking up to Malcolm's apartment, I stopped and pressed my ear to the door.

Silence. I knocked, ready to run if I heard any movement. Nothing. I wiggled one of Dad's fancy devices in the keyhole and the lock popped. With a slight turn, the door opened.

I slipped in like a night shadow.

Twenty-five

I SWEPT THROUGH MALCOLM'S apartment like a small whirlwind, opening drawers, rifling through closets. There had to be something. A phone number. A picture. A diary. Or maybe chocolate chip cookies from his mom—if the story about his family were true. I stormed through his bedroom, closets, and kitchen looking for something, anything. About Aimee. About me. About Jolie. Something to tie the pieces together.

After about half an hour, I plunked down at the table. I had to stop thinking like Nancy Drew, searching for clues in the cupboards. He was too good to leave information about my family exposed or to leave a picture of Jolie's prisoner under a magnet on his fridge.

I sank into one of his kitchen chairs. Who was Malcolm? I mean who was he really?

"Why, Malcolm?" I closed my eyes, willing the walls to whisper his secrets.

I started thinking about his connection to Jolie and their connection to my mom, but then my thoughts turned to the gray flecks in his eyes and the curious way he studied me. His burning touches on my arm and the gentle whisper of his lips on my skin. I shook the memories away. He was probably faking it all anyway.

A laptop. That's what I needed. Better yet, a cell phone, but he was too smart to leave that lying around. I opened the closet doors and shined my flashlight into it. This was where he'd kept our disguises. Maybe he kept laptops in here too.

Nothing.

I stopped rushing around and let my eyes wander the kitchen, taking in everything slowly, not missing an inch. And there it was. Sitting next to the coffee maker. His laptop. How had I missed it?

I gently opened it and pressed power. Someone like him would have passwords, right? I tried everything. Email. Internet. Everything was locked down. He was good. I opened a folder left on the desktop. Immediately a document popped out at me.

Bent.

My. Last. Name.

He had a file on me. The mouse hovered over the file. All I had to do was click on it. Did I really want to know what he had on me? On my family? Hell, yeah. I clicked on the file.

No pictures of me walking across a street like I expected, or my mom at the Eiffel in her disguise, or even my dad, hair slicked back, wearing shades. Instead there was a picture of just some normal-looking guy in khakis. I scrolled down but the text was complete gibberish. Encrypted. I couldn't read it if I tried. My life had been reduced to a bunch of squiggles and a picture I didn't recognize.

A high-pitched giggle from outside Malcolm's apartment cascaded over me like confectioner's sugar. I ran to the door and peeked out. Malcolm was stumbling up the stairs with some blonde hanging off him. His roving hands encircled her waist, and he kissed her neck as they lost their balance and almost fell. They paused halfway up the stairs, and he whispered in her ear, nuzzling her neck. Seriously. Get a room. Except, they were about to get one. In Malcolm's apartment.

In less than three seconds, I slammed the laptop shut and crawled into the tiny closet that wasn't meant for people. Just as I slid the doors shut, they waltzed into the room.

"Soooo," Malcolm drawled. "Would you like a drink to top off the evening?" *Was he drunk?*

"Sure," oozed her sugary voice.

Glasses clinked. I had to separate my emotions from the job at hand and be heartless so the ache in my chest would go away.

"Why don't we have some fun and play a game?" Malcolm's voice was sultry and suggestive. I doubted he had Connect Four in mind. The voice that had once caused my heart to flutter now made it race with fury. Man whore.

"Ooh, sounds naughty," the blonde replied. "I love it. What do you have in mind?"

All I could picture was strip poker.

"It's a game I call Truth or Lie," Malcolm said, and I could picture the gleam in his eye and the curve of his lips.

"Poo. That doesn't sound like fun."

"Let me explain." Chairs moved against the floor. I was sure she didn't need much convincing. "I say something about myself and you have to decide if it's the truth or a lie."

"Ooh, and if I'm right, then you take off an article of clothing."

"And take a shot."

Great. I knew it. A stripping and a drinking game.

"You start," Malcolm said.

"Okay." More giggles. "Last summer I climbed Mt. Everest."

That was so obvious. She clearly just wanted to get naked.

"Lie," Malcolm answered.

"How'd you know?" Giggles.

There was silence as I was sure the shot was poured and an article of clothing cast to the floor. She probably didn't start with her socks. I hoped her bra was old and ratty.

"My turn." Malcolm paused, probably trying to subdue the temptation to rip off all her clothes and skip the foreplay. "I come from a long line of assassins, going back hundreds of years."

My mouth opened slightly in shock. A family of assassins? Right. I taught him everything he knew about being a secret agent. Or so I'd thought.

More giggles. "Lie."

"How'd you see through me?"

I tried my hardest not to picture him ripping off his shirt and revealing his impeccable pecs, which I'd seen before.

"I'd love to move the game to the bedroom," she said.

"Tsk. Tsk. It has to be something about yourself."

Silence. As I'm sure she racked her empty head for something to say.

"I giggle when I'm nervous."

No, really?

"True," Malcolm said.

I sat through various questions about family pets, siblings, childhood, and embarrassing moments. I could have learned more about Malcolm, but most of the words dribbling from his mouth were lies. Eventually, it all became white noise as I studied the grime on the inside of the door.

When they stopped rambling and laughed and moaned, heading away from the kitchen and toward the bedroom, I couldn't take it anymore. I eased open the sliding door without a sound and crawled out, my body stiff and sore. With a scathing look toward the bedroom, which I hoped Malcolm felt burning a blister onto his probably naked butt, I snatched the laptop from the table and put it back on the counter.

"I think you might be taking Spy Games a little too seriously."

I jumped a mile then whipped around. Malcolm stood at the edge of the kitchen, like a cat about to eat his favorite meal.

Where the hell was a frying pan?

Twenty-six

"I. . . UM. . . STOPPED BY to talk about Spy Games. Then you showed up with her." I jerked my thumb toward his bedroom. "I felt stupid, so I hid in the closet."

Malcolm flashed a wry grin, like he didn't believe me.

"When you weren't here, I decided to upload the info to your laptop." So lame.

"Where's the flash drive then?" he asked.

I smiled and cheese practically fell out my mouth it was so fake. "Darn. I forgot it. I'll have to get it to you tomorrow."

"What is going on?" the blonde said in her cute little French accent and slung her arm over his shoulder in an attempt to drag him back to the room.

"I have something I need to take care of. Maybe we should call it a night." He leaned back and whispered in her ear. She gave me the evil eye before kissing his cheek.

"You live close enough to walk?" Malcolm asked as he followed her to the door.

"No worries. I will call friends. *Bonsoir.*"

The blonde left and the door clicked shut. Malcolm turned and blocked the doorway with his body.

Major adrenaline kicked in, causing my body to tremble. Somehow I had to get him away from the door so I could get out of here. I swiped the counters looking for something to throw at him but he was too clean. A cupboard hung partly open. I grabbed a plain white dish and held it out like a shield.

Malcolm stepped closer. "We need to talk."

"Yeah right," I said. His kind of talking probably meant torture of some kind.

"Give me one minute and then I'll let you leave." He poured on the innocence and charm with his little-lost-boy expression. "Please?"

"Fine." I kept the plate up not really sure how it could protect me but it was better than nothing. "Talk."

He moved away from the door. "What are you doing sneaking around my place? And don't give me the same line about passing on information on Spy Games."

"What are you doing asking so many questions about my mom?" I clenched my teeth and settled in for a fight.

He reached toward me as if to grab my hand but I stepped back and waved the plate like it was some kind of medieval sword. "Not one step closer until you answer."

"I was just trying to get to know you. Is that so wrong?"

Any other girl might have been fooled, but Mom lied for months about her scrapbooking, which now I doubted if she ever cut even one piece of paper or glued one button into a book. After all that, I could now recognize the signs of a professional liar, the perfectly blank face and the relaxed shoulders and the casual pose. I was so tired of being lied to. So tired. "The truth. Now."

He sighed. "I like you and wanted to get to know you better."

My arms slightly trembled. The emotion built in my chest until I yelled, "LIAR!" In one bold move I threw the plate against the wall. It splintered and crashed to the floor. In the few seconds it took for him to register my actions, I booked it toward the door. The smell of old carpets teased me from the hallway. It was the smell of freedom. I was almost there.

Until he grabbed my arm and yanked me back into the room.

I struggled, but he was too strong. "What do you want with me? Just tell me."

Not letting go of me, he kicked out a chair with his foot. "Sit."

"No way."

He dragged me over to the closet where he grabbed a stray piece of rope that looked familiar.

"Nice rope you got there."

He grimaced at the reference to his framing Peyton, which was another thing I didn't understand. After he pushed me onto a chair, he tied my arms in the back. I got in a few good kicks.

"So now I'm your prisoner? What the hell is going on, Malcolm?"

"You're not my prisoner." He grew agitated and fumbled in a kitchen cupboard.

"Could've fooled me."

"I don't want you running away before you hear me out." He poured water into a small coffee maker then stood staring at it. Every few seconds, his hand would run through his hair in the typical show of male frustration. Finally, he sat at the table across from me and opened his laptop, probably to catch up on his daily blog reading about how to be a jerk or how to lie to a girl effectively.

Minutes later, late-night coffee percolated. The smell filled the small kitchen and I kept thinking about the words I'd overhead from the freezer in Jolie's. They talked about my mother. "I want the truth."

He poured a cup of coffee but never took a sip. He placed it down too hard on the table. Coffee sloshed over the sides. "The thing is...I can't tell you the truth. Just, please, stop poking around in Pouffant's affairs for your own good."

"I can't," I whispered. "I want to find my mom...and Aimee. You've got to understand that."

He nodded. "I swear I'll never hurt you, but I can't promise that others won't. Please, just go about your way and act like a normal teen."

His words sounded familiar. That was exactly what Mom had said to me. Bingo. That was the last thing he should've said. Now I knew for sure that somehow this was all connected. If I kept my nose to the trail, I'd find my mom, but Malcolm had to think I'd given up. I let out a loud sigh. "Fine."

He didn't say anything. Seconds or maybe minutes passed. Finally, I couldn't take it anymore, and my eyes wandered over to him. His eyes peered into mine, open and honest, then dropped to my mouth. My heart rate spiked. Jiminy crickets, he was spying on my family. How could he look at me like he wanted to kiss me?

"What about the girl?" I tried to keep the hurt from my voice.

He moved into the chair right next to me and pulled it up, so his knees surrounded my legs. I closed my eyes.

"Savvy."

"What about the girl?" I repeated.

He kissed my cheek. "You don't have to worry about her."

My body and heart were traitors to what I knew in my mind. That we couldn't work out. That I was an assignment. That he was a liar and refused to tell me the truth.

He brought his lips inches from mine. "Do you still have that damn serving tray up your shirt?"

Nothing registered on my face, but he'd gone too far mocking my highly refined methods of defense. I'd wanted to play dumb the whole time, but I needed to push and get a reaction. It had nothing to do with the fact that he had my insides tied into knots.

The anger and hurt I felt bubbled up, and I didn't have the desire to play games with him anymore. I spit out the words. "I know you work for Jolie and you're keeping secrets. And you probably kidnapped Aimee too."

My words spurred him on as if he didn't care I knew his secrets. That's where my plan went wrong. He reached around behind me, pressing his chest against mine. With a flick of his wrist, he untied the ropes from my arms.

"You win." He picked me up off the chair and put me on the kitchen table. With one suave move, he whipped the serving tray out and let it clatter to the floor. He moved in to kiss me, but I pushed him away. My plan was backfiring. He was supposed to get mad, not get turned on.

"So you admit it?" I asked.

"I admit nothing."

"Then I'm done here." I gave him one final push and scrambled off the table, straightening my hair and doing my best to smooth my shirt. "I'll see you later."

"Savvy."

"Skip it. I'm not interested."

"You don't understand."

"Oh, I understand everything. You're a man-whore and all that word implies. And I mean in more ways than in the bedroom sense. You also whored yourself out to Jolie for pay, while pretending to help me find my friend."

I needed to leave before I hurt the poor guy. "I'm so outta here," I said.

Halfway through the doorway, I heard him shout out, "The girl. She used to work for Jolie."

I stopped. That sick feeling I'd gotten my facts wrong sat in my gut. "What do you mean?"

"I hung out with her tonight and brought her up here to sneak in some questions about Jolie." He gripped the back of the chair. "For Aimee. I'd hoped the girl knew something about her or had seen her on the job."

I narrowed my eyes. "Did she?"

He lowered his head. "No."

"Pfft. Right. I'm sure it was torture for you, cross-examining her."

I turned my back and let his words run through my mind. It was hard to believe his night of seductive words and groaning had turned out to be nothing more than a spy mission. On my behalf. Should I believe him? I wasn't that stupid, but he didn't need to know it.

He crossed the room and grabbed my hand. He didn't say anything at first but ran his fingers through my hair to tuck it behind my ear. "I'm afraid you'll take it a step too far...and try to spy on Jolie by yourself. I want you stop the games and work with me."

"Hmm." I was willing to play along and see where this went, but I couldn't say I trusted him. He rubbed his thumb over the skin of my wrist then kissed the red marks the ropes left behind. "I still have questions before I can trust you."

He nodded. "Go ahead."

"Did you have anything to do with Aimee being kidnapped?" I asked.

"No."

"Are you working for Jolie?"

"Yes. I'm supposed to be spying on you, but I'm pretending in order to gain his trust and figure out if he has Aimee."

"How come you didn't tell me this before?" I shot out.

"Honestly?" He slid into the chair. "I didn't want to scare you."

"Hmm." His story had more holes than Swiss cheese. "How did he trust you so quickly?"

"I'm a good worker. I earned his respect quickly."

I rubbed my chin. I didn't trust him for half a millisecond, but I needed him to believe I did. I needed to find out more about Jolie. And why they were talking about my mother.

"Okay, fine. Deal." I stuck out my hand, and we shook on it.

He really shouldn't have believed anything I said. Guess I'm a liar too. Because the only way to get to the truth was to spy on the big guy himself. Jolie Pouffant.

Twenty-seven

THE NEXT AFTERNOON, I sipped my latte, letting the creamy hot liquid calm my nerves. I pulled my hat low, to hide my face. The atmosphere at *Les Pouffant's* was just what I needed to think about Aimee: the chatter of French, the smell of cinnamon, and the presence of my enemy.

Peyton hadn't kidnapped Aimee. Malcolm and Jolie had purposely led me to believe he had. In *Les Pouffant's* there was a musty smell coming from the basement. Possibly a good place to keep prisoners. Jolie didn't want me to focus on him. Bingo!

My only lead was Jolie. What mysteries was he hiding? Was he possibly connected to my mom and the money? What did he know about Aimee? Why was he spying on me? Thoughts swirled in my mind like creamer in coffee. It was time to get to know the person behind the name. And I could only do that by shadowing him, spying on him, hoping he'd get careless and expose information.

I moved across the street from *Les Pouffant's*, waiting for Pouffant to leave for the day. He must live in a grand mansion out of the city, so I was prepared. I had money for the Metro or to hire a cab if I needed to.

After my fifth or sixth latte, Pouffant exited with his coat and hat. He chatted with customers, instructed a new waiter, and then took off down the street at a brisk stroll. Time for action. He must be off on some devious mission of death.

With 007 music playing in my head, I slipped in and out of the crowds, just far enough behind the target that if he looked over his shoulder, I'd melt in with the masses. I tracked him from the streets to the Metro and then back to the streets until finally he stopped before a house. It wasn't too big or too small. White shutters at the windows winked at me in a friendly sort of way. Pansies lined the walkway up to the front door. And the grass needed to be cut. Quite normal.

I stopped and hid behind a tree with my legs crossed because the five lattes had caught up with me. This did not look like the residence of a master criminal. There had to be some mistake. I pulled the binoculars from my bag and narrowed in on Jolie as he approached the front door. I almost could see the confectioner's sugar still lingering in his twisted beard.

The door opened. But before I could see who welcomed him, he quickly stepped into the house and shut the door. Was this his house? Or was he visiting someone? Only one way to find out. And I'd never felt like such a criminal.

After waiting a few minutes, I sprinted across the street to a hedge of bushes dividing the house from the neighbor's. When my breathing got back under control, I dashed across the small yard until I reached Jolie's house. I leaned against the siding, expecting his voice to ripple across the yard, yelling at me. But I didn't hear anything like that. His stern voice echoed from the backyard. Feeling the need for stealth, I crawled along the side of the house. Huddling next to a bush, I wrapped my coat around me, wishing it could completely hide me, wishing I could steal inside and use their bathroom without them knowing.

I leaned my head against the house, not looking, just soaking in the sounds. Their stream of French washed over me. No English. As I sat wondering why I thought this would be helpful and feeling totally useless at solving the mystery of Aimee's disappearance, I listened more carefully. The voice of his companion was familiar, but I couldn't quite place it. They didn't seem to be having a friendly conversation. They were debating, words pinging back and forth at each other. The door slammed and someone went inside. I dared to peek around the corner.

Jolie squatted low to the ground and held his hand out with some crumbs on it. A chicken pecked at the ground. A chicken? Who has chickens for pets? But then I looked past Jolie. A tiny henhouse stood in the back of the yard, and several hens with brown speckled breasts were wandering free. He spoke to it in soothing tones and tried to get it to eat from his hand.

"Squawk, squawk," Jolie imitated the hen.

I choked on my saliva. This was the man behind the name? In his own environment, he seemed human, almost normal, other than acting like a bird. The door shut and an older woman walked down the steps. On the top of her head was a bun of white hair, wisps hanging down. Her back was to me. I held my breath, waiting for her to turn. She poured him tea and placed a plate of cookies on the table, and then she stood off to the side as if waiting for a command.

Her voice plucked my heartstrings. My body froze. It couldn't be. How could I not have recognized it? She turned and confirmed my worst fears. Marie, Aimee's grandmother was Jolie's house slave, a servant, feeding him gingersnaps and mint tea. I clasped my hands together to keep myself from hurdling the bushes, grabbing a potted fern and knocking him out. How dare he keep an elderly lady captive? And someone as sweet as Marie? The lines on her face seemed deeper, and her shoulders hunched over a bit more. He'd better be treating her right. Images of her locked in her room with barely any food made me dig my fingers into the ground. Were those the same clothes she wore when I visited her with Malcolm? Maybe she was kidnapped later that day?

I fought the urge to sneak through the window for proof. Was Aimee inside? Only yards away from me? While Jolie munched on cookies—and hopefully pulled out a filling or something terrible like that—I could be sliding in between the shadows of the house, saving my friend. But wait. Dad would never believe me without proof.

I had proof! I pulled my phone from my pocket and with one touch put it on camera mode. Without looking, because that's how good spies do it, I aimed my phone around the corner of the house to capture Jolie and Marie together. Proof. Or the start of it. I'd come back tomorrow, rescue them both, and head to the police with evidence. I'd be a hero.

A strong hand grabbed my wrist.

Twenty-eight

WITH A QUICK BUT strong yank, someone pulled me from my hiding spot. I tumbled and landed on my stomach, face in the grass, right next to a hen pecking at seeds. Would Jolie believe I was lost? He kicked out a black wrought iron chair.

"Please, join me."

Should I make a run for it? Use the potted plant? Or stay calm and draw on my Spy Games experience to pull information from him without him even knowing it, like taking candy from a baby.

His voice held fake enthusiasm. "How nice of you to drop by. How timely. We have cookies and tea."

I pushed onto my knees and squinted up at him through the glare of the setting sun. His full, curly beard still held crumbs from his day in the kitchen. His clear blue eyes were smart and didn't miss anything. Like the picture I took. He held the phone in his chapped hands and flipped through my pictures, including ones of Aimee. I searched his face for any recognition.

He nodded and smiled then tossed the phone on the table. I had a feeling the pictures of him and Marie were deleted. I sat on the edge of the chair and tried to catch Marie's eyes but she stood off to the side, looking at the ground. He spoke to her in French, and without a glance in my direction, she walked inside. How dare he? But then I remembered my mission. I needed to be suave, gentile, and sophisticated.

"These cookies look delicious. Is that your neighbor who baked them?"

He waved his hand. "Pfft. *Non*. We have always had this tradition. Meet after work and sip tea while talking. Do you have such traditions with your family?"

"Um. Yeah, sure." I racked my brain.

We used to. Back when Mom lived at home in Pennsylvania, and we were a family. But since we'd arrived in France it was all about Spy Games. Our traditions revolved around the latest gadgets for listening in on a conversation or how to put the biggest scare into clients. The last words Mom spoke to me were directions to burn the package, which I didn't do. I did miss one tradition I'd started in Paris.

"I used to meet my close friend Aimee for croissants every morning."

His mustache twitched before he stroked it into obedience. "Ah yes. At my café. You two met at *Les Pouffant's, non?*"

"*Oui.* I mean yes. We used to." My determination slipped a bit.

"Traditions, meeting with friends and family that is the *joi de vive.* Nothing more important than family. You agree?" His eyes narrowed in on me.

"Yes. I agree. I'd do anything for a friend." Was he threatening me?

He pushed the plate of cookies closer. "You see. We are not that different."

A chilly night breeze ruffled my hair, carrying the smell of late-blooming flowers from the edge of the yard. He and I? Not that different?

"What happened to your friend? I have not seen her there."

What happened? How dare he? Any resolve I had to be 007 disappeared.

"I thought you might know something about that. Considering you're making her grandmother be your servant."

"*Excuse moi?*" He puffed his belly out a bit more.

I gripped the sides of the table and stared him down. "Yes. I know the truth. I know Marie. I would know her

198

gingersnap cookies anywhere." I stood up and inched toward the side. "I know Aimee, her granddaughter. I know the two of them disappeared last week. And now I know you're a liar."

Tinges of red appeared on his neck and cheeks. He spluttered a bit. "Girl, you do not know what you are talking about."

"Yes, I do. I demand you release them. Now. And my name is Savvy. Savvy Bent." My voice quavered a bit, and my threats seemed silly as the hen pecked at my feet.

Jolie roared with laughter, great big bouts that dwindled down to chuckles. When he finally stopped, tears streaming into his beard, he took one look at me and burst out laughing again. "My dear. You are quite amusing."

I stopped inching away. "You are a washed up pastry chef heading past his prime. Release the prisoners, and I won't report you to the police."

His boisterous laughter made my blood run cold in my veins.

"I'm serious." I put my hands on my hips for emphasis.

Suddenly he was by my side, his fingers digging into my arm. "You can call the police if you'd like. I'll even give you your phone back." He whispered in my ear. "It will be a waste of time. The police know me and would never doubt a famous chef."

I snorted. "They probably know you because you paid them off."

"Possibly. But playtime is over. My interest in you is waning. Thank you for the brief entertainment."

He pulled me toward the back of the yard, his footsteps quick and sure. His agility amazed me. I pulled back, realizing that he might be more dangerous than his rolipoliness let on.

"Well, thanks for the cookies. My dad's expecting me home."

He grunted his disapproval as we reached the back of the yard. The henhouse was a dingy gray and a distinct odor wafted between its walls. I wrinkled my nose.

"Did you want me to make you scrambled eggs for dinner? I'd be happy too."

I regretted the words as soon as I said them. He opened the door and pushed me toward the small opening. I pushed back.

"I don't think so," I grunted, but his powerful grip steered me toward the small house. This was it. I'd be locked up with the hens for probably the next week living off raw eggs. He didn't think twice about keeping a prisoner, which was more proof he'd taken Aimee and Marie captive. Okay so they weren't chained in the basement, but something was very wrong.

Jolie and I were caught in a push and shove battle. With one last shout, I let a kick fly, hoping to catch him in the stomach. But he grabbed my foot and with a twist that sent pain shooting up my leg, he pushed me into the house and slammed the door.

I pounded on it. "You can't keep me in here."

"I won't keep you forever. Just a little payback for the tranquilizer dart."

I went silent. What could I say?

"What? No smart answer to that? Yes, I know all about that." The latch clicked. "Why don't you think about how wrong your actions were, and I'll be back later."

I was alone. In a henhouse. I still had my phone, but who was I going to call? Dad? No way. Malcolm? Impossible. I'd told him I wouldn't spy on Jolie. Basically, I had no one.

Feathers ruffled and one hen jumped to the dusty floor. Were hens protective of their eggs? Would they attack? Had Jolie left me to die at the claws of a bunch of chickens? I wanted to send a quick text to Stephen King. I had the perfect idea for his next horror novel. Crazy pastry chef collects prisoners like keepsakes and tortures them with the smell of chicken poop.

A cobweb brushed against my cheek, and I let out a tiny scream. I pressed my back up against the door, ready to kick any flying poultry that came at me. With a wave of my arms, I tried to shoo the hen away. She cocked her head and stared at me. I could see through its beady eyes to the small workings in its teeny brain. It was debating if I was a threat or not.

I pasted on a cheesy smile. "Squawk! I'm a friend. No worries. I won't touch your eggs no matter how hungry I get. I promise."

After a three-second stare down, she turned and pecked at a non-existent corn kernel on the floor. I breathed a sigh of relief now that the immediate threat of death by pecking had disappeared. I leaned my head against the strong but rickety door, no longer caring about the cobwebs or the chickens. So much for my 007 act. I never claimed to be a great spy and this proved it. While thinking about my mom, her strange words, and Malcolm's double-dealings, I must've dozed off because when the door opened and I tumbled backward down the small ramp, I wasn't prepared.

At all.

Twenty-nine

I SCRAMBLED TO MY FEET. Marie stood over me with a finger to her lips, pointing to the side yard. "Leave. Quickly."

I searched her eyes but found nothing that revealed the truth. "What's going on? Are you okay? Is Aimee okay?"

She shook her head. "You must leave now. I must get back inside."

"But. . ." I tried to argue, but she forcibly pushed me away.

When I heard Jolie call to her from inside the house, I took one last look at her warm eyes before running.

The next morning, I was ready to go. But this time I was prepared. Water bottles, granola bars, camera, binoculars, hairpins, Band-aids, and a crowbar. If I were going to end up in a dirty henhouse again, I'd have the basics. I strode into the kitchen, confident, in control, ready to take on the world of espionage with the best of them.

Dad sat at the kitchen table buried in the newspaper as usual. I poured a cup of coffee, black this time. I didn't need a sugar crash later in the day. The steam coated my face in warmth.

"Any more shootings?" I asked.

"Thankfully, no. But I've pulled shooting blanks at our clients from the program, for now, until this dies down."

I bit into an apple and munched. "Good idea."

Every morning, any time Dad and I bumped into each other, Spy Games became the topic of the day. I could change and let him into my life by talking about Malcolm, or about Mom. But if I brought those subjects up, and Dad asked questions or we fell into a serious talk, I'd have to lie. I don't think he'd do well with, "Oh, by the way, Mom could be an assassin," or "Yeah, funny thing, Malcolm is spying on our family and a pastry chef might have it out for me," or even worse, "I have thousands of dollars stuffed in my closet." Yeah, no. He had experience running a business, and anything I said he'd blow off as paranoia. Or he'd take over and lock me in my room. No way.

I played his game. "How's the new route coming along? Are we ready for Spy Games this weekend?"

He flipped down the newspaper and gave me the eye, suspicious that I even cared. I don't blame him because most of me didn't. It was called deflection. Let's talk about you so we don't talk about me. And he always fell for it.

"It's great. We're all set for this Saturday. I think the new addition will be perfect. I'm thinking of expanding even more, trying for a game every weekend instead of twice a month."

"Money?" I asked, suddenly feeling guilty about the hidden wads of cash, and remembering the phone call I'd heard from under his bed.

But I had no idea where the money came from. What if I used it and then found out it was stolen and some mad man with muscles the size of a truck came after me and broke my kneecaps? No thanks.

"Well, yes. And it will be good for the business. Get the word out." His eyes flicked to the clock on the coffee maker and then to the front door.

"Expecting someone?" I finished my apple and tossed it into the trash.

Dad nodded to the fridge. "There are some leftover pancakes in the fridge if you want them."

"Thanks." I warmed them up in the microwave, not falling for Dad's trick of changing the topic. Maybe I learned my conversational tactics from him. While dowsing them in syrup, I said casually, "So, someone stopping by? Gray? Nancy?"

Dad coughed and lifted the newspaper. "Spy Games business."

"Don't think," I stuffed pancakes in my mouth, "that I can't see what you're doing."

"What?" Dad feigned shock.

"That's right. Vague answers. What do you want me to do?"

A smile lit up his face. "I thought you'd never ask."

Someone knocked on the door.

"And perfect timing," Dad said. "Come on in!"

Malcolm entered, and I about peed my pants. Good going, Dad.

Thirty minutes later, Malcolm and I stood outside the Notre Dame cathedral. Tourists brushed past us to enter the old church, but I wasn't ready. Again, the cobblestones got to me. I loved them. I lifted my head straight back and stared up at the stone structure carved with so many saints and intricate details. Incredible. That might be why I barely noticed when Malcolm slipped his arm around me.

"You ready?" he asked.

If history could be carried on a breeze, it rushed and swirled around me. The sounds of ancient priests, the clip clop of horses, the ring of the giant bell I knew was hidden in the cathedral's towers.

"Can you imagine?" I whispered.

"What?" he whispered back.

"Being here, living here. Sometimes I'd love to touch the iron fence, the right one, and I'd travel back in time."

"That sounds great, but I have to work this afternoon. And we're on a mission for your dad."

Right. I shook it off along with Malcolm's arm.

"Let's go."

As we walked under the arches, I felt the crowbar press through the backpack into my back. I shouldn't have to use it if I played the game. And if Malcolm didn't act suspicious.

Again, an overwhelming sense of history in the black and white checkered floor and the vaulted ceilings washed over me. The long halls and the muted light filtering in through the stained glass windows made me whisper.

"I don't think this is going to work for Spy Games."

"Why not?" Malcolm spun, his outstretched arm pointing to the interior. "I think it's great. Another big tourist place."

"Yeah, but it's a church. Isn't it wrong to play games here? And we have to pay to get to the towers. Dad's looking to cut costs."

We paid the fee and headed toward the start of the spiral stairs.

"That's what your dad said when I suggested we check this place out—"

"This was your idea?" I stopped in my tracks, right at the bottom of the stairs.

A chill descended into my bones. He set this whole thing up? Since I didn't trust Malcolm, I had to look at the deeper reason he brought me here. I knew he didn't care about Spy Games.

"Isn't this the church famous for the hunchback?" I asked.

"Yes, exactly. That's why I think people will love it, especially Americans."

That hunchback was held prisoner in the towers overlooking Paris. Held prisoner. Was this a veiled threat? Or was I being too melodramatic? All of a sudden every tourist pointing a camera in my direction became the enemy. Every man in a suit coat with a Bluetooth in his ear became a possible assassin. What if Jolie had goons following us with plans to shoot me down with a special camera? It's been done before. I could end up in something worse than a smelly chicken coop. Like a coffin. After they extracted whatever secret information they thought I had embedded deep in my psyche.

Adrenaline rushed through my limbs, and I wanted to whip out the crowbar, just in case. I took a deep breath and forced myself to climb the stairs. From the outside, I had to look like I was enjoying myself, out on a date with a cute boy. I grabbed Malcolm's hand and swung our arms like we were an innocent couple in love.

He sneaked a glance at me and smiled. In that moment, I wanted to tell him everything. About the money, the Extravaganza, that I had no clue what they wanted to know. That I wasn't a spy, that I wasn't a danger to anyone. A part of me trusted him, trusted the nice boy who planned picnics and wanted me to be safe.

"What?"

Then I remembered his conversation with Pouffant, his willingness to spy on me. "I was just thinking how we've got a lot of stairs to climb. Let's get started."

We climbed around and around and around. The stairs were endless. My legs burned.

"How much longer?" I puffed out.

"We're almost halfway. Trust me, the climb is totally worth it. Even if we don't use it in Spy Games, you've got to make the climb at least once."

"I'm not sure about that. There's no way we can do this for the games. Just climbing the stairs will take two hours!"

I stopped to rest. An echo of footsteps behind us also stopped.

"Okay," I said, "Let's do this."

After a couple minutes, I stopped. Again, a few seconds later, the footsteps behind us stopped too. We were being followed.

Thirty

"COME ON," MALCOLM CALLED over his shoulder. "We're almost halfway. And there's a small café!"

I ran to catch up with him. I might not have any real spy skills but I was a teenage girl with a healthy dose of gut instinct, and my gut was telling me to get the hell out of there. Fast. At the same time, my chest ached deep inside. I couldn't ignore the overwhelming sadness that he probably didn't really like me when I was totally crushing on him.

At the tiny but adorable café halfway up, I begged off to use the bathroom. Locked in the stall, I sat on the toilet and brought my legs up to my chest. I took little comfort in the feel of the metal tray pressed against my chest. A plan formed. Escape here, go to Jolie's and rescue Aimee and Marie. Have Jolie arrested and go to the Extravaganza to complete Mom's mission. And then forget all this ever happened.

First, I had to escape. I went to the door of the bathroom and peeked outside, hoping to find Malcolm waiting for me with two drinks. But what I saw confirmed my fears. He stood with his back to me at a postcard rack. A man in a suit coat stood a couple feet away. Malcolm passed him an envelope, probably a payoff. They were talking to each other, acting like two strangers, who just happened to meet up in an ancient church. My feet itched to sprint across the room and down the stairs to freedom, but what if more goons waited down in the hallways, hiding behind statues, arms ready to grab me. I sprinted the only place left to go. Up.

And up.

And up.

The rest of the four hundred stairs.

Fear chased me, always a step away, ready to grab me. Finally at the top, I collapsed in a corner and curled into a ball. Every footstep on the stairs, every echo of a male voice, my heart rate spiked and visions of my death played with my emotions.

I stayed huddled against the cold comfort of the mighty cathedral and hoped God was watching out for me. The grimacing demon and other winged gargoyles sent shivers through my body. I pictured Jolie's face carved into one of them, complete with wings, horns, and glowing red eyes. The devil himself.

After rubbing the cramps out of my calves, I stood and limped over to the wire mesh surrounding the entire top of the tower. Paris spread out before me with its stone buildings, lush gardens, and the Eiffel in the distance. How many more times would I be running for my life in this city until I found answers? Did Paris hold something against me? Did my terrible accent offend her? No. I wished it were that simple. We were here because of Mom's apartment. Mom. That was who this all came down to. My trouble started when I opened the package. All the pieces were connected to her secrets and lies. Jolie, Malcolm, and Aimee. Not sure how they were all connected, but I'd start with rescuing Aimee and Marie.

The golden sun rested in the lower half of the sky, but I couldn't find warmth in its rays. A permanent chill had descended on my shoulders. I straightened up, needing to brave the world outside the cathedral and book it over to Jolie's before he came home. Surely, Malcolm had left. I clomped, ran, walked, dragged myself down the four hundred stairs, only stubbing my toe twice and tripping three times. Before leaving the cathedral I searched the area, and only when I made sure there was no sign of Malcolm or his buddy, I grabbed a latte at a small café across the street. The hot liquid trailed down my throat and spread its desperately needed warmth through my body.

I texted Dad saying the mission had failed. The cathedral was a no go for Spy Games. Then I got on the Metro to head back closer to home, walking distance from *le maison de Pouffant*. The house of Pouffant. Was that even his home? I didn't know. And I didn't care as long as I found Aimee.

At the house, I peered around the hedge, trying not to bump into the sharp twigs. The place seemed empty—no muted lights through the window, no clinking of teacups from the backyard—nothing that I could hear or see. I gripped the straps of my backpack and studied the house. No sneaking around this time. The best way would be to act natural, like I belonged. The neighbors wouldn't question a visitor opening the backdoor. No slinking or acting like a criminal.

With quick, sure steps, I marched across the small side yard to the backyard not even glancing at the henhouse. I peered through a window. No one. I hesitated at the backdoor and listened. Confident Jolie wasn't home, I stepped inside into the lingering smell of cinnamon. Not surprising for the house of a pastry chef.

A girl's jacket lay across a worn plaid loveseat. A small piano wedged in the corner had music for the theme song from Harry Potter on the top. A chess game sat on the table, half played. Framed pictures of family were on the wall. My chest tightened as memories from Pennsylvania rushed back. Family times with my mom and my dad. Happy times. Even if they weren't perfect. I wanted that back. Being in Jolie's home, which felt cozy and happy, pricked my heart.

Enough. A good spy does not let emotions cloud her mission. Not wanting to wake up a snoozing pastry chef, I crept through the downstairs. The living room led to an open but tiny kitchen with room for a table for four.

"Marie?" I whispered, then scolded myself. I needed to sweep the whole house and be smart about this. The stairs were at the back of the kitchen. I tested each wooden step before putting my entire weight on them. At the top, I could go right or left. I poked my head in the door on the right. Must be Jolie's with the clean room and professionally made bed. Pouffant did not pass over the details, which scared me.

I tiptoed across the tiny hall. A car door shut outside. Voices. Familiar ones. My body froze up, and I couldn't get my legs to move. Fear of getting caught spread like wildfire across my skin and I had to force a swallow. A tiny sob escaped. Why didn't I bring rope to escape out the second story window? Or a smoke bomb?

The front door opened, and a current of French streamed into the house, up the stairs, and wrapped around my head, entangling my legs. I was trapped, too afraid to move in case they heard me. Maybe they'd returned for their sweaters before going back out to dinner.

The stairs creaked.

Damn. My body unfroze and survival instinct took over. I shimmied into the bathroom and whipped back and forth for a spot to hide. The closet filled with towels and sheets was too small. A voice cleared on the stairs. A deep growly voice, one that I recognized.

With a gulp, I stepped behind the flowery curtain into the shower stall and tried to control my breathing so I didn't sound like a girl terrified for her life. I could see the outline of the sink and toilet through the curtain and realized that anyone could see me too. I slithered to the bottom of the tub and lay down, my legs bent and turned sideways.

Jolie whistled in the hall.

Thirty-one

PLEASE, PLEASE GO INTO THE BEDROOM.

Jolie didn't. The floor creaked outside the bathroom and I closed my eyes, wishing I could disappear. The whistling entered the bathroom, and I cringed. I heard a zipper.

Oh no. I shuddered as he relieved himself. Brief thoughts of whacking him over the head with the crowbar passed through my mind but then he zipped his pants back up. I held my breath and silently prayed. I begged forgiveness for anything and everything. The last argument I'd had with my mom before she left, my snobby disdain for Spy Games, and my treatment of the clients, for not being a better friend to Aimee by asking more personal questions, and for eating the last package of Oreos Dad had brought over from the States, and then telling him a mouse had gotten to them. If I made it through this, I'd confess to everything.

My breaths were short and shallow, but when his chapped hand with hairy knuckles appeared over my head, they stopped altogether. I don't usually notice hands. But this one could be my downfall, and it hovered inches from my face. I closed my eyes, waiting for him to grab my ponytail and drag me out. Instead, the knob squeaked and the pipes shuddered to the life. Two seconds later, tiny pricks of freezing water struck my face, arms, and pierced my clothing. I gasped for my breath. A shower? He was taking a shower? His pants landed on the floor outside me. Oh crap!

Water streamed into my mouth and dripped into my ears. Terrible foreboding images flashed through my brain, scarring me forever. I did not want to see a pastry chef, this pastry chef, in the nude, with everything all hanging in the freeze. I mean breeze.

Someone rapped on the door and shouted. They sounded rushed and upset. I prayed again. My lips moved in silent confession as I tried not to choke on the water. This time, I confessed to all my deep, dark hidden secrets, like not telling Dad the truth about Malcolm and our date when it happened, and stealing his tracking devices to spy on Peyton.

"Zut alors!"

The water shut off. Jolie pulled on his pants. My body trembled violently.

The girl on the other side of the door kept yelling through it. Jolie spit out directions and rushed out of the bathroom. Something had happened. The hand of God in their lives. To save me. And I was supposed to be the hero.

They clomped down the stairs, and I sucked in air like I would never breathe again. Hairs were plastered to my head, and I felt like a drowned rat. I probably looked like one too. I listened for the front door, and then waited for what seemed like hours, shivering, trying to get warm.

When the house quieted and the panic faded, I crawled out of the tub, not caring about leaving my wet footprints. Everything clicked. The jacket. The Harry Potter music. The girl's voice. I rushed down the tiny hall, barely staying on my feet and crashed into the girl's room. While fumbling through her desk, I thought back on the family pictures hanging in the living room. Many were old black-and-white photos of unsmiling ancestors. But many showed the growing up of a girl with blonde curls.

I swayed on my feet, goosebumps popping out on my already-cold and shriveled skin. How could this be? I ripped open a second drawer, fighting back tears, looking for more current pictures. Finally, I found the tip of one poking out underneath a deck of cards. I pulled the photo out. My heart splintered.

Aimee and Jolie stood, with their arms around each other, smiling, happy, close. Aimee and Marie weren't prisoners. They lived here. With Jolie. They were family.

I couldn't rip my eyes away from the photo. My friend smiled adoringly up at her grandfather. The crinkle in the corner of her eyes that I always loved when we joked about Spy Games brought a tightness to my throat. The picture slipped from my fingers and I slumped to the floor, blinking away tears. Our entire friendship was a lie.

Did she even care about me? Us? Memories flashed of my times with Aimee, whispering secrets, laughing over silly things like the ugly hat some person was wearing at the table near us. I'd felt guilty because our relationship seemed focused on me. When she'd disappeared, I'd partly blamed myself for not asking more questions and digging into her life more, like a friend should. But maybe, just maybe, that was how she'd wanted it.

No questions. No deep conversations—unless they were about me. No visits to her real home here with Jolie "the great" Pouffant. I couldn't even begin to think about the implications of this information, and the ripple effect it had in what'd happened since Malcolm and I were first shot at. I didn't want to think about it. I couldn't.

Everything seemed to close in on me—the puffy pink pillows on her bed, the cute kitten posters on the wall, the

220

flowered wallpaper. I scooted back across the wooden floors, ready to run, escape, and eat donuts for the next two hours. After scrambling to my feet, water still dripping from my hair and clothes, I ran down the stairs and into the kitchen. On the bottom step, my foot slipped in the river following me, and I fell flat on my face.

In front of a giant hole in the floor.

Jolie's dining area off the kitchen had morphed into a gaping hole. My eyes widened as I took in the room. The table was turned on its side and shoved in the corner, the chairs stacked, and the carpet rolled back. I got to my knees, crawled over to the bell-shaped hole, and peered into the inky black darkness.

Warm, musty air, thick and heavy rose up from the hole. A rusty metal ladder clung to the side of the rocky wall. Did Jolie and Aimee go down there? Why? I knew what I should do. I should get my freakin' ass out of there and walk—no run—straight to my dad and tell him everything. I mean everything. But what secrets were they hiding down there? This might be my only chance to find out the mystery surrounding my close friend, or ex-close-friend. And more importantly, how it was all connected to my family and me.

I couldn't be foolish about plunging into a dark pit that probably didn't lead to a nice, lighted cellar. Light. I needed a flashlight. All the spy gadgets and granola bars in my backpack wouldn't help me in what were probably the catacombs under Paris. Weren't these secret entrances totally illegal? I opened their kitchen drawers completely guilt-free and dug around until I found a flashlight.

After one last glance into the dark hole, I sent up a pretty shallow prayer and wondered if I'd ever see daylight again. Time to suck it up. I climbed down and down. My backpack weighed a ton and dripped water with every step. My legs trembled, and my heart pounded as the light from Jolie's kitchen disappeared.

I clenched the flashlight in my teeth and kept peering down, but the ladder didn't seem to end. Dizziness overwhelmed me, but I fought it off with every foot of the stone circular wall that passed. What did they store down here? Prisoners? Stolen gold? Extra pastries?

Finally, I reached the bottom. A narrow hallway opened up before me. I tiptoed through it, terrified with each step that a rat would run over my feet or worse I'd bump into a skeleton or something. The dull, flickering flashlight cast weird shadows and barely penetrated the darkness.

The passageway was short and opened into a small cavern. Niches carved into the walls held candles with small flames lighting the way. Water seeped from the limestone walls. A thick tree-trunk-like pillar of stone held up the ceiling, and the room branched off into two different hallways. I followed the one lit with candles and shoved the flashlight into my backpack for later.

I crept along the best I could, avoiding the mud. A layer of dust clung to my wet clothes and face. With every step, I strained to hear voices. But I heard nothing, only my ragged breathing and muffled footsteps. I trailed my fingers along the small hills and valleys of the wall. Then I heard the unmistakable voices of Jolie and Malcolm. Arguing.

Except it was in French, damn it.

Thirty-two

MALCOLM BEING DOWN HERE didn't surprise me at all. Jolie and Malcolm were thick as thieves, evil twin brothers. I shut out my broken and confused feelings and focused on the moment. I needed a plan.

Think. Think. Eventually, they'd return and go back up the ladder to Jolie's kitchen. Had Malcolm been with him? Or was there a separate entrance and Malcolm met him? I needed to hide, so after they left I could figure out what the hell was so important they had to conduct business five or seven, maybe ten stories underneath their cute little cottage.

Several small pillars of stacked stones were in the cavern, but nothing was wide enough to hide behind except for the hole in the wall behind one of them that was big enough for me to crawl into. While their angry voices drifted from the other room, I crept across the floor, weaved between the pillars, and reached the hole. My skin crawled like a zillion ants were marching over my body. What was in here? Did animals live down here? Like zombie rats that had morphed into larger creatures with sharper teeth?

Their voices drew closer. I practically dove into my hiding place, elbows and knees slamming into the knobby surface. My head banged into the rock-hard ceiling, and I bit my tongue to avoid crying out. I crawled to the back of the hole and curled into a ball, hoping, praying, they wouldn't see me. The crowbar in my backpack jabbed into my spine.

Malcolm and Jolie passed by like ghosts from the past, their shadowy images looming over my hiding place. Out of the darkness, Aimee appeared. Her hair seemed a bit on the fritz and her face was pale, but she was there! She was safe! A part of me wanted to crawl out and give her a big hug, letting her know I'd never believed that stupid cover story, and say she'd have to be a lot smarter to fool me in the future. She continued to talk, a crease appearing on her forehead.

Jolie lifted his arms in exasperation. Malcolm shifted onto one leg and kept glancing at the passageway like he wanted to exit stage left. But why? Crawling, like vermin in the deep, dark, hidden places of Paris fit him perfectly. My eyes were drawn to the way his hair fell below his eyebrows. His lips were pressed together as if he wanted to speak his mind. His face was pale, almost sickly, like he was nervous. Go Malcolm. Tell them you're through with them! I wanted to send telepathic messages to his brain convincing him to make better moral decisions. A black T-shirt matched his black jeans. He looked quite the spy. His hand rested on a coiled rope on his belt.

I looked twice, wanting to pull out my flashlight. The rope glimmered in the soft light. But ropes don't usually take on a gleam in candlelight. Blood rushed to my face as I realized it wasn't a rope, but a whip. An Indiana Jones whip. My jaw tensed and my teeth ground together as I held back the urge to vomit all over their feet. There must be a practical reason Malcolm would need a whip down here. For example, maybe they found a large rodent-like creature with fangs. Or maybe Malcolm was practicing to become a cowboy and go back to the States and compete in rodeos. I mean it's not like you can practice that kind of thing in daylight without someone suspecting you had a prisoner locked in your basement.

Oh, crap.

A prisoner. A whip. And he carried a small tool chest in his other hand, probably filled with corkscrews, pliers, and nail files. Construction tools were candy to someone like Malcolm. Someone like Malcolm. Jolie was paying Malcolm to torture a prisoner? Why? What kind of trouble could a pastry chef get into?

I studied the yellowish hue of Malcolm's face. Was he the tough guy he pretended to be? Or had he gotten involved in something he couldn't get out of? The splinters that used to be my heart broke into more splinters. Malcolm had never made me promises. So we'd shared a kiss. Big deal.

He entered the conversation and motioned toward the hallways. They split off. He headed down one tunnel, and Jolie and Aimee the other. But before Jolie swept from the room he blew out all the candles. Just what I needed. Creep factor.

I pulled out my handy dandy flashlight and flicked it on, ready to go rescue a prisoner. A scream rose into my throat as I bit down on my hand. The gaping eyes of a skeleton, embedded into the stones, stared at me from the ceiling. A creepy crawly feeling attacked my body until I jumped into action. The knobby stones dug into my knees and I shined the light down at them. Bones and more bones. Knees and elbows of the dead poked through. I remembered feeling the hills and valleys of the walls. Bones. I breathed in and out trying not to cry and puke at the same time. I flashed my dim light against the walls. I caught the reflection of gaping jawbones, nasal cavities and skulls. I was in a crypt!

I scrambled out of my hiding place, which was more like a tomb of some kind. I shuddered in an attempt to shake off the imagined feeling of bony fingers tracing down my spine or tickling my toes. The breath of past souls on my neck pushed me into the next room, where I promptly dropped to my knees not caring about the dead body parts in the walls. They couldn't hurt me. A sob formed deep in my chest. A chair sat in the middle of the floor. An empty chair. With frayed ropes around it.

Was the prisoner dead? Had they been arguing about how to get rid of the body? I remembered the crease on Aimee's forehead. She would have more than a crease if someone had died. Maybe. I smiled. Maybe the prisoner escaped. That was why they went down the tunnels. To search for the prisoner!

My body shivered as my wet clothes pressed against my skin. I pulled out my phone and snapped a picture of the chair, the frayed ropes, and the cavernous room. A sudden image popped into my mind—as if ever since I saw the empty chair, my brain had been working in the background, humming, buzzing, searching for clues from the past week and a half. I remembered the fear in Mom's eyes when she talked to me at the Eiffel Tower. That felt like a century ago. Had she been hiding from Jolie? Maybe he knew about the package and the instructions to shoot him, so he grabbed Mom and tortured her for information. And that's why Malcolm infiltrated Spy Games and my family. Because Mom wasn't talking. My fingers curled into a fist.

Footsteps echoed from the tunnel. His muffled voice called out to his partners in crime. I needed to get the hell out and put the puzzle pieces together over a creamy latte and powdered donut, but I couldn't go back the same way. I had no choice but to run through the tunnels and hope I didn't get lost.

Without looking back, because I didn't want to slam into a wall, I sprinted through narrow tunnels and low-ceilinged caverns. I brushed against limestone walls and sloshed through squishy mud. My legs moved with the fear of a whip wrapping around them at any second, or kissing my back. I kept my eyes trained right in front me because I had no desire to see the faces, or the lack of faces, of the dead staring at me, telling me I'd never find a way out, that I was doomed to wander these catacombs and eventually join their skeleton crew.

I wasn't exactly in run-through-the-catacombs shape. Every time I stopped to heave out a couple of breaths because the thick air seemed to suck it from me, I heard them. Muffled footsteps. Panicked French from more than one person. They were after me.

I ran. Every footstep jarred my body. The walls blurred. Sweat dripped into my eyes and stung. What would they do to me? If they tortured me, I couldn't be as strong as Mom. I'd cave at the first sight of the pliers heading toward my teeth or at the first snap of the whip. But if it was information on Mom they wanted or her secrets, I wouldn't be able to tell them.

Then they'd take it the next step and break all my fingers, one by one.

A sob rose up from my chest causing my throat to burn. A pool of light shimmered up ahead. Escape! I stumbled the last few steps to a circular set of stairs going up, up, and up. My legs still ached from my climb up the tower in the Notre Dame. These steps made those seem like chocolate cake. Never ending. I pushed and pushed.

This was absolutely crazy. Why had I ever complained about posing as an art student at the Louvre or dealing with wannabes like Peyton? Spy Games was nothing compared to the real thing. And I wasn't even a real spy, just a determined teenager. Almost at the top, voices echoed from below. Malcolm and Jolie. I stopped, my foot in midair. With my hand cupped around my ear, I turned toward the voices.

"*C'est reediculus!*" Jolie peppered Malcolm with words.

They continued back and forth, their words coming out in surges as they made their way up the stairs. I should go, but listening was too tempting. I heard my name and Extravaganza. Great. Talking about me again. Really. I'm not that interesting.

Jolie hmphed. Malcolm kept talking. He said my name again, and I dug my fingers into the stone wall. What else would he share about me? He didn't know that much.

He slipped into English. "You don't have to worry about her. Classic case of a girl abandoned by her mommy and trying to make up for it by pretending to be Martha Stewart."

I hid my gasp. Is that how he thought of me?

Malcolm continued. "She has some skill from working for her dad. But overall." He paused, probably to breathe. "She is not capable of infiltrating your organization."

Jolie's voice grew louder and more suspicious but he didn't switch over to English.

Malcolm laughed out loud between wheezes. It turned my insides. Malcolm was someone different for everyone. For Dad he was the loyal staff member, knowledgeable in all areas. For me he was the flirty coworker and loyal friend—or he acted like it. For Jolie? A hired spy. Did he care about me at all?

As they kept talking, I stood straighter, trying to control my rage at Malcolm's cheap shots at me. At his lies. At his cowardice in not taking the high road but rather doing Jolie's dirty work.

The conversation dwindled, and Malcolm asked in a threatening voice. "What would you like me to do with her? You've barely tapped into my skills since hiring me."

And then Jolie spoke in English, loud and clear. "Take care of her."

I gasped. I know, it's so cliche, but what did he mean? "Take care of her." Was that a death threat? Forget Peyton. He was a little lost lamb grazing in a meadow filled with wild flowers. A pompous jerk and a tad bit too emotional. But he would never make death threats on innocent teen girls.

That's when I realized Jolie and Malcolm had stopped conversing about their evil plans of elimination. No voices echoed up the stairwell. Finger by finger, I pulled my hand away from the wall. Slowly, I lifted my foot off the stair and backed up. The stair shuddered.

I bit down on my lip until I tasted blood. What if they exterminated me right then? Stuck me in a freezer. Permanently? Would Malcolm do that? He said he wouldn't hurt me, but I couldn't take my chances. When their steps pounded below, I dropped any pretense of a subtle get-away. I burst up the stairs like there was only one pastry left on the shelves. Up, up, and up. Legs burning and pain shooting through my chest. At the top, my shoulder banged against a door as I fumbled with the knob.

I flew through the passage with no idea where I'd end up.

Thirty-three

THE HALLWAY. THE DIRTY cobwebby hallway. I sprinted down it and up the small set of stairs. Freedom was close. I whipped open the door leading into *Les Pouffant's*. The *maitre d'* stared at me from down his long, pointy nose. Angry French voices followed me, footsteps thumped. I slammed the door shut. I had to get out of there. As in last week.

The manager grabbed my arm. All the chefs turned and stared at me with their beady eyes. Their arms froze in position with frosting tubes in their hands. I must look like a total catacomb-zombie-freak, covered in drying dust and grime. They advanced toward me, so I did what any panicked girl caught spying on a famous French pastry chef would do. I kicked the guy in the shins. A girl's toes are her best weapon! He let out a howl and in the process let go of my arm. I ran from kitchen, pushing waiters and chefs to my right and left.

"Zut alors!" and other French niceties got lost in the crashing of pans and dishes.

Cakes splattered against the wall. Cream-filled pastries smeared into perfectly manicured French mustaches. I left them behind and sprinted out the front door.

Young couples in love cast strange looks like I was a bit cuckoo. And maybe I was.

"Arrête!" Someone yelled behind me.

Of course, I had no plans of stopping. Darkness shadowed the tables and the streets. I ducked under the old-fashioned-looking lights with large bulbs strung across the outside of the shop. I tried not to bump tables and knock over the vases holding roses as I weaved between them. I fled the scene, wishing I'd run all those fivers and tenners Dad had asked me to do. My breath wheezed out like an old air-conditioner on its last life. I dodged and ducked tables and Parisians out for a stroll. The doorways of cute little boutiques blurred past me as I ran.

I leaped over miniature poodles. I tried my hardest not to look behind me. At this point, Jolie with his Santa belly wouldn't be the one chasing me. Malcolm would be. Even though we'd kissed that didn't mean squat in his world. He kept telling me he was spying on Jolie for me, but every word out of his mouth down in the basement of Jolie's shop said otherwise. He was too convincing for a waiter.

Lies. Lies. And more lies. Everything about him was a lie. All the lies made me doubt anything he'd told me. Would he ever hurt me? I wasn't sure anymore.

With every step, the muscles in my back sent shooting pain up my spine in anticipation of a hand about to clamp down on my neck. But it never came. At least half a mile away, I prayed I'd be safe, slowed down, and tried to hide behind a group of older woman out for a shopping trip. At a crosswalk, I strode between two businessmen until I was safely on the other side.

I had to stop and rest. My lungs burned, so I plopped down on a hard wooden bench.

Malcolm was nowhere in sight. I breathed a deep sigh of relief and let out a couple deep sobs. I'd made it out. Jolie wasn't shoving me into his freezer. If I was lucky, Malcolm and Jolie didn't even know who it was spying on them from the stairs.

I let my head fall back and stared up between the tree branches. I stifled a laugh. Everything I hated about being a spy I had become. I hated butting into other people's business and living life like a trapeze artist, constantly afraid of falling and dying. I hated lying to people as much as I hated being lied to. I hated being sneaky. Except when I kinda liked it. Mom had never been honest with me. Like mother, like daughter. I guess.

Hands gripped my shoulder and I felt his breath against my ear before he whispered.

"Why hello there. What happened to you?"

Thirty-four

MALCOLM PLOPPED ONTO THE bench next to me and casually crossed his legs, his arms extending to the sides. He played with the ends of my hair, twirling it between his fingers.

I choked and froze. I could've been a statue carved hundreds of years ago.

"No. Seriously. You look..." He took my appearance in, his eyes roving up and down my body. The grimy face, my hair half dried and caked with dust, and my clothes still damp from my surprise shower and trip through the underworld of Paris. "...like you've been dragged through the mud. Literally."

I bit my bottom lip so the words building, screaming to get out, wouldn't. I had questions I wanted to beat Malcolm over the head with until I got answers. Questions about everything. His alliance with Jolie. My mom. Whether he liked me or not. I pressed that one deep down into my

237

subconscious. I didn't want the answer to it, because then I'd have to admit that my emotions had been manipulated. While I'd pretended to be the ultra-cool spy, he'd been slipping through the backdoor, raiding the privacy of my heart.

He tugged at the strand of my hair, nudging me to answer. I peeked sideways at the emotion radiating from his face, the caring look in his eyes, the way his head tilted to the side, his lips. Oh, those traitorous lips. He acted like he cared, but underneath he was probably terrified I could expose him.

Spies act cool, calm, and suave in any and all dangerous situations. And this was a tricky one. He had to know I'd been down in the catacombs, especially if he'd followed the trail of water I'd probably left in my wake. He wanted to know what I knew.

"Okay, I'll try another one. Where did you disappear to yesterday? You never came out of the bathroom at the Notre Dame. I had to sneak in and look for you. And that's dangerous territory entering a girl's bathroom."

The splinters of the splinters I used to call my heart could not break any smaller.

"Major girl problems." I lied like a pro.

"Oh."

That shut him up. Always a good excuse.

"Why didn't you call?"

Crap. "My phone was dead."

He pulled his arm back. "I don't believe you."

"That's fine. Don't."

My arm twitched, and I had to grab onto it to stop myself from slugging him a good one. How could he ask me these questions? We both knew the answers.

"If you're feeling up for it, I found this great bookstore with an incredible café next door. The tarts have gotten top reviews. You'll love it."

He continued rambling on about this perfect date we should go on. That night. Both my fingers clenched into fists. My neck tightened. The blood raced beneath my skin, roiling and boiling at this boy's balls. Did he think I couldn't see through his act? That the "date" was his attempt to lure me into a trap, so they could squirrel me away somewhere, tied up to a chair with nothing to look at but the bones of the past?

"And then we could talk a bit more about Spy Games this weekend. In two days, I'll be a spy. I might need some last minute tips."

"Will you just stop?" The words came out louder than I'd meant, but I couldn't take it anymore. I needed answers. Even if they weren't what I wanted to hear.

He uncrossed his legs and jiggled them up and down. "I'm sorry. You must be tired of talking about Spy Games. It's just it's my first time, and I'm a little nervous."

I whipped around in my seat, my glare piercing through his act. Screw his act. I wasn't a spy. I didn't have to act like one.

"Stop." I choked out. "I don't want to play this game anymore. Tell me about my mom. Do you have—"

He put a finger to my lips. "Shh."

"Don't touch me." I jerked my head away. "Okay. You want to talk about something else. Fine. Let's talk. Why did you ask me out that first night? Was it to spy on my family?"

My voice cracked and trembled, threatening to betray my real feelings. But the words came pouring out, unbidden and free. I grabbed his shirt and pulled him close.

"That's fine if you were paid to spy on my family. I don't get why because we're a broken family from Pennsylvania. But you had no right to lead me on, to act like you cared, to become my friend, to kiss me."

And then I couldn't help it. The fear and rage coursed through my limbs, spreading and gaining speed. I punched him in the stomach. He doubled over.

"Good one," he said in a strangled voice. "For a girl."

"I'm not joking. You can't make this go away with a joke and a laugh."

I punched him again. In the arm, the chest, until my fist hurt. He didn't fight back. He took it, took in all my feelings of hurt and betrayal. Finally I slumped over and put my head in my hands, not wanting to look at him.

He stiffened. "Fine, you want the truth now?"

I didn't answer, but waited, not looking, with my eyes closed, and my heart shielded.

"I tried my hardest to keep you away from Pouffant. But you refused. I tried to distract you and to warn you to stay away. But you wouldn't. You nosed around in things you know nothing about. I know that now. Because if you knew the truth, the real secrets behind all this, you wouldn't be so careless and stupid."

I was stunned. Too stunned to form thoughts, never mind words.

His voice lowered. "I'm sorry if I confused you. I thought your flirtations were part of the game. You started it. You got yourself into this."

His words slipped past the cracks in the shield around my heart, the place he always managed to infiltrate. One question burned there. I might've started it, but did he care about me at all? And I didn't even care about any romantic feelings. I mean was he my friend or not? Because at this point the friendship part was hurting a lot more.

And then it was as if he'd read my mind. "I don't want to hurt you. But you need to know the truth. This whole thing, you and me, flirting and having fun, has been a game, a charade, a distraction. I played along. I pretended to like you."

Any shred of hope and dignity that once bloomed inside me, shriveled up and died. He was right. I was playing a game I knew nothing about and should've stayed away from. I should've played my little role in Spy Games, believed Aimee's note about traveling, and not questioned anybody.

Right. I didn't think so either.

"And this is my warning to you. Stay away. And you might get away with your life." His words left a trail of dread wrapping around my body. "Stop asking questions. Stop pestering Pouffant. I'll make up something to keep the big boys away from you. I'm a good liar. As you know."

Those were his last words to me before he got up and strode briskly away. I watched his back, his confident strut, like he was the master of this game. He never looked back, not once.

I stayed on the bench and leaned back, looking up at the trees and the innocent leaves being tossed back and forth by the breeze. My body felt depleted, empty of any emotion. I'd been through the wringer. In that one conversation I'd gone through fear, anger, hurt, betrayal, heartache, and back to anger. When I looked back to the road, Malcolm had disappeared into the crowd.

At home, I slipped in through my bedroom window, leaving a trail of dirt against the outside of the apartment. But that was better than through the living room. No lights were on, so I hoped Dad was out on official Spy Games business. The games were in two days, but I only cared about one thing. A shower. My grimy skin could just feel the pelting streams of hot water washing away the fears and memories of the past day, especially the skeleton memories. I slipped out of my clothes and stuffed them into a bag to be incinerated.

The shower cleaned my body, but no matter how hot I ran the water, the fears remained, wedged in my mind. One word pounded in my heart. Mom. Mom. Mom. Maybe she had good reasons for not being around. Like being held prisoner in the catacombs. I prayed she'd escaped from the clutches of the mad pastry chef. I could barely think, never mind say his name.

With wrinkled skin and wearing comfy clothes, I flopped on my bed and drifted off.

At some point in between sleep and wake I jolted up in bed. My room was pitch black.

Someone was in the house.

Thirty-five

SHOES TAPPED ON THE kitchen floor. I held my breath. Heat pricked my skin, needles running up and down my arms. Dad normally slams the door and talks to himself. Who was in our apartment?

I slid out of bed, grabbed the heaviest book on my shelf, and stood to the side of my door. My legs shook so hard I could barely stand. Drawers opened in the kitchen. Papers shuffled. What did Jolie or Malcolm think we were hiding? Could they really think we were spies? What a joke.

The floor creaked right outside my door. He wasn't wasting any time. The door opened. Slowly. I raised the book above my head. As soon as the door opened all the way, I screamed and whammed the book at the intruder.

"Savvy!" he said with a grunt and wrapped his arms around me. Except it didn't feel like Malcolm. Or sound like him.

"Dad?"

He let go of me. I scrambled away and flicked on the light.

"Savvy, what are you doing?"

"I was trying to sleep."

And then I got mad. Like really mad. I threw the book on the floor, threw my hip out and crossed my arms. If someone usually slams the door and grumbles on entering, then he should always slam the door and grumble.

His eyebrows went up. "What's wrong?"

"Why are you creeping around the apartment like you're a burglar or something?"

"I didn't want to wake you in case you were sleeping."

"Oh." I uncrossed my arms and let them hang at my sides. "Sorry. I'm a little tired. Only because I've been training people for Spy Games." *And trying to stay alive.*

"Come on into the living room. We need to talk."

I stumbled over to the couch, desperately trying to squash the desire to tell Dad that these could be his last moments with his one and only daughter. But he always found a way to make my confessions seem foolish. I sat on the edge of the couch and pulled a frayed pillow into my lap. I wanted to rewind time, before my parents started arguing almost every night. That summer we'd made fires out in the fire pit and roasted marshmallows. We'd talked, laughed, done family-like things.

Dad rubbed his temples. Finally, he looked at me but still couldn't find my eyes. "It's about Spy Games."

The lines around his eyes were deeper and he seemed to have the weight of the world on his shoulders as he hunched over. He sighed and waited almost a minute before speaking. I pulled about fifty threads out of the pillow.

"After tomorrow, I give you my official blessing to leave Spy Games. I promise I'll stop trying to live my dreams through you. I'll stop talking about West Point, and I'll stop forcing you to pretend you're a spy."

"Dad...." I didn't know what to say.

Was I that much of a failure that he didn't want me on Spy Games anymore? I'd screwed up at the Louvre, but I'd make up for that. He'd see.

"And one more thing." He squirmed like a child who's stolen a cookie from the cookie jar. "I've been lying to you."

What? I stared at him. Dads don't lie. They always tell the truth and set the example. Right?

"I know how to communicate with your mother. I haven't, but I know how." He pulled at the threads of a frayed pillow too. Tears stung my eyes. He knew?

"But, but. . ." I couldn't finish.

"I've been selfish and didn't want to share you, especially after she left without offering you a choice. Of course, I love having you here, but if you'd rather be with your mom, I can work it out. I haven't been much of a dad lately. You could be back in the States next month or earlier."

"Oh, okay." My chest deflated.

How could I possibly tell him that mom probably wouldn't answer the phone? That she might never see daylight again? I couldn't. Not without telling him about my recent spy missions. And then just like that, he turned and left.

There it was. Proof. I'd messed up big time with Dad. I trudged back to my room and curled up into a ball in my closet near the box of special mementos. Standing in open view in front of windows didn't seem very wise given the circumstances. I flipped through the box of gadgets, thinking back on how my life had changed in two weeks. My emotions veered back and forth between rage at Malcolm for tricking me and extreme fear for my mom.

The door creaked open. "Savvy?"

"What?" I crawled out of the closet and sat on my bed.

Dad studied me. I mean really looked at me. He opened his mouth several times before spitting out what was on his mind. "Do you want to stay here? With me?"

Tears burned. Dad had been the one to stay, to provide, to burn the mac and cheese for me. He wasn't perfect, but he cared.

"Yes," I said, my heart blooming and filling some of the hollow spaces in my chest.

His whole body seemed to lighten and the wrinkles smoothed out. The smile on his face radiated and was like salve on my heart. He wanted me!

"Terrific. But I'll still try and communicate with your mom."

"Why did she leave?" I blurted out, testing him.

"Those are questions only your mother can answer." He stepped closer. "I know it's hard, without her around." He sat on the bed and put his hand on my shoulder. "But you're strong. If you can survive my cooking, you can survive anything. You're a fighter. Don't forget that."

He kissed my forehead, then he left with a fresh spring in his step. Wow. I was on dad-daughter-bonding overload. He believed in me. Even though I'd screwed up, numerous times, more times than he even knew, he believed in me. The anger and fear faded and morphed into something new and different. Determination.

Then I saw the hat. The spy hat. The wonderful, glorious black hat Dad gave me as a gift. Laughter bubbled up from some creepy twisted place inside of me because I shouldn't be finding a spy hat the least bit humorous. I crouched down on the floor and ran my fingers across the folded edge. It wasn't so bad. At least it wasn't zebra striped. Right?

And then there was the box of spy gadgets from bugs to audio-recording devices to code-breaking books. But many more lay in the box, screaming out the same message. They almost vibrated. I ran my fingers over them, and the pulse shocked my fingertips and spread like wildfire up through my arms. A switch in my brain flicked on. I'd been doing it.

All along, ever since the fateful night that I'd made the decision to tie up Malcolm, I'd been doing what I swore I'd never do. I thrived on danger. I took risks. I wore disguises and listened in on conversations. Oh. My. Holy. Spy. Pants. What did I ever have against spying anyway?

I moved to the edge of the bed, my body tense, racking my brain on how to rescue my mom and make things right. The Extravaganza was this Saturday, the same exact time as Spy Games. I couldn't be in two places at once. I needed to be at the Extravaganza. I'd probably never know what Mom was supposed to do there, not if she'd been taken hostage. But I had to go. The answer came quickly in the form of the person I'd offended the worst. Peyton. I'd ask him to help me in Spy Games to make up for my mistakes.

I'd been playing the game wrong, boldly stepping into this chaotic mess like I had a right, like I was immune to getting hurt. I needed to play a different game, one that didn't include clumsily spying on people and breaking and entering houses. I needed to stop thinking of being a spy as James Bond and 007 and all that. Spies could be normal people. Like me. Innocent people who drew on their strengths of normalness. I needed to embrace my allies instead of leaning on my enemies.

For the first time in a long time, the cobwebs in my mind cleared, and I felt purpose. I could find some answers and free my mom. At the same time, I could make up for my mistakes by taking action and making Dad proud. Step one in Operation Save Prisoner?

Training.

Thirty-six

I HAD ONE DAY to train and be ready for Spy Games.

I grit my teeth to pull out another ten sit-ups. When that was done and my stomach muscles allowed me to move again, I hopped to my feet. I stood outside in the tiny front yard, hoping our neighbors in the apartment building wouldn't peek out their windows.

I jumped back and forth and shook out my arms like a boxer would before a match. I might not have done my job before, but I would do it now.

Do fifty more push ups and twenty lunges, my internal trainer shouted.

I did them.

Harder. Don't quit. Don't slow down.

I didn't.

The chill in the air encouraged me to move. After completing a series of karate kicks and floor drops and ninja turns—that I totally made up—I did them again. And again.

Thirty minutes later, after rolling in the grass, kicking like the Karate Kid, and leaping like a ballerina, I dropped into the grass and groaned. Sweat soaked my shirt and dripped off the sides of my face.

Holy cow! I couldn't keep training like this or I wouldn't be able to walk to the Extravaganza finals the next day. I hobbled back to my room and dragged the box out of my closet. The guilt that hung over this box could finally leave because for the first time, it would get put to good use. Dad gave me this when we arrived in Paris as a welcoming gift. It was one of the many things he'd done to get me excited about his spy venture, but I don't think I'd ever looked through the whole thing. I dug down for the book on breaking codes. At the bottom of the box, I found a silver case. I'd never seen this. I opened it and my mouth dropped open. A switchblade? With shaky fingers, I flicked it and a sharp knife popped out.

Holy freaking hell. Um, yeah. I closed it back in the case and shoved it to the bottom of the box. Then I found the book. After racing back to the kitchen the best I could on my sore legs, I slapped down a page of basic code breaking.

Code breaking 101. You have five minutes.

I attacked each one like I was going for Olympic gold, scribbling furiously, a smile spreading across my face. If only Dad could see me. When the time was up, I sat back with satisfaction. The days of starting off a training day at *Les Pouffant's* were over. What would Aimee think? She'd laugh and say, "About time." I closed my eyes and pictured Aimee's infectious smile, the one that used to greet me every morning. We'd chat and joke about Spy Games. Truth was I missed her.

An hour later, with a black scarf wrapped around my neck and wearing dark, inconspicuous clothing, I studied Peyton's apartment building. It felt like years ago that Malcolm and I crouched in the bushes waiting for the right moment to break in, using my oh-so-sly methods. I kinda missed those days when Malcolm and I would flirt and do spy stuff together instead of against each other. And that was only a couple of weeks ago.

When I'd called Peyton, his phone number had been disconnected. I contemplated how he might react to my surprise visit. He could call the police. He could tie me up and stuff me into a closet. Or he might just take my offer and help out during Spy Games. My way of an apology on the path to becoming a better Spy Games staffer and daughter. Only one way to find out.

Each step across the street and into his apartment building caused a crack in my confidence. This guy hated me.

In front of his door, instead of slicing the pie or nonsense like that, I knocked. And waited.

And waited.

And waited.

I knocked again. The idea of breaking in tempted me. I mean I hadn't turned my back on spying, just on my laziness when it came to working for Dad. I knocked once more. And the door opened a crack. Hmm. This wouldn't be breaking in, just popping in for a friendly Spy Games hello. Especially if I tripped and my toes nudged the door open all the way and I just kinda fell into the apartment.

Oops! I fell forward. How clumsy of me.

But it didn't matter. The apartment was empty of everything but the furniture. Empty. As in no signs of people living there. No trash. No half-empty coffee cups. No loaf of bread on the counter. I scoured the apartment. The nose strips were gone. The books, the maps, everything. It was like Peyton never lived here. Bummer. But I'd tried. I shrugged it off and went home to gear up for the next day.

After a restless night's sleep, the morning of the Extravaganza and Operation Save Prisoner dawned. In the back of my closet I found a pair of black leather pants I'd packed for the Paris nightlife. I pinned the flower/audio-recorder to my shirt. Then I pulled out the switchblade and tucked it into my sock. Just in case.

254

I was a spy. But not the cold-hearted, sneaky kind who worked for profit. I'd be different. The kind of spy who saved people. The kind who solved problems and rooted out the bad guys because they were bad, not because of how much I got paid. I'd be a daughter and rescue my mom. And I'd make my dad proud. I'd run my first tenner in five months even if it killed me. And then, I'd be...a spy like me.

At nine a.m. on the dot, I creaked open the door to the warehouse. On time. Gray Chalston wasn't even here yet. Dad studied his notes. I stared at him in awe. His hair was perfectly styled, not for vanity, but so it wouldn't fall in his eyes while in the field. Maybe it was the only way to control his hair or maybe no one ever told him he used a bit too much gel. Nancy and Malcolm entered from the side, with Frankie on their heels. Dad nodded at them as they took their spots around the table. For some reason, I couldn't make myself walk forward. I couldn't move from watching them through the crack in the door.

I mean how hard was this? I'd been doing it for months. But that was when I didn't care. I wiped my sweaty palms on my pants, and sudden panic hit me. Maybe I shouldn't have worn these pants. They did make my butt look a little big. And the hat was totally dorky. What was I thinking? Call me delusional. They'd probably take one look at me and laugh. I should've got here before anyone else arrived. Too late.

I watched as Nancy chatted gaily with Malcolm. They laughed like old friends. God, he was cute. And a flirt. He'd once turned that killer smile on me, and where had that gotten me? Nowhere good. He'd tangled up my heartstrings, made me care.

They all cast nervous glances at each other. Waiting for me. Dad pulled a clump of gel from the side of his hair, stalling, probably waiting for me to disappoint him. It was time. I clutched my throat. Was it closing up? I stepped back from the door and took several shallow breaths. Cool air breezed across my face and hair sending goosebumps down my arms. I thought about Aimee. Mom. And Dad. All his hopes and dreams in me. Deep breaths. They needed me. I could do this. I could find and rescue my mom. After one more giant breath, I grabbed the door and opened it again.

Malcolm ran right into me.

Thirty-seven

"WHAT ARE YOU DOING out here?" Malcolm asked.

"Nothing." Why didn't I memorize some cool spy lingo?

With a flip of my hair, I faced him, channeling the coolness factor of an iceberg. His eyes widened and traveled up and down my body. I glared at him, trying to hide my reaction. He backed up. I brushed past him and strode across the warehouse toward the others, shoulders back, head up, chest out. My black boots clomped on the cement. My spy hat slipped, and I pushed it back into place. Dad opened his mouth but no words came. A noticeable gleam filled his eyes.

"Welcome, Savvy." He finally managed to say.

Minutes later, I was clicking into my cables and tightening the ropes. The metal rafter was firm beneath my feet, and I simply refused to look down. My legs still felt rubbery from my three-mile run, which had dwindled into a jog up and down the street. Start small. That was key.

Gray nodded in approval. After his introduction speech, Dad boomed out the names of the staff. Frankie dropped down first then Nancy until it was Gray, Malcolm, and me. My eyes flicked over to Malcolm's. I couldn't read his expression. His steely gray eyes caught mine and held them for a few seconds.

Gray interrupted. "Malcolm, your turn."

He flew down to the cement floor in his hot spy glamour, much to the awe of the clients.

Gray nodded. My turn.

Dad's voice boomed, "And here's Savvy!"

Without a thought, I jumped, my arm straight out, my head held high. The wind rippled through my shirt and my eyes teared up. I clenched the ropes until my feet landed on the cement. I think I even got a few gasps myself. Damn. Soon, Jolie Pouffant would regret the day he messed with Savvy Bent.

I breezed through my informant job at the Eiffel Tower. I handed out clues with confidence. I stayed focused. This round was not about a hostage. One of the clients was a mole, a double agent, and the rest of the clients had to find the stolen Da Vinci, while digging for the mole. Extra points for the team who could name the double agent. I could. Malcolm. But that only counted in my book, and I wouldn't be receiving any prizes.

With a sigh, I realized my job was done, but my real work had yet to begin. I texted Dad to let him know I had monthly girl issues but would make it to the final debriefing. When I arrived at the Extravaganza, I stood on the side street. The small groups of musicians played music and whisked me back to the 1800s. Mimes with their sad faces acted out their dramas. Sellers cried out and promoted their homemade goodies. The smell of apples and cinnamon floated in the air. It all brought me back to the first Extravaganza, where I'd hoped to find Aimee but learned Malcolm was a double agent, where I'd met Jolie and learned he was a nefarious pastry chef. And then, where I shot the guy with a tranquilizer dart.

Today would be different. Today I'd save my mom.

I wandered past the tables, searching for a table with the number 14. Magnificent entries surrounded me. *Les Pouffant's* was on my right, closed for the day. A sense of unease sapped my confidence. Nothing ever went right for me in that shop, and me and pastry shops were usually best buds.

I found my table at the far edge of the blocked-off street, but when I saw it, my fists curled into balls at my side. While I'd finished up my work for Spy Games, Jolie's minions had destroyed my entry. It looked like something from a Tim Burton movie. And not in an artistic way. Gold, silver, and red frosting bled across the white paper tablecloth. The wires that held the cupcakes were twisted and deformed with sharp edges sticking out. Even the cupcakes with a creamy fillings had been slashed, their guts spilled. From what I could tell it had been a masterpiece of little cakes placed in the formation of the Eiffel Tower. Emotions whipped through me like the wind, tearing at my insides. Shock. Surprise. Sadness. Anger. But the one that stayed with me, lodged in my throat, was fear. If Jolie had no problem destroying something he loved—pastries—what would he do with me?

I cracked my knuckles. The fun and games were over. Time for stage one. Infiltration.

Problem. A security guard blocked the door to Jolie's bakery. Well, he probably was a security guard, dressed in dark colors and wearing sunglasses. I needed a distraction. With my large purse on my shoulder, I smeared frosting from the ruined Eiffel Tower á la cupcake onto my arms and a dab on my nose so I'd look like one of Jolie's pastry minions. I ran along the perimeter of the Extravaganza then rushed up to the door of the bakery and jerked the knob back and forth. The guard approached, liked I hoped he would.

"*Arrête!*" His voice was sharp and commanding.

I motioned to the frosting, mentioned Jolie's name, and pointed into the bakery. The guard narrowed his eyes. I contorted my features into something I hoped looked like panic, which didn't take much effort. He nodded and strode off. I pulled out the gadget that unlocked doors, stuck it into the keyhole, and wiggled it around. Nothing.

I glanced over at Jolie's table. The guard was just reaching him. Damn. I wiggled harder, but nothing happened. I changed hands and kept trying to force it to work. Snap! The gadget broke. I'd have to talk to Dad about investing in higher-quality devices, if he was really serious about this whole spy thing.

Using my purse, I was about to punch a hole through the door when a shadow blocked the sun and a chill whispered across the back of my neck. I froze. Rough hands gripped my arm and whipped me around. Jolie.

"Um, *Bonjour*?"

Thirty-eight

JOLIE DIDN'T EVEN CRACK a smile. Instead, he unlocked the door and pushed me into the bakery. Okay, not quite the way I'd envisioned this happening. He gave me a final push, and I broke my forward momentum by slamming my hands against his front counter.

I kept my back to him. A torrent of French filled the shop. Normally, I love the French language but not today. He continued to yell, his words falling on me like pieces of glass. Technically, I was the more innocent of the two of us. Then he switched to English.

"How dare you?" he roared. "I tried to convince my partner you were not an innocent victim in all this. You are a conniving spoiled brat."

"Don't hold back," I shot out.

He waved his hands in disgust. "I would never let my granddaughter talk like that. And I never would have worked with your papa if—"

I flipped around. "Worked with my dad? What are you talking about?" That made no sense. No way would Dad work with a homicidal pastry chef.

"He asked me to be a part of his Spy Games. Quite ironic, don't you think?"

The knowing smile on Jolie's face reflected the truth. He knew I knew about him, and he didn't care. I fiddled with the flower pin on my shirt, a gift from Dad, pressing the record button.

"Yes, quite, considering you're the spy," I said.

He laughed, a deep belly laugh.

My anger went from simmering to rolling waves. "It won't be funny when you're convicted and put in jail."

Tears streamed from his eyes. "Little girl. You know nothing."

"I know a lot," I shouted. "I know you hired Malcolm to take Aimee's place so you could spy on my family."

"HA!" The word burst from his mouth like a gunshot. "Oh, you have brought me so much entertainment these past weeks I do not know whether to get rid of you or to hire you onto my staff."

"I am not some sort of joke. This is serious." I stopped myself before blurting out that I was here to rescue Mom.

He wiped his eyes. "Eh. When the night we'd planned for your kidnapping went up in smoke, I made other plans."

"I don't believe you." I racked my brain and couldn't think of any near-kidnappings. No men in dark clothing. Nobody offering me candy. Nothing.

"Let me explain." He took a bow.

And they call Americans obnoxious.

"Malcolm was a plant."

"Duh." Okay that sounded totally childish. "I know he took Aimee's spot to get to me."

"Wrong!" He burst out again, laughing. "He was a plant at *Les Pouffant's*. He was never a struggling waiter in need of cash. He asked you out on a date and romanced you because I paid him to."

Right then and there I became a piece of pastry dough, punched and slammed around until there was no air left in me. I had my suspicions, but to hear it stated out loud made it real. Too real.

"Why so pale? Malcolm is way out of your league my dear. Forget him. He will bring you nothing but heartache."

"But why?" He'd tried to kidnap me before I even had any thought about entering the pastry contest? "I'm a nobody."

He nodded. "True. But I needed to make sure. Do not worry you passed the test."

I stepped closer to him. "You needed to make sure about what?"

"That is classified." He made the motion like he was zipping his lips.

My anger went from rolling waves past boiling to the cracking stage. "You're not the only ones with secrets, Santa Claus."

"Please, enlighten me."

"I know things about you too. I know about your precious Aimee. And I know your secret in the basement."

Jolie stopped blabbing, his words dried up. Slowly, a change came over him. His mustache twitched and he ran the back of his hand across the bottom of his beard. His nostrils flared and his face turned the color of a brilliant sunset. His chest heaved in and out, and he stepped closer, pushing his face in mine.

"How do you know about that?" His breath smelled like peppermint and sugar.

It felt really good to have pulled something over on him. "Sorry. I'm not at liberty to say."

"What?" he blasted out.

My body trembled under his roar. I straightened my back and stood firm. No fear. "Life's not so funny when you're the one being fooled, is it?"

He growled and pushed me away in disgust.

"Honestly, if Aimee knew what a big bully you really are, she'd probably never talk to you again. So, why don't you hand my mom over to me, and I'll leave. And you can forget all about me."

A devious smile pranced across his face. "I know nothing of your mother."

I looked out the window and gasped. *"Zut alors!"*

Quick as lightning Jolie fell for the oldest trick in the book and whipped his head around to see what happened. I reached into my large purse and grabbed my taser. With one quick thrust I aimed for his big belly. But he wasn't as stupid as he looked. He caught my wrist inches from his belly. His grip tightened on my arm until I groaned in pain.

"You want to play with the big boys? *Non*? Then I will treat you like one." He twisted my wrist around and jammed the end of the taser into my side.

Bolts of electricity entered my body, zaps of pain shot through my limbs. I felt numb. I hit the floor with no chance of blocking my fall. Drool wet the side of my cheek. Jolie's evil cackle filled the air and settled deep into my soul. My body twitched.

He grabbed my wrists and dragged me across the floor. I mumbled out words of protest. My head lolled back and we passed the glass case with fresh pastries and entered the kitchen. A door creaked open, and he brought his face close to mine. The smell of peppermint washed over me.

"You can't fool me. I know your family has been watching mine. First your mother, then you, and finally your father drawing me into his Spy Games. I will take your family out before they can finish me off."

With that, he gave me a push down the stairs.

Thirty-nine

I SCREAMED AS WOOD jabbed, poked, and whammed into every part of my body all the way down the steps. Finally the world stopped spinning, and I lay on the floor. Throbbing pain racked my body. The dull glow from a flickering light on the ceiling blurred in out of view. I focused. Cracks ran down the plastered walls and grit was on the floor. Jolie's last words were burned into my mind. My family wanted to take him out? Huh?

The door was shut and probably locked at the top of the stairs. Pouffant actually did me a favor because just a short jaunt down the passageway and I'd be at the catacombs. But he'd be back with his minions. He wouldn't leave me alone with access to his underground tunnels filled with his secrets. I had to save Mom and then keep running and exit through Jolie's house. I think I could find it again. I hoped.

With a groan, I stood up. The room spun, and I waited for my vision to clear. My fingers traced a path through the grime on the walls as I headed toward the door in the back. Creepy crawlies ran up and down my spine the closer I got. I turned the knob and stared down into the never-ending darkness.

I pulled a flashlight from my pack and made my way down. The steps passed under my feet quickly, winding down and around until I reached the bottom. Flashing the light ahead of me, I ran through the tunnels, ignoring the cobwebs and bones. I tried to remember the path I took the last time, but all the walls and tunnels looked the same. With each turn, fear of failure weighed on my shoulders, heavier than the thick air pressing in on me. As the tunnels twisted and turned, I realized there were no forks or turns. It was a straight shot. I sprinted/hobbled harder until I burst into a cavernous room.

"Mom!" I called as loud as I dared.

If my life were a reality TV show, glitter and confetti would drop from the sky and the crowds would cheer. With arms open wide, a cheesy grin on my face, I dreamed of running into her arms. We'd escape into the sunshine, maybe stop at a café and sip a few lattes. I think I even smelled whipped cream and a bit of hazelnut. But I didn't find Mom. I came to a halt and stared in shock.

A man sat slumped over in the chair, snoring gently. Fresh ropes bound his ankles and hands. Dirty clothes hung off his body. The pants were tan, maybe? I tiptoed closer, afraid to wake him but knowing I needed to. Why this man? I expected Mom. Did this mean Mom was out free and clear? Or did they have her tied up in a separate cavern. The mystery doubled.

He murmured in his sleep, but I couldn't understand him. After a glance back toward the darkened tunnel, I gently shook the man's shoulder. Once, and then again. Finally he lifted his head and tried to focus on me. His eyes were so dark brown the whites appeared very white. His face was pale from a lack of sun, and his hair fell to his ears in an uncombed mess. Underneath the dirt and grime, he probably wasn't too much older than me.

"You," he whispered.

I took a step back. *Me?* I got down on my knees. "You know me?"

"It's you. You're real." He had a heavy accent I didn't recognize, but he spoke perfect English.

He tried to move his arms, and his face flashed with pain. What was I thinking?

"Let me untie you. I'm so sorry."

I moved to his back and pulled out the knife tucked into my sock and under my pant leg. With one slice, his hands were free and then his feet. He rubbed his wrists and then reached out to me. He ran his fingers down my hair.

"Long and black. I knew it."

I let him touch me because clearly he wasn't in his right mind.

"You don't know me, sir."

Compassion surged through me. The last time I was here. The empty chair. He must be the prisoner who'd escaped. Obviously, he hadn't made it. He probably hadn't eaten a proper meal in forever.

"I don't know how long you've been here but we need to go." I tried to help him up. "I know a way out."

"I can't believe it's you." He stared off, and the start of a smile tugged at his mouth. His eyes grew moist, but he shook it off. "No. I need to talk to you."

His eyes cleared and he glanced down the tunnels. "They will come. I'm not strong enough to escape. But you are. And you must. I've been waiting, staying alive, for you."

Crap. The guy was having delusions from dehydration. I pulled out a water bottle and held it up to his lips.

"Drink." I tipped the bottle. "Then you'll see."

The water spilled down his throat and the sides of his mouth, making dark prints in the floor of the cavern. He choked and pulled away.

"Thank you. Thank you. You've been too kind. That's enough. You need to listen." He slipped into a different language.

I gently gripped his arm to help him stand and lead him away. Our time was running out, and I couldn't just leave him here.

"Come on, let's go."

He pulled away and spoke in English again. "No. You must know!" His eyes held a hint of desperation and he grabbed my arms with newfound strength. "I've been hiding the truth. I left my brethren. I risked everything. To find you. To tell you. To save your life."

Clearly this guy wasn't going stop. "Fine. Tell me. But make it quick. We have angry French pastry dudes coming after us."

"That is not important. You have more dangerous enemies than Jolie." His voice grew scratchy, probably from lack of talking during his captivity.

"More water?" I offered the bottle again.

"No. No. Not now. A few years ago I had visions. I kept them to myself and did nothing because they made no sense. I saw fire—great flames—leaping toward the ceiling. For many nights, I stood at the edge of the vision and felt a rush of warm wind. I thought the wind was from the fire. But then the vision changed, and a set of large wings were above the fire, fanning the flames, making them hotter, brighter, and bigger. And you were there."

"Okay, listen." This guy seemed nice and all but being a hostage had affected his mind. "I think the air down here has gotten to you."

Was that muffled footsteps I heard? "They're coming. We have to go. Now!"

"No! I must tell you!" His voice rose to a frantic pitch. "I tried to tell the brethren about my visions and that you needed help, and they mocked me."

"Now I know you've got the wrong girl. I'm here to save you, not the other way around." This guy had completely lost his marbles.

"At first I thought it wasn't important either. As time went on," his voice dropped low and he glanced around, "the vision changed again. This time, the fire faded. All that was left were the charred bones of the dead. You were gone."

I tried to lead him out of the room but this guy was much stronger than he looked. He gripped my arm and pulled me close so I felt his breath on my face. His voice came out raspy.

"I made the mistake of telling the brethren about the new vision. This time they took my words very seriously. When I left, they followed me. They know your family has been part of a centuries-old struggle that has led to bloodshed. They will come after you."

He coughed and drew a ragged breath, then continued, "They let me leave, because they knew my visions were from a higher power. I am meant to save you, so I am forever at odds with my brethren."

A voice rang through the cavern, sounding like a gunshot. "Aha! And you thought you could get away?"

Forty

BOTH THE PRISONER AND I turned. Jolie's hired gun, the *maitre d'*, stood in the doorway. He leaned against the wall, chest heaving, sweat dripping like he'd just taken a shower.

"You girl, have become too much trouble," he growled. "And your boyfriend doesn't seem to be able to get the job done."

The prisoner pulled me behind him. The smell of body odor drifted off him, but I didn't care. The rough texture of his shirt hit my cheek, and it clicked. The photo on Malcolm's laptop flashed back to me. It was him. Could this guy be telling the truth? He sounded completely off his rocker.

"You cannot save her!" The *maitre d'* stated with confident conviction. "And you cannot save yourself either. You have been too much trouble for the master. You both have run out of time!"

The barrel of a revolver faced us along with the menacing glare of a butler with an anger-management problem. Time seemed to freeze. The butler went on, but I blocked him out. I couldn't believe this was happening. Not to me, nice Savvy Bent. The girl who never picked a fight, and who almost always followed directions. Spying for the good of others was one thing, but staring death in the face snapped something inside me. My fingers curled even tighter around the knife still in my hand, and I switched it open.

The prisoner whispered out of the side of his mouth, "I'll distract him. You run."

My legs twitched with the desire to follow his directions, to turn and flee up the stairs. To run away, search for Mom, or to go get Dad. Then I could go into therapy and hypnosis and brainwash the memories away. But no. Not this time. No more running from the truth. My truth.

The butler waved the gun at the prisoner. "Back on the chair."

I gripped his shirt, not letting him go. The knife felt red hot in my hand, a burning that needed to be released. I switched the knife to my right hand. With left arm, I shoved the prisoner to the side. The butler's piercing black eyes caught mine, and he grinned. I whipped my arm over my head and let the knife fly. It soared toward its mark at the same time the revolver went off.

Instinctively, I screamed, dropped to the ground, and curled into a ball, waiting for a burst of pain. But I felt nothing. Thankfully the butler was probably better at serving pastries than shooting a gun. Someone groaned.

I crawled over to the prisoner, fearing for his life. I patted his legs and up to his torso, then saw the dark red stain spreading through his shirt. He'd been shot in the side.

"Oh my God. Oh my God." I smoothed his hair away from his face.

His chocolate eyes were kind, but reflected pain as he turned them on me.

"My time has come. I need to finish. Almost done." His breathing became quick and labored.

"No!" I pulled out my Band-aids and fumbled with the wrapper.

Something had to help. This man did this for me, or so he'd said. Even if he was crazy and had lost it, I couldn't let him die for me. No one had done that before. I just wasn't that important. Someone groaned again, but not the prisoner.

The butler was curled into a fetal position. The knife stuck out of his side, and blood seeped through his fingers. My body prickled with the heat of guilt and the dread that followed. What had I done?

"Is, is he doing to die?" I stammered, clutching the prisoner's arm, forgetting the Band-Aids. Spying on someone was one thing, but killing a man? That was completely different. I didn't want murder on my resumé.

"That doesn't matter. Listen."

All I could see was the red stain, spreading, growing.

"I don't know what happened," I started babbling and couldn't stop. "Something just came over me when I saw the gun pointed at us. I'm not the kind of the girl who stabs men in catacombs or anywhere for that matter. The most violent thing I've done is to kill ants, but you should've seen them overrunning our kitchen, swarming over the leftover candy canes. Yes, it was probably my fault."

Finally, I ran out of words and grabbed his hand. I traced the chapped, worn skin trying to give him warmth, to let him know I cared. I looked into his eyes. They were still full of compassion. He wasn't judging, just waiting. His body relaxed as his words poured forth, and peace spread across his face. He mumbled about finding my mom, arriving in Paris, and then Jolie finding him. Finally he stopped, but his face was pale. I didn't say anything. I was wrapped in his words, hoping, wishing he knew where to find my mom.

He choked and blood dribbled out the side of his mouth. I pressed harder against his shirt to stop the bleeding.

"Jolie thought I knew about your family. He kept asking. I didn't say a word." He could only manage short sentences. Not a good sign. "One night. I knew. The place. The fire. And I saw you caught in a bloody tug-a-war. I need to tell you. You must—"

A high-pitched scream interrupted his story. And it wasn't mine.

Forty-one

AIMEE HAD ENTERED, headlamp on, carrying a tray of food.

"You!" she shouted.

"You!" I echoed back.

We fell silent, staring, barely acknowledging the secrets that had torn us apart. Her frizzy blonde hair was pulled back in a ponytail. She placed the tray on the floor.

My shock grew. I had absolutely no clue what was going on. My fingers curled into tight balls and anger shot through me like lightning. It felt like years had passed since I'd seen her. I'd been shot at, I'd sneaked and spied, and I'd been cooped up in a hen house.

"You've been feeding him?" I whispered.

I wanted to say so much more as the questions piled up.

"*Oui.*"

Aimee grabbed the napkins. She ripped the man's shirt and pressed the napkins to his wounds.

"What happened?" she asked sharply, but then she gasped at Jolie's man lying on the floor and the revolver several feet away.

My voice wavered. "I hoped my mom was down here. But I found him."

"Has he been talking?"

"Yes. But I think he's lost it."

Aimee didn't say anything as she worked quietly, cleaning up the man's wound the best she could. Her forehead creased in thought, like she had a lot to say to me. Rage built on days of worry simmered underneath my thinning veil of patience. Would she tell me the truth?

My voice turned sharp and prickly. "Where the hell have you been?"

Her movements became fast and jerky, but she still did not answer. Oh, but I had lots to say.

"I thought you were gone! Missing! Kidnapped by that lunatic Peyton! I didn't believe your note for one second and did everything I could to find you. All I needed was proof, a real note, a goodbye, face-to-face. Was that too much to ask?"

She wrapped the man's wounds with precision, her lips pressed tight together.

"Answer me!" My voice rang out loud and clear.

I pushed her shoulder, angry, trying to get her to say something. Anything.

"Or are you fabricating your story, your lies, just like your grandfather, the great Jolie Pouffant? Maybe you can tie me up, too. Heck, why stop there? Go after my dad and mom too."

"Enough!" Aimee dropped everything and rushed at me.

Her arms wrapped around my middle and she pushed. I landed flat on my back, and the air whooshed out of my chest. I reached up, wrapped my fingers around her ponytail, and yanked her off. We struggled, pushing and shoving, rolling in the dirt. My face pressed into the floor. I managed to flip around and twist her arm behind her back. She wiggled out and we locked arms, unable to move each other. Finally, we let go and flopped down side by side, spent, and breathing like racehorses.

"Why?" I asked, desperate to understand the lies that surrounded me and pressed against me and freaked me out even more than the bones and skulls in the walls.

Why had Aimee pretended not to know Jolie Pouffant? Why wouldn't she tell me? Why did she take off? And if Jolie was a criminal what did Aimee know about it?

"I had my reasons." Her voice sounded close to breaking.

Tears might have streaked my dirty cheeks but I didn't pay any mind. "I thought you were gone. I thought you were in trouble. I lied to my dad and broke rules so I could find you. You were my friend. And you lied. The whole time. I know about you and Jolie."

"I know." She couldn't look at me. Guilt was etched across her face.

The prisoner spoke softly, his calm words filling the air like the glow of a burning candle. "Tell her. Everything."

Aimee pushed up but wouldn't look at me.

"There is no time." She grasped his hands. "You must see a doctor. We wasted enough time already."

"Tell her." He closed his eyes, his chest barely rising and falling.

"Tell me what?" My words sounded like an accusation. I stood to my feet, ready for round two. "Do you know where my mom is? Did your crazy grandfather lock her up too?"

Aimee shook her head sadly. "If my grandfather had anything to do with your mother, I know nothing." Her voice grew desperate. "But he is in trouble."

I snorted. "Like I care."

She rubbed the prisoner's hand but her words were for me. "I do not expect you to care for my grandfather. But it has to do with you, too."

My body sagged, and the last bit of anger trickled out. I didn't know how much more truth I could take.

"I'm listening," I said, broken but dreading what was coming next.

"Months ago, my grandfather started acting jumpy and nervous. He said it was nothing, but I poked around and listened to his phone calls."

She stopped and her head dropped to her chest. Tears splattered against her chest.

"Go on," I said, my anger slowly dissipated. What was our connection? The prisoner squeezed her hand and reached for mine.

Her voice was a whisper. "I think someone was threatening his life. I was afraid he would die. Soon."

My frustration rose. "What does this have to do with me? And my mom?"

"My grandfather thought your mom had something to with it. That she was here to take his life, because she was watching him. But then she disappeared, and you and your dad arrived. I joined Spy Games to spy on you and your family. I thought your dad might pick up where your mom left off."

I choked on my argument. I thought about the camera and all the money someone had sent my mom. Was she an assassin?

"So why leave without saying goodbye?" I asked.

"My grandfather found out I was working for your dad and was furious. He forced me to disappear." She snapped her fingers. "No goodbyes. No explanations. Just the letter. Then he hired Malcolm to take my place."

"My family is not dangerous." At least not me and Dad. Mom used to go on a lot of trips. I thought they were for her scrapbooking business. But maybe they were official trips to kill people.

"I tried to tell my grandfather that, but he would not believe me. And then you started poking your nose around where you should not. That did not look good."

She narrowed her eyes.

"It was always about my mom," I murmured.

I didn't know whether to be furious, happy, or sad. The conflicting emotions whirled inside me, pulling me one way and then another every few seconds. The prisoner groaned.

Aimee put her arm around his back. "I must get you to help."

He pulled me close again. His ragged breaths were filled with pain. He tried to talk but his words jumbled together and he spoke nonsense. Aimee put a hand to his face.

"He is burning up. He must go now."

I put my hand behind him to help her. This man had risked everything, and he might lose his life, for me. As much as I wanted to hear more of Aimee's explanation, I had to hear the rest of his story.

"No." She pushed my hand away. "I need your help."

What? "There is nothing I can do to help you. I want to help him!"

Tears filled her eyes once more. "I need you to save my grandfather. Please? I can bring this man to a hospital. I speak the language. But I cannot do that and save my grandfather."

I stared at the prisoner, the pain etched in the lines on his face, the weariness of weeks of captivity. He'd put himself last, and me first. A girl from a vision who he didn't even know existed until today. He had faith. But could I trust Aimee?

"You do not trust my grandfather, and you are right. Jolie does not always make the right decisions. He has a bit of a temper." She twisted her hands, not able to meet my eyes. "He is probably involved in something illegal but I know nothing about his business. I am still your friend. I am like you." She lifted her head. "Trying to save my family."

Her words sank in deep, taking root and reminding me of all the reasons I'd lied or done something wrong. At the Extravaganza preliminaries, someone, still didn't know who, had me shoot Jolie with a tranquilizer. Had that been a warning for him? Maybe today at the finals, they'd finish the job. Maybe instructions were waiting up at the table for me. Maybe I'd be a distraction, while some hired gun finished the job. Or maybe it was my mom who would be doing the killing. I had to know.

"Fine. I'll go see what your grandfather is up to, but only if you'll see that this man gets treatment and money to leave the country."

Aimee opened her mouth to speak but a gunshot rang out, echoing in the small chamber.

This time, we both screamed.

Forty-two

THE SHOT GLANCED OFF the wall with a spray of dust. The butler was crawling toward us, the revolver hanging from his hand. I didn't have time to think, just react.

I'd watched just enough spy thrillers with my dad. My leg shot out and caught the butler in the face. One more kick, and his weapon skittered across the floor. His head fell to the floor and he didn't move, knocked out.

"Is he one of the bad guys?" I asked.

"I do not know." Aimee shook her head. "I will come back later for him. Quick. My grandfather is in trouble. I can feel it."

I grabbed the heavy revolver and shoved it down the back of my pants just in case. It felt bulky and obvious. "One more thing. In my apartment, in my bedroom closet is a whole lot of cash. If I don't make it, take half and give it to this man to leave once he is well. Then take the other half and leave it for my dad, for Spy Games."

She nodded. I stood, unable to turn around and leave. She was still my friend, and this was goodbye, possibly forever. She pulled me into a hug and whispered in my ear.

"I am sorry. For everything. For not letting you know somehow that I was okay. For not telling you the truth from the start. "

We clung to each other, both of us reliving the memories, the laughter, the sharing we'd experienced in our short friendship. She was my first friend in France, and I didn't get nearly enough time with her. I wanted to apologize for not asking more questions, for not insisting she tell me about her life. Instead I'd let her distract me and had focused on my problems. Now I wanted to hear about all her troubles with her grandparents, and her memories of her parents before they died. But the words stuck in my throat. Before I could respond, she kissed my cheeks and left with the man leaning on her. I never learned his name. We parted. Probably forever.

At the doorway, the man turned. "Stay safe. Protect your life."

I ran back through the tunnels, my thoughts confused, my heart aching. I stormed up the stairs, down the hallway, up more stairs, and burst into Jolie's kitchen.

Empty.

My feet felt rooted to the ground. My mind was back in the catacombs, reliving my knife-throwing and the crimson spreading across the butler's crisp white shirt. I could've killed him. I leaned over and rested my hands on my knees, breathing in and out, in and out. Holy crap! I had a revolver sticking out the back of my pants.

I couldn't think about everything he'd said, his visions, my death. Maybe he had breathed catacomb air for a wee bit too long or had his stories mixed up. I had to focus. Aimee wanted me to save her grandfather. Everything I'd worked for I had to turn away from—vindication, justification, all of it. But for some crazy reason, it felt right. I yanked off the flower pin on my shirt and crushed it under my heel, our recorded conversation gone forever, any incriminating evidence destroyed.

At the front door, I paused, scanning the Extravaganza. I needed to mix with the people. The crowds milled, the dancers danced, the singers sang, the mimes mimed and none of them knew the truth. I slipped out the door and joined the flow.

A crowd of people strutted past. Old and young, male and female all dressed in black trench coats and yapping nervously. Spy Games? A shiver ran through the core of my body. Why were they here? I thought about the times I'd zoned out at staff meetings. I thought about Dad's plans to include a well-known businessman after the Louvre disaster. I thought about Jolie bragging how he was going to work for my dad. How? I wasn't sure.

The teams flooded the street and sidewalks. Amidst the dark sunglasses, baseball caps, old-man hats, trench coats, and pea coats, I didn't spot Malcolm. He was supposed to be working for Spy Games. Dad had put him in charge of a group because of his "spy look." Please.

The groups weaved in and around the reporters and mimes looking for someone. One spy client waved his arms and shouted Jolie's name to his group. My dad had asked Jolie to be an informant and hand out clues? Then Jolie had told the truth. He was working with my dad. This was so not in the plans. Damn.

The news Jolie had been spotted rippled through the teams. Three of them approached him like school children gathering around the most popular kid. They jostled for position. Their greedy hands reached forward hoping to touch his apron or grab the clue. I wanted to sprint forward and pull them all back, let them know that Spy Games had turned dangerous—as in life-or-death dangerous. But my feet wouldn't move, and I watched, helpless, numb from all the surprises thrown at me.

One group, led by a tall man with silver hair—another wannabe—arrogantly pushed his way past the reporters and through the jockeying crowd. He strode up to the great pastry chef who would propel him to victory. He spoke to Jolie, and received not even a look or a wave of the hand. Red crept around the guy's collar line and up his neck. What would he do? In front of his group, leading the charge, would he tolerate being ignored? He cleared his throat and spoke again. Spy Games' clients pressed in on them.

Jolie took a deep breath and turned, his body expanded to full height and breadth. French sputtered out of his mouth. Too bad he was too annoyed to speak in English. Another client in a trench coat approached Jolie who threw his hands up in the air in defeat. His face turned redder and redder as the spies all called out for the clues. And then out of the corner of my eye, I caught a flash of dark hair.

Malcolm.

Forty-three

I LEFT JOLIE FOR the moment and inched my way through the crowd, closer and closer, squeezing between two reporters huddled in conversation. I grabbed a tray of pastries and lifted it up in front of my face, a pitiful attempt at camouflage. The few pastries on it weren't even stacked high enough. So with the confidence of a trained F.B.I. agent, I made my way to all the contestants' tables, and when they weren't looking, I grabbed a pie, a cake, or some kind of pastry to build my tower.

I absolutely could not let Malcolm see me.

About ten yards away, I peeked around a strawberry tart. Malcolm was shaking his finger in the face of a street mime with black lips and black triangles above and below his eyes. I gripped the tray to prevent myself from dropping it and running. Taking baby steps, I moved as close as I could without being obvious. I turned my back and listened. The tower of pastries wobbled a bit. The frosting shone in the sun. My arms strained under the weight.

"What the hell is your problem?" Malcolm snarled.

"Just watching out for you."

"Go back home. You haven't left me alone since I found her."

The mime laughed. "Does someone have a little crush? Do you know how dangerous that is? Thank God I'm here. To get the job done."

Malcolm lowered his voice, and I couldn't hear.

I pushed through the crowds a bit further. How did Malcolm know the mime so well?

The mime spoke. "Do you have the guts to follow through, or should I?"

Follow through? My arms shook harder, and I almost dropped the tray. Was Jolie in danger? Or was I? Aimee counted on her grandfather. She loved him. She needed him. In one big flood my feelings toward Jolie changed. I wanted to save him for real.

"Back off," Malcolm threatened. "I got this. And I'll take care of the girl too."

The colors and sounds of the Extravaganza swirled around me. The classical music started to sound like something from a horror movie—the part where the main character gets killed. The sugary smells made me feel sick.

The *M* word sat in the back of my throat, and I had to take in deep breaths.

I rushed away on wobbly legs, scared I'd give in to my impulse to slam my tray of delights into their faces. Why would the mime be following Malcolm around? Why would they want to murder Jolie? And what girl would they be taking care of? Me?

Jolie's voice roared above the crowd. He held out his arms in a lame attempt to ward off the Spy Games' teams. But he must have had enough, because with a grand flourish, he reached into his coat and threw what had to be the next clue into the crowds. The papers fluttered in the breeze, dancing over the heads of the spies.

In a mad frenzy, they rushed forward, knocking over reporters, grabbing at the air, desperate for the clue. He never should have underestimated the competitive drive and determination of the people that sign up for Spy Games. I never would again. My eyes widened as a couple of the clues completed whirly birds and landed gently on the top of Jolie's entry to the contest.

Silence gripped the crowds as the last clue landed. It was a perfect distraction for me to talk to Jolie, whisper words of warning in his ear. I crouched, but as I approached, men in tuxedos closed in on me. Jolie's minions. Who else could they be?

They stood in a perfect line, not saying a word, their faces unreadable. I half expected them to start kicking up their legs in a line dance they were so perfectly organized. Did they spring from the cobblestones? Maybe it was coincidence. I waved my hand at them, gesturing I needed to get through.

"*Excuse-moi!*"

They didn't blink an eye. Damn. I was stuck.

"Savvy?"

I whipped around. Dad? The lines on his forehead looked like mountain ridges.

"Hey, Dad!" I forced a smile and waved, a tad bit relieved.

They couldn't drag me away, not with Dad to protect me. He eyed the line-up of men in tuxedos and leaned closer to me.

"What is this all about?" he asked.

"What do you mean?" My voice sounded like Alvin the Chipmunk.

"This." He pointed to the mountain of pastries on my tray.

"Oh, that. I, um, entered the pastry contest."

He would be proud if he knew the truth. I had finally become everything he wanted me to be. I was sneaky. I lied to him about not feeling well, and I'd rubbed shoulders with a bad guy.

He pointed to the crowd of Spy Games clients all grasping at the paper clues.

"Please tell me you don't have anything to do with this."

"I don't. They all arrived at the same time. Promise."

The line of Jolie's men stepped closer, their top hats blocking out the sun. Dad eyed them while pulling me a few steps away.

"Is there something you're not telling me?" he asked.

Time for the truth. If I could face down bad men and save a prisoner, I could face my dad.

"I'm sorry." I searched his eyes, looking for some hint of understanding or compassion. "When you wouldn't believe Aimee had been kidnapped, I stole into your office to find out where Peyton lived."

Dad's mouth formed an *O*, and he surveyed the scene with a knowing look.

"While I was looking at your files, you came back, and I overheard you talking about money troubles so I entered the Extravanganza. I won first place and advanced to the finals. There's prize money, and if I win, you can have it all."

The words seemed useless and my voice dropped to a whisper. "That's why I lied earlier about not feeling well."

The crowd screamed. Dad and I turned and watched. The moment of reckoning had arrived. The group of clients had jumped at the remaining clues on top of Jolie's mountain of elegantly displayed fruit tarts in the shape of a dove or a pelican. Some kind of bird.

"*Mon Dieu!*" Jolie dove at the crowd with his arms spread, pushing the crowds away from his masterpiece.

Okay. I felt a tiny bit bad. As the spies-in-training struggled over the clues, they gave no regard to the tarts. In a matter of seconds, they were covered in an assortment of colors. Strawberry juice dripped off their hands like blood. It could've been a rated R violent movie scene. Dad gripped me in a hug. I tensed, ready for the lecture.

"I'm proud of you, Savvy."

I pulled away. "Say that again?" He had to be kidding.

"I'm not saying you did everything right. But you took risks. And that man has been the most stubborn mule to work with. He deserves it."

I smiled. Dad didn't know the half of it. Jolie gave up on his tarts. He stood with his back to us, his shoulders heaving. His body trembled. I tried to step back, but the wall of minions blocked my way. Inch by inch, Jolie turned around. He searched the crowds, back and forth, until his eyes landed on me. He shoved the reporters and his fans to the side and stormed over to me, his eyes flashing.

And that was when I fully grasped the old cliché of, "You can't have your cake and eat it too."

Forty-four

FRENCH EXPLETIVES BURST FROM Jolie's mouth and burned through the air and into the minds of the crowds. A mish-mash of red, green, and blue frosting stuck to the front of Jolie's belly like encrusted jewels. His fingers were curled into fists. I had to warn him. His life was in danger.

"Savvy. What did you do?" Dad asked in a low voice.

I spoke out the corner of my mouth as Jolie advanced through the crowds, the cameras and press following him. "Nothing really." *Just stole his pastries. And freed his hostage.*

"Um, Savvy?"

"Not now, Dad. Evil is nigh."

"Your tray."

Zut alors! The whole middle section slid forward. Reaching around with a forceful shove, I pushed the whole masterpiece back into place.

"You!" With one word, Jolie commanded my attention.

I slowly faced him while the tray balanced precariously on my arm. "I'm sorry, sir."

Jolie narrowed his eyes. "It is too late for that."

A man with curly hair pushed through the wall of people. He gripped a digital tape recorder and a pencil stuck out from behind his ear. Jolie moved his killer glare to the reporter. I swallowed what little spit was in my mouth and tried to find the courage to tell Jolie he was in a lot of trouble. Like someone might try to plant a bullet in his chest.

Jolie spoke in rapid French and the reporter backed away, cowering. To my right at the perimeter of the contest, Malcolm moved closer to us, slipping in and out of the crowd like a stealthy predator. I scanned the mass of people until I found the mime to my left. I didn't know what he had to do with Malcolm yet, but he was connected. That I knew. He did his mime thing, and with every exaggerated motion, he moved in. Possibly for the kill. I had to get close enough to talk to Jolie without anyone else hearing.

I goaded him. "Mr. Pouffant, I understand we've had our differences, but really, if you were to be honest, you'd see that I was not the aggressor in this unfortunate situation."

Jolie chuckled and faced his fans. They echoed a forced chuckle. "Silly girl." He made a cuckoo sign, like a fourth grade boy would to a girl who teased him. "You do not know what you are talking about."

"Yes, I do." I stepped closer to him and lowered my voice. "Your life is in danger."

As Jolie laughed hysterically, Malcolm and the mime closed in. My limbs trembled and blood pumped through my heart so fast it scared me.

"Um, Savvy?" Dad whispered. "The cakes!"

I didn't take my eyes off Jolie, while keeping the pastries balanced. It seemed rather silly that I gripped the pastries as if they could protect me. *Use the revolver,* a tiny voice inside my head commanded. The cold metal of the barrel pressed against my lower back, hidden away.

Dad stepped forward. "Now, now, Mr. Pouffant. I'm sure we can work things out here like reasonable people."

Jolie's eyes flashed. "Reasonable? You Americans are not rational. Your daughter attacked me earlier with her zapper. How is that for rational?"

Dad hooked is arm through mine and pulled close to me. "Is this true?"

"Yes." I was done lying. "But only so I could search his shop."

Jolie eyed the pastry cakes on my tray. "And she is stealing cakes for an entry."

My face burned. "Only because you destroyed my entry before I even got here. Don't you dare try to deny it."

"Like you had a chance of winning? That is a joke."

Why did I want to save this man?

Dad puffed out his chest. "My daughter can bake a mean birthday cake. Watch it."

My throat tightened. He'd stuck up for me. That rarely happened. Ever. During Spy Games, I always disappointed, always made the wrong choice, always caused a scowl to cross his face.

"Way to go, Dad," I whispered.

"Oh, how touching." Jolie smirked. "I do not have time for this petty back and forth." He signaled to his guards. "These people are disrupting the Extravaganza. Escort them to the exit."

The power-hungry pastry chef, beloved by his country, running illegal scams of some kind behind his wall of scones and croissants, turned his back to me. But I had to make him believe me. Jolie's goons ripped Dad away from me.

"Savvy!" Dad cried.

He fought against the men holding his arms. When the crowds started murmuring and even more attention swung onto Jolie, he motioned to the men to stop dragging my dad away.

The tray weighed on my arm and on my mind. I grabbed a hunk of cake. Blue, green, and white squeezed between my fingers. It felt squishy.

"Hey, Jolie!"

Right as he turned, I threw it. It was a silly, two-year-old thing to do, but I couldn't help it. The man infuriated me. And I had to warn him.

The cake landed in Jolie's beard and dripped onto the front of his shirt. He reached his hand up only to smear the colors into his beard. Slowly, his hand went from his beard, to the frosting on his shirt, and down to the sides of his pants. His fingers twitched. He shifted back and forth between his feet as if ready to run or attack. A low growl sounded in his throat and rose to a loud pitch. He rushed at me, arms outstretched, aiming for my neck.

I waited until the last second and then slammed the tray into his face.

Forty-five

CAKE SPLATTERED THE GROUND. A tart smeared into Jolie's hair. Veins in his neck bulged. Sweat dripped down his face and mixed with the frosting stuck in every crevice. With one swoop, he grabbed a hunk of cake from the ground. Two seconds later, warm cake hit my eye. I gasped and wiped it off. Huffing and puffing, he took a step toward me but slipped in the confectionary delight. With a flutter of his arms, he fought gravity and lost, landing on his rump.

I hated the guy and the evil part of me surged forward and wanted to let him get killed. Aimee's smile flashed in my eyes. And her laugh. I caught sight of dark hair. Malcolm. *Use the revolver*, the tiny voice commanded again. With my hand shaking, I reached toward my back and curled my fingers around the part sticking out. I couldn't think about right or wrong.

Jolie spluttered and gasped, wiping frosting from his eyes. Three of the men in tuxedos pushed me aside and rushed to their boss. Two dragged my dad away toward the exit. I'd lost sight of Malcolm and the mime. But they were there. Possibly taking aim.

Shoot the revolver. Cause a distraction.

I pulled out the gun and aimed at Jolie. Maybe just shoot him in the knee. But what if I missed? Or hit someone else? My hands shook. Frosting made my fingers slippery. With a small sob, I let go. The revolver clattered to the stones and I kicked it under a table. But I still had to save him.

I grabbed an apple tart, somehow untouched in the chaos. With a battle cry, I leaped at Jolie and landed right on top of him. My knees landed on his stomach. I smashed the tart smack dab in the middle of his face. As I bent down to whisper in his ear, a shot rang out.

Everyone screamed and dropped to the ground. The bodies blurred around me, piling up like it was a mass murder. I couldn't tell if I was screaming or not. My throat hurt. Frosting and tears stung my eyes. A sob poured out of me. *It wasn't me.* I didn't shoot it. Jolie shoved me off of him, and I landed on the cobblestones. My leg throbbed as if a thousand pastry knives were jabbing into it over and over again.

I crawled away from the scene, dragging my leg behind me because it refused to cooperate. I dug my elbows into the grit and pulled forward, my knees scraping the stones. I needed to get away, find my dad. That was it. He'd whisk me back to Pennsylvania and put me back together. He'd take care of my cuts and bruises, and then we'd play Chess. Or talk about how we'd work together to get Mom to come back.

"Dad!" I sobbed.

He had to be here. Not too far away. Just up ahead. The crowd ignored me. They focused on their beloved idol and their own safety. Most people made a mass exit toward the main streets. They hurdled over me and on me. Feet trampled, landing on my back, my head, my arms. My nose smashed into the ground. No one stopped to help. No one bothered. No one cared.

I struggled to get to my feet. Someone brushed into me. I collapsed to the ground and crept forward, painful inch by painful inch. The spots returned and my breath came out in gasps at the fire shooting through my leg. I shivered even as the sun beat down on me. I shouldn't be here. I never should have been. I should have stayed in Pennsylvania.

I stopped moving and rested my cheek to the warm stone. I smelled dirt. I remembered gardening with Dad as he pointed out which leaves were weeds and which were the herbs. A raspy noise gurgled from my throat. I didn't recognize it. My shoulders shook. Arms hooked under my shoulder and rolled me over. The face was fuzzy but I saw Dad's dark hair. His face was blurred.

"Dad!" I sobbed. "I'm sorry. I should've told you everything."

My leg burned. I jerked away. But he held me tight and wrapped something around my leg.

"I'm sorry but this is going to hurt." He put his arms underneath me and scooped me off the ground. Away from the crowds and the jabbing feet.

Dizziness and nausea rushed over me, and I cried.

"Shh. You'll be fine."

Through the pain, my mind locked in on his voice. It wasn't Dad.

Forty-six

ADRENALINE SHOT THROUGH my body. "Why?" I groaned. I wanted answers. Why did he pick me up when he could have left me to die? Why did he smile at me so tenderly at times when I was just an assignment?

While holding me, Malcolm talked into his earpiece, telling someone to meet him. Probably calling in the big guns to get rid of me. This was not how I planned on spending my last minutes on earth. I figured on old age, still living in the 'burbs, watching TV reruns. No one in the town would have pegged me for death by assassin.

Dad. I'd never get a chance to explain everything. I'd never get the chance to yell at Mom and hear her say she was sorry. I tried to lift my head but it felt like a dead weight pulling me down. I struggled to get out of Malcolm's clutches and mumbled empty threats.

"Shh. Don't try and talk," he murmured.

"Don't let anyone kill me."

He didn't say anything. My head rolled side to side as he walked. I flashed in and out of awareness. Next I knew, a bridge appeared next to me, and a jolt of pain stabbed my leg. Steps. I smelled the tangy waters of the Seine. He lowered me to the stony ground. My eyes fluttered wider.

"Don't try to escape," he said.

I tried to call for help, but my voice came out hoarse and raspy. He pulled out a knife, and Dad's words rolled through me. *Fake it until it's real.* Okay. I was brave. I was a fearless warrior who would never give up. Call me, ninja.

With a quick kick of my good leg, I made sure my jab landed right in Malcolm's gut. He struggled against the momentum and fell backward. I tried to scramble to my feet, but excruciating pain caused spots to tango in front of me. I shook it off and took a deep breath. I'd crawl away if I had to.

He grabbed my foot. I screamed and kicked him off. Three seconds later, his arms wrapped around me. The floodgates opened and I beat against him with my fists.

"I know. I know all about you." My words came out a sob. "I know Jolie hired you to spy on my family because someone wants him dead, and he thought my family had something to do with it. But he's just a pastry chef and makes the best croissants, and then I realized that someone must be trying to kill me too or my mom and it must be you but that doesn't make any sense because I know you wouldn't hurt me."

I took in a ragged breath as my body heaved, tears running, nose sniffling.

"I wouldn't hurt you. Now shh. I need to remove the clothing so we can see if the bullet is in your leg." He laid me down gently. "Don't move."

My eyes widened. Bullet?

"Yes, you heroically jumped in front of a bullet to save Jolie. Why, I have no idea." With short, jerky movements he rubbed a cloth over his knife.

"I was going to shoot him," I whispered. "But I didn't." My leg. The gut-wrenching pain made me want to puke.

"You took the bullet meant for Jolie."

I didn't plan on saving Jolie like that, just cause a distraction so the creeps couldn't get a clear shot. Material ripped as Malcolm's knife cut through my right pant leg. The leather from the most expensive pair of pants I owned fell to the ground. A shadow fell over us and a familiar voice tickled my ears.

"Hey, isn't that why you called me?"

Peyton. Peyton? Malcolm handed him the knife.

"Whoa, whoa, whoa!" I shouted.

My life had become a funhouse full of mirrors. Peyton grinned a normal, nice, warming smile. Gone was the swaggering, cocky jerk who had participated in Spy Games.

"Hey there, darling. Bet you never expected to see me again." He poised the knife above my leg. "I have to dig around a bit. This might hurt."

I pushed back and tried to squirm away.

"He's here to help." Malcolm gripped my arms so I couldn't move. "Let him. He's much better at this than me."

I held my breath. Pain like a thousand fireworks exploded in my leg.

"You're lucky. The bullet wasn't in too far. This will sting."

He dabbed some kind of liquid fire on me that I swear burned a hole through my leg.

"What the hell?" The pain seared my skin, and I felt like the fiery flames of hell were punishing me for my lies.

"I'm cleaning it. Hold on. I'm almost done." Peyton focused on my leg, his hands gentle but confident. He unrolled a bandage and wound it around my leg.

I flinched. "Why? I don't understand."

My world had gone topsy-turvy. In my world, Peyton had packed and gone back to the States. In my world, Peyton and Malcolm weren't buddies who called each other in a pinch.

Peyton smiled at me again but spoke to Malcolm.

"Man, you can't stay here long. The police are crawling all over the city." He slapped Malcolm on the back. "Good luck." He turned back to me. "Sorry about all that fuss and trouble I caused you. Nothing personal."

Warmth hung like a halo around Peyton. He winked and then disappeared up the stairs. He was not the same man from Spy Games. Or he'd had me completely fooled.

"Guess you want some answers, huh?" The knife still lay at Malcolm's side.

"That would be nice." My leg throbbed but I clenched my teeth because I needed the truth.

"Peyton is a friend of the family. I called him in to distract and lead you away from Jolie." He bit his lip. "And to threaten you, so I could save you and earn your trust."

His answer clicked, and Peyton's uncalled-for rage and drama made sense. But how and why Malcolm knew Peyton dropped to the bottom of my list of questions. "I saw you." My words grated and tension throbbed between us. "If you didn't shoot me, who did?"

His face showed no emotion as he finished adding extra tape to my leg. He'd used me. He'd pretended to romance me just to spy on my family. He'd lied to me when he knew where Aimee was the whole time and then he tried to act like the hero in "searching" for her. Lies. All of it.

But in another time, another year, another life, maybe in a regular high school in the middle of Pennsylvania somewhere, in the midst of cheerleaders and chem labs and Spanish tests, we might've been friends. Maybe we would've dated and gone to the movies or for ice cream. We would've had a normal first kiss. He wouldn't be a hit man. I wouldn't be a wannabe-spy still living with her dad, who screws everything up.

"Answer the question. Who shot at me?"

"That was my brother. As the mime."

He lifted my head and sloshed water down my throat. It streamed along the sides of my face. With the bottom of his shirt, he wiped off any frosting from my skin. Brother? And then it all came together. The mime I'd seen on our date at the Parc des Buttes. And at the Extravaganza.

I wanted answers, needed answers, but the whole day was crashing down on me. My thoughts swirled together and turned into a blurry haze. "Malcolm?"

"What?"

"Who are you?"

Forty-seven

MALCOLM DIDN'T ANSWER ME but sat with his arms resting on his knees. His gaze lingered on the rippling water. "When did your mom first contact you?"

"Pfft. I don't know what you're talking about."

He turned toward me, and my heart squeezed—out of fear or attraction I wasn't sure.

"I know all about your family," he said.

I laughed and not in a jokey sort of way, then winced as pain shot through my leg.

"I don't know anything about yours." *Except that his brother likes to dress like a mime and try and kill people.*

"You don't want to know." He looked bitter.

I guess I wasn't the only one with a dysfunctional family. He reached into an inside pocket and pulled out a small flask.

"This might help with the pain."

My heart completed a set of short, staccato beats. Was this some sort of cathartic release he was experiencing? Tell me the truth, heal me, and then let his brother kill me?

"Malcolm." He knew. I could see it in his eyes. It was time. "Just tell me the truth."

He opened the flask and handed it to me. I tipped my head back and the liquid scorched my throat and burned in my chest. He inched closer.

"Do you know anything about your mom's work?"

"Not really. She's a scrapbooker." I highly doubted that was true. Mom worked a lot, spent late nights locked away in her office, and frequently left on trips.

He took a swig. "Tell me about her."

"She's one more person who's not what they seem." After taking another sip, my body already felt the effects. "What do you know about my mom?"

And then he gave the typical cryptic response. "I wish I could tell you, but that would only put you in danger."

"Right." I stared at his profile, his strong jaw line, desperately wanting to believe he cared and was telling the truth, but I was seeing only the tip of Malcolm. "I don't know where to find my mom. How can I protect myself if I don't know what's going on or why people are after me?"

He turned his eyes on me and really looked at me, as if he could see past all of my charades and self-defense. A battle raged on his face. He clearly didn't know how much to tell me.

"Our families are enemies. They have been for centuries. My family takes care of future leaders or politicians that will lead our world away from a united front, those people who will cause damage to our world."

I gulped. Take care of? I was pretty sure he meant take care of permanently. "What about my family?"

"Are you sure you want to know?"

"Yes." I think. I mean how bad could it be? Right?

"Your family, your mom's side of the family, will do anything to protect those persons in danger. Regardless of their criminal activity or moral bent, your mom believes in the sanctity of life."

We fell silent as I soaked in his words. The truth. Finally, the truth. My mom wasn't an assassin. My mom wasn't an assassin. My mom wasn't an assassin. Those words danced in my head and in my heart, lifting my spirits. She saved people.

"Even though your great grandmother and your grandmother knew my family, my dad, my brother, and me; we didn't know where to find you and your mom. Until recently."

Malcolm grimaced and I took this to be bad news. Especially for me.

"How'd you find out?"

"We laid a trap." There was no smirk on his face this time. "My dad chose a completely innocent man who had dabbled a bit in criminal activities—but no one we would ever look at—and we made it look like he was our next target."

My heart broke at how their trap had affected Aimee's life. "Pouffant?"

"Yes. It was a carefully laid trap for your mom first and then you. We planted the package and the money."

"But why did you try and kill him if he was innocent?" Not only were they crusaders with a twisted mission, they were just plain old mean.

"If my brother, Will, wanted Jolie dead, he would've been dead." He picked at his fingernails and glanced at me. "He was probably aiming for you before you jumped on Jolie. He shot at us on our date and at the park too—as a warning to me."

"What about the prisoner? How does he fit into all this?" I asked.

"Jolie figured out he was friends with your mom and nabbed him for insurance."

"Don't say anymore. I get it." When my mom meddled and tried to save Jolie, they figured out who she was, and then she disappeared from my life to go into hiding. That's why she told me to burn the package, to not get involved. Too late. A crazy laugh bubbled up. The whole scenario sounded like some unbelievable story that belonged on *Dateline* or something.

"Great. I've got people trying to kill—"

He pulled me to him and his mouth covered mine. I fought him back at first but he wouldn't let go and my defenses crumbled. Heat washed over me as his kiss deepened. His body pressed into mine. I stifled a tiny groan of pain and pleasure. The vodka had pretty much numbed any feeling in my leg. His kiss deepened again, and it was better than eating a triple peanut butter chocolate ice cream cone in Pennsylvania or skinny-dipping in the creek when it reached 100 degrees.

His kiss softened. He was gentle and loving, like he cared. His hand grazed my cheek. His past, my past, our families all faded. It was just me and him. Malcolm and Savvy. Two teens.

My heart broke a little bit. I don't even know why. Maybe because I could add one more person to the list of people I cared about who would betray me and leave me. One more person I cared about more than they did me.

His hands slid down my back to the hem of my shirt. In one suave lift, my shirt was off. My hands roamed across his chest, exploring. He tenderly ran his fingers down my arm, and I shivered.

He whispered in my ear, "God help me, you're beautiful. Even with frosting in your hair."

The words sank in and something broke. The cracks in my heart that I'd plastered and put Band-aids on tore open. Emotion flooded out and filled every inch of my body. My face was wet with tears.

He pulled away and kissed them. "In my line of work, you can't care about anyone too much. It can get you killed."

"That's good, because I don't care about you. The tears are purely a post-traumatic side effect of getting shot." At least I was pretty sure my life wouldn't end tonight.

Malcolm rubbed his thumbs under my eyes. I leaned into him for another kiss, not wanting to admit my feelings or forgive. His soft lips were warm and inviting. He pressed his mouth against mine harder, and a thrill ran through my insides. He pushed me back, kissed my cheek, and whispered in my ear.

"Savvy Bent, don't you ever let anyone hold you back. You're the most amazing girl I've ever met."

"I could've told you that from our first date," I teased. "Or when you first asked—"

He kissed me again, then pulled away, leaving me breathless.

"You and me. Our families. Just being with me puts you in danger." His voice held a note of sadness and regret.

At that moment, I didn't care. I pulled him back to me, needing to feel him against me. I held him tight, close to me, as if that could fix everything. His warmth spread through me like wildfire, igniting, growing, burning away the rest of the fear and tension.

He broke away. "I wish I was half as strong as you are. I mean it. You've made me question everything in my life. My family. Their line of business. I want to leave it all. But I can't. Not yet."

"We can get past this. Somehow."

"Not if you want to stay alive." His face changed, from soft and passionate to hard and determined. Sirens grew louder. "I can't let you get hurt. I won't let that happen."

In one swift movement, he pulled my arms behind my back. Something cold and metal clamped around my wrists. "The judge pronounces you guilty."

I yanked away. Somehow, I didn't think the cuffs were for fun. The high school scenario of two teens fooling around dissolved. My body quickly cooled off, and I tried to ignore the fact my shirt laid in a crumpled mess on the ground beside me. Malcolm's eyes twinkled and he stood up.

"You. Wouldn't. Dare."

Forty-eight

"OH, BUT I WOULD." Malcolm smiled.

He unsnapped my spy pants and gently pulled them off so as not to hurt my leg. It was too hard to kick my legs again without shooting pain.

"Gee, thanks."

He cleaned up any mess from Peyton wrapping my injury, then brushed my hair out of my face. "You didn't think I'd forget, did you?"

Blood rushed to my face. "But, but my leg! Shouldn't you bring me to a hospital or something?"

"I'm sure someone will find you soon."

"But, but, my dad! He'll worry. And he'll hunt you down!"

"I'll be gone." He punched numbers into his phone.

Fear rose in my throat and clamped down on my vocal chords.

"I'll hunt you down!" I threatened.

"I'll be disappointed if you don't." He leaned forward and pressed his face into my hair, then he dropped his head and tried to kiss me. But I turned away. He started to leave, but I was still desperate for answers. I trembled, trying to build the courage to ask what secretly my heart wanted, needed to know. The words barely made it past the lump in my throat.

"Am I just an assignment to you?"

"I sent the package to your mom's apartment knowing she wasn't there, hoping to draw her out of hiding, and testing you to see if you would take her place. When you did, it made you look guilty, but as time went on I was convinced of your cluelessness even though others weren't."

"You didn't answer the question."

"Yes, you are, I mean were..." but he couldn't say the words. Instead, he said, "Savvy. You have to believe me. When I first asked you out, I didn't know any of this. About our families and the age-old battle. Nothing. By the time my family filled me in, it was too late. But it's not too late for you. Walk away from all this and forget about me. Live a normal life."

Bitterness settled on his shoulder like a winter wind. "Trust me. Because next time you might not be so lucky."

Then he turned and walked away. Probably forever.

Not long after, the sirens grew louder in the distance.

Dad must be worried sick, and I couldn't bear to think about Malcolm and the lasting effects of his words. I glanced

322

at the bandage on my leg. How soon would the vodka wear off? Would I be able to walk home? I had to try.

I pushed up onto my feet, balancing delicately on my good leg. I couldn't easily forget that I was in my underwear and bra. I desperately wished I were wearing my new Victoria's Secret bra, which was folded neatly back in my drawer. It would be near impossible to get home without anyone seeing me. Maybe I'd end up on a YouTube video, get like a million hits, and wind up on TV.

I limped up the stairs, wincing at every step. The green grass and paths with scattered trees and benches stretched in front of me. Couples held hands while chatting happily and strolling innocently. Families dragged tired kids back to the Metro. Businessmen strode through without even a glance at their famous tower. This was going to be impossible.

Suck it up.

I took a deep breath and with my head held high, I half-walked, half-hobbled away from the Eiffel. My hands were still cuffed behind my back. At first the stares, the giggles, the crazy looks, the disgusted eyebrow waves got to me. I tried not to look at anyone and kept my eyes forward, thinking about home. That was my goal.

Ask for help. Right. Like anyone would believe my story. It wasn't one I could explain in one sentence. I'd need more like six months.

I made it to the road and started down the sidewalk. Unless someone was looking for me, it was dark enough that the average driver wouldn't notice me. The shadows were my friend.

Cooler air prickled my skin. I thought about summer nights in Pennsylvania after a tough afternoon of pulling weeds. I'd bike down to the creek, shed my clothes, and wade into the ice-cold water. I'd fall backwards, and the current would envelop me and wash off the dirt and grime from the day. I always rose clean, refreshed and ready for more. So here in the streets of Paris, the musical sounds of the most romantic city on earth washed over me, lifting the guilt from not being the perfect daughter, sifting away the anger that somehow Mom was to blame for all of this, and chipping away at the fear I'd never see Malcolm or Aimee again. Or ever hear the rest of the prisoner's story.

At least I'd survived.

Sirens wailed in the not-so-far distance, their warning echoing throughout the city. My heart banged against my chest like it would punch out in just a couple of beats. Sweat dripped down my sides. I hobbled a bit faster, regardless of the blood now seeping through my bandage and dripping down my leg.

Several cars screeched to a stop on the road next to me. A huge spotlight swept back and forth until it stopped on me. Talk about embarrassing.

"I didn't see anyone running! Your guy must be somewhere else!" I yelled in a raspy voice.

The spotlight stayed on me. Men in uniform rushed at me from all sides. With guns. Pointed at me. Oh. My. Holy. Spy. Pants. They were after me. I couldn't breathe. My chest stopped rising and falling. They didn't seem to care I couldn't breathe. One man, carrying a shield—I guess because I looked just that dangerous—grabbed my arm and threw me against the nearest car. The cold metal shocked the skin on my stomach.

When he realized my arms were cuffed, he dragged me out into the street. The cops had set up a roadblock—I guess in case all my minions came to my rescue. People poked their heads out of their cars, hoping to catch a glimpse of the hardened criminal. I mean the person must be quite a danger to society to need so much back up. Right?

The uniforms crawled all over me. It was like I was in a mosh pit, except my destination was the back of a cop car. The vodka must have worn off because the pain in my leg returned full force. I leaned over and puked. I heard a bunch of expletives in French. Cold words bounced off me. Rough hands grabbed at me until I was pushed into the car. I didn't think it was a free ride home. I yelled for my dad. I asked where they were taking me. I struggled but the pain felt like they were starching their shirts on my leg.

They slammed the door shut. Two cops sat in the front, the mesh cage separating me from them. The car zoomed through Paris. I must be pretty important to have an escort. I pressed my head against the cool window and watched the city as it blurred past me. Tears pushed at my eyes but I refused them. I would be strong. I didn't know how they found me or why they thought I was so bad. Maybe the same reason Mom didn't want to fight for me. I doubted my prank on Malcolm had ended up with him in the back of a squad car.

He said I was beautiful. Right. Like I believed him. Malcolm was a sneak and a liar. Not only one more person just to leave me, but to leave me practically naked, bleeding, and handcuffed. I guess I deserved it.

The cop driving the car gripped the steering wheel in a death grip. Somehow I had to explain that I'd saved Jolie Pouffant and his prisoner. The guy I'd knifed was an accident, self-defense.

"I thought I told you to burn the package and not get involved."

My heart stopped beating, and I looked into the rearview mirror. Stern eyes met mine. The cop took off her pointed hat and long brown hair spilled down her back. Mom! So many words burned in my throat, wanting to be spoken. So many questions.

The second cop took off his hat and turned toward me. I couldn't forget those warm chocolate eyes. The prisoner.

"You're lucky I found you."

"Mom?" I croaked.

Her lips pressed together, but her eyes stayed on the road. Then she spoke.

"We're leaving the country."

...to be continued in *Heart of an Assassin*

Note from the author

Thank you so much for reading A Spy Like Me.

Several years ago when planning my next novel, I heard the advice to write what I'd like to see on the shelves. And I wanted a fun spy story set outside of America with a teen girl who wasn't trained for the job. What would that look like? How would a life of espionage change her?

If you enjoyed *A Spy Like Me*, I'd love to hear from you. You can contact me through the contact tab on my blog at laurapauling.com.

About Laura

Laura writes about spies, murder and mystery. She's the author of the exciting Circle of Spies Series, and the time travel thriller, HEIST. She's a former elementary teacher and currently lives in New England. After spending time reading books to her kids and loving a good plot turn, she put her fingers to the keyboard. Don't ask her about the unfinished quilts and scrapbooks in her attic. Stories are way more exciting. She writes to entertain and experience a great story...and to be able to work in her jammies and slippers.

Visit www.laurapauling.com for more information on her books and to sign up for her newsletter.

Also by Laura

Circle of Spies Series

A SPY LIKE ME - Book 1

HEART OF AN ASSASSIN - Book 2

VANISHING POINT - a novella - Coming fall 2013

TWIST OF FATE - Book 3 - Coming fall 2013

Other works

HEIST - a time travel thriller

Printed in Great Britain
by Amazon.co.uk, Ltd.,
Marston Gate.